Lucian the dreamer

J. S. Fletcher

Lucian the dreamer

The present edition is a reproduction of previous publication of this classic work. Minor typographical errors may have been corrected without note; however, for an authentic reading experience the spelling, punctuation, and capitalization have been retained from the original text.

ISBN: 978-1-64439-369-7

CONTENTS

CHAPTER I

The railway station stood in the midst of an apparent solitude, and from its one long platform there was no sign of any human habitation. A stranger, looking around him in passing that way, might well have wondered why a station should be found there at all; nevertheless, the board which figured prominently above the white palings suggested the near presence of three places—Wellsby, Meadhope, and Simonstower—and a glance at a map of the county would have sufficed to show him that three villages of the names there indicated lay hidden amongst the surrounding woods, one to the east and two to the west of the railway. The line was a single one, served by a train which made three out-and-home journeys a day between the market-town of Oakborough and the village of Normanford, stopping on its way at seven intermediate stations, of which Wellsby was the penultimate one. These wayside stations sometimes witnessed arrivals and departures, but there were many occasions on which the train neither took up passengers nor set them down—it was only a considerable traffic in agricultural produce, the extra business of the weekly market-day, and its connection with the main line, that enabled the directors to keep the Oakborough and Normanford Branch open. At each small station they maintained a staff consisting of a collector or station-master, a booking-clerk, and a porter, but the duties of these officials were light, and a good deal of spare time lay at their disposal, and was chiefly used in cultivating patches of garden along the side of the line, or in discussing the news of the neighbourhood.

On a fine April evening of the early eighties the staff of this particular station assembled on the platform at half-past six o'clock in readiness to receive the train (which, save on market-days, was composed of an engine, two carriages, and the guard's van), as it made its last down journey. There were no passengers to go forward towards Normanford, and the porter, according to custom, went out to the end of the platform as the train came into view, and held up his arms as a signal to the driver that he need not stop unless he had reasons of his own for doing so. To this signal the driver responded with two sharp shrieks of his whistle, on hearing which the porter turned away, put his hands in his pockets, and slouched back along the platform.

'Somebody to set down, anyway, Mr. Simmons,' said the booking-clerk with a look at the station-master. 'I wonder who it is—I've only booked one up ticket to-day; James White it was, and he came back by the 2.30, so it isn't him.'

1

The station-master made no reply, feeling that another moment would answer the question definitely. He walked forward as the train drew up, and amidst the harsh grinding of its wheels threw a greeting to the engine-driver, which he had already given four times that day and would give again as the train went back two hours later. His eyes, straying along the train, caught sight of a hand fumbling at the handle of a third-class compartment, and he hastened to open the door.

'It's you, is it, Mr. Pepperdine?' he said. 'I wondered who was getting out—it's not often that this train brings us a passenger.'

'Two of us this time,' answered the man thus addressed as he quickly descended, nodding and smiling at the station-master and the booking-clerk; 'two of us this time, Mr. Simmons. Ah!' He drew a long breath of air as if the scent of the woods and fields did him good, and then turned to the open door of the carriage, within which stood a boy leisurely attiring himself in an overcoat. 'Come, my lad,' he said good-humouredly, 'the train'll be going on—let's see now, Mr. Simmons, there's a portmanteau, a trunk, and a box in the van—perhaps Jim there'll see they're got out.'

The porter hurried off to the van; as he turned away the boy descended from the train, put his gloved hands in the pockets of his overcoat, and stared about him with a deliberate and critical expression. His glance ran over the station, the creeping plants on the station-master's house, the station-master, and the booking-clerk; his companion, meanwhile, was staring hard at a patch of bright green beyond the fence and smiling with evident enjoyment.

'I'll see that the things are all right,' said the boy suddenly, and strode off to the van. The porter had already brought out a portmanteau and a trunk; he and the guard were now struggling with a larger obstacle in the shape of a packing-case which taxed all their energies.

'It's a heavy 'un, this is!' panted the guard. 'You might be carrying all the treasure of the Bank of England in here, young master.'

'Books,' said the boy laconically. 'They are heavy. Be careful, please—don't let the box drop.'

There was a note in his voice which the men were quick to recognise—the note of command and of full expectancy that his word would rank as law. He stood by, anxious of eye and keenly observant, while the men lowered the packing-case to the platform; behind him stood Mr. Pepperdine, the station-master, and the booking-clerk, mildly interested.

'There!' said the guard. 'We ha'n't given her a single bump. Might ha' been the delicatest chiny, the way we handled it.'

He wiped his brow with a triumphant wave of the hand. The boy, still regarding the case with grave, speculative eyes, put his hand in his pocket, drew forth a shilling, and with a barely perceptible glance at the guard, dropped it in his hand. The man stared, smiled, pocketed the gift, and touched his cap. He waved his green flag vigorously; in another moment the train was rattling away into the shadow of the woods.

Mr. Pepperdine stepped up to the boy's side and gazed at the packing-case.

'It'll never go in my trap, lad,' he said, scratching his chin. 'It's too big and too heavy. We must send a horse and cart for it in the morning.'

'But where shall we leave it?' asked the boy, with evident anxiety.

'We'll put it in the warehouse, young master,' said the porter. 'It'll be all right there. I'll see that no harm comes to it.'

The boy, however, demanded to see the warehouse, and assured himself that it was water-tight and would be locked up. He issued strict mandates to the porter as to his safe-keeping of the packing-case, presented him also with a shilling, and turned away unconcernedly, as if the matter were now settled. Mr. Pepperdine took the porter in hand.

'Jim,' he said, 'my trap's at the Grange; maybe you could put that trunk and portmanteau on a barrow and bring them down in a while? No need to hurry—I shall have a pipe with Mr. Trippett before going on.'

'All right, sir,' answered the porter. 'I'll bring 'em both down in an hour or so.'

'Come on, then, lad,' said Mr. Pepperdine, nodding good-night to the station-master, and leading the way to the gate. 'Eh, but it's good to be back where there's some fresh air! Can you smell it, boy?'

The boy threw up his face, and sniffed the fragrance of the woods. There had been April showers during the afternoon, and the air was sweet and cool: he drew it in with a relish that gratified the countryman at his side.

'Yes,' he answered. 'I smell it—it's beautiful.'

'Ah, so it is!' said Mr. Pepperdine; 'as beautiful as—as—well, as anything. Yes, it is so, my lad.'

The boy looked up and laughed, and Mr. Pepperdine laughed too. He had no idea why he laughed, but it pleased him to do so; it pleased him, too, to hear the boy laugh. But when the boy's face grew grave again Mr. Pepperdine's countenance composed itself and became equally grave and somewhat solicitous. He looked out

3

of his eye-corners at the slim figure walking at his side, and wondered what other folk would think of his companion. 'A nice, smart-looking boy,' said Mr. Pepperdine to himself for the hundredth time; 'nice, gentlemanlike boy, and a credit to anybody.' Mr. Pepperdine felt proud to have such a boy in his company, and prouder still to know that the boy was his nephew and ward.

The boy thus speculated upon was a lad of twelve, somewhat tall for his age, of a slim, well-knit figure, a handsome face, and a confidence of manner and bearing that seemed disproportionate to his years. He walked with easy, natural grace; his movements were lithe and sinuous; the turn of his head, as he looked up at Mr. Pepperdine, or glanced at the overhanging trees in the lane, was smart and alert; it was easy to see that he was naturally quick in action and in perception. His face, which Mr. Pepperdine had studied a good deal during the past week, was of a type which is more often met with in Italy than in England. The forehead was broad and high, and crowned by a mass of thick, blue-black hair that clustered and waved all over the head, and curled into rings at the temples; the brows were straight, dark, and full; the nose and mouth delicately but strongly carved; the chin square and firm; obstinacy, pride, determination, were all there, and already stiffening into permanence. But in this face, so Italian, so full of the promise of passion, there were eyes of an essentially English type, almost violet in colour, gentle, soft, dreamy, shaded by long black lashes, and it was in them that Mr. Pepperdine found the thing he sought for when he looked long and wistfully at his dead sister's son.

Mr. Pepperdine's present scrutiny passed from the boy's face to the boy's clothes. It was not often, he said to himself, that such a well-dressed youngster was seen in those parts. His nephew was clothed in black from head to foot; his hat was surrounded by a mourning-band; a black tie, fashioned into a smart knot, and secured by an antique cameo-pin, encircled his spotless man's collar: every garment was shaped as if its wearer had been the most punctilious man about town; his neat boots shone like mirrors. The boy was a dandy in miniature, and it filled Mr. Pepperdine with a vast amusement to find him so. He chuckled inwardly, and was secretly proud of a youngster who, as he had recently discovered, could walk into a fashionable tailor's and order exactly what he wanted with an evident determination to get it. But Mr. Pepperdine himself was a rustic dandy. Because of the necessities of a recent occasion he was at that moment clad in sober black—his Sunday-and-State-Occasion's suit—but at home he possessed many wonderful things in the way of riding-breeches, greatcoats

4

ornamented with pearl buttons as big as saucers, and sprigged waistcoats which were the despair of the young country bucks, who were forced to admit that Simpson Pepperdine knew a thing or two about the fashion and was a man of style. It was natural, then, Mr. Pepperdine should be pleased to find his nephew a petit-maître—it gratified an eye which was never at any time indisposed to regard the vanities of this world with complaisance.

Mr. Pepperdine, striding along at the boy's side, presented the cheerful aspect of a healthy countryman. He was a tall, well-built man, rosy of face, bright of eye, a little on the wrong side of forty, and rather predisposed to stoutness of figure, but firm and solid in his tread, and as yet destitute of a grey hair. In his sable garments and his high hat—bought a week before in London itself, and of the latest fashionable shape—he looked very distinguished, and no one could have taken him for less than a churchwarden and a large ratepayer. His air of distinction was further improved by the fact that he was in uncommonly good spirits—he had spent a week in London on business of a sorrowful nature, and he was glad to be home again amongst his native woods and fields. He sniffed the air as he walked, and set his feet down as if the soil belonged to him, and his eyes danced with satisfaction.

The boy suddenly uttered a cry of delight, and stopped, pointing down a long vista of the woods. Mr. Pepperdine turned in the direction indicated, and beheld a golden patch of daffodils.

'Daffy-down-dillies,' said Mr. Pepperdine. 'And very pretty too. But just you wait till you see the woods about Simonstower. I always did say that Wellsby woods were nought to our woods—ah, you should see the bluebells! And as for primroses—well, they could stock all Covent Garden market in London town with 'em, and have enough for next day into the bargain, so they could. Very pretty is them daffies, very pretty, but I reckon there's something a deal prettier to be seen in a minute or two, for here's the Grange, and Mrs. Trippett has an uncommon nice way of setting out a tea-table.'

The boy turned from the glowing patch of colour to look at another attractive picture. They had rounded the edge of the wood on their right hand, and now stood gazing at a peculiarly English scene—a green paddock, fenced from the road by neat railings, painted white, at the further end of which, shaded by a belt of tall elms, stood a many-gabled farmhouse, with a flower-garden before its front door and an orchard at its side. The farm-buildings rose a little distance in rear of the house; beyond them was the stackyard, still crowded with wheat and barley stacks; high over everything rose a pigeon-cote, about the weather-vane of which flew countless pigeons. In the paddock were ewes and lambs; cattle and horses looked over the wall of the fold; the soft light of the April evening lay on everything like a benediction.

'Wellsby Grange,' said Mr. Pepperdine, pushing open a wicket-gate in the white fence and motioning the boy to enter. 'The abode of Mr. and Mrs. Trippett, very particular friends of mine. I always leave my trap here when I have occasion to go by train—it would be sent over this morning, and we shall find it all ready for us presently.'

The boy followed his uncle up the path to the side-door of the farmhouse, his eyes taking in every detail of the scene. He was staring about him when the door opened, and revealed a jolly-faced, red-cheeked man with sandy whiskers and very blue eyes, who grinned delightedly at sight of Mr. Pepperdine, and held out a hand of considerable proportions.

'We were just looking out for you,' said he. 'We heard the whistle, and the missis put the kettle on to boil up that minute. Come in, Simpson—come in, my lad—you're heartily welcome. Now then, missis—they're here.'

A stout, motherly-looking woman, with cherry-coloured ribbons in a nodding cap that crowned a head of glossy dark hair, came bustling to the door.

'Come in, come in, Mr. Pepperdine—glad to see you safe back,' said she. 'And this'll be your little nevvy. Come in, love, come in—you must be tired wi' travelling all that way.'

The boy took off his hat with a courtly gesture, and stepped into the big, old-fashioned kitchen. He looked frankly at the farmer and his wife, and the woman, noting his beauty with quick feminine perception, put her arm round his neck and drew him to her.

'Eh, but you're a handsome lad!' she said. 'Come straight into the parlour and sit you down—the tea'll be ready in a minute. What's your name, my dear?'

The boy looked up at her—Mrs. Trippett's memory, at the sight of his eyes, went back to the days of her girlhood.

'My name is Lucian,' he answered.

Mrs. Trippett looked at him again as if she had scarcely heard him reply to her question. She sighed, and with a sudden impetuous tenderness bent down and kissed him warmly on the cheek.

'Off with your coat, my dear,' she said cheerily. 'And if you're cold, sit down by the fire—if it is spring, it's cold enough for fires at night. Now I'll be back in a minute, and your uncle and the master'll be coming—I lay they've gone to look at a poorly horse that we've got just now—and then we'll have tea.'

She bustled from the room, the cherry-coloured ribbons streaming behind her. The boy, left alone, took off his overcoat and

6

gloves, and laid them aside with his hat; then he put his hands in the pockets of his trousers, and examined his new surroundings.

CHAPTER II

Never before had Lucian seen the parlour of an English farmhouse, nor such a feast as that spread out on the square dinner-table. The parlour was long and wide and low-roofed, and the ceiling was spanned by beams of polished oak; a bright fire crackled in the old-fashioned grate, and a lamp burned on the table; but there were no blinds or curtains drawn over the latticed windows which overlooked the garden. Lucian's observant eyes roved about the room, noting the quaint old pictures on the walls; the oil paintings of Mr. Trippett's father and mother; the framed samplers and the fox's brush; the silver cups on the sideboard, and the ancient blunderbuss which hung on the centre beam. It seemed to him that the parlour was delightfully quaint and picturesque; it smelled of dried roses and lavender and sweetbriar; there was an old sheep-dog on the hearth who pushed his muzzle into the boy's hand, and a grandfather's clock in one corner that ticked a solemn welcome to him. He had never seen such an interior before, and it appealed to his sense of the artistic.

Lucian's eyes wandered at last to the table, spread for high tea. That was as new to him as the old pictures and samplers. A cold ham of generous proportions figured at one side of the table; a round of cold roast-beef at the other; the tea-tray filled up one end; opposite it space was left for something that was yet to come. This something presently appeared in the shape of a couple of roast fowls and a stand of boiled eggs, borne in by a strapping maid whose face shone like the setting sun, and who was sharply marshalled by Mrs. Trippett, carrying a silver teapot and a dish of hot muffins.

'Now then, my dear,' she said, giving a final glance over the table, 'we can begin as soon as the gentlemen come, and I lay they won't be long, for Mr. Pepperdine'll be hungry after his journey, and so I'm sure are you. Come and sit down here and help yourself to an egg—they're as fresh as morning dew—every one's been laid this very day.'

The boy sat down and marvelled at the bountiful provision of

Mrs. Trippett's tea-table; it seemed to him that there was enough there to feed a regiment. But when Mr. Trippett and Mr. Pepperdine entered and fell to, he no longer wondered, for the one had been out in the fields all day, and the other had been engaged in the unusual task of travelling, and they were both exceptional trenchermen at any time. Mr. Trippett joked with the boy as they ate, and made sundry references to Yorkshire pudding and roast-beef which seemed to afford himself great satisfaction, and he heaped up his youthful visitor's plate so generously that Lucian grew afraid.

'Cut and come again,' said Mr. Trippett, with his mouth full and his jaws working vigorously. 'Nothing like a good appetite for growing lads—ah, I was always hungry when I was a boy. Never came amiss to me, didn't food, never.'

'But I've never eaten so much before,' said Lucian, refusing his host's pressing entreaty to have another slice off the breast, or a bit of cold ham. 'I was hungry, too, or I couldn't have eaten so much now.'

'He'll soon get up an appetite at Simonstower,' said Mrs. Trippett. 'You're higher up than we are, Mr. Pepperdine, and the air's keener with you. To be sure, our children have good enough appetites here—you should see them at meal times!—I'm sure I oft wonder wherever they put it all.'

'It's a provision of nature, ma'am,' said Mr. Pepperdine. 'There's some wonderful things in Nature.'

'They're wanting to see you, my dear,' said Mrs. Trippett, ignoring her elder guest's profound remark and looking at her younger one. 'I told them Mr. Pepperdine was going to bring a young gentleman with him. You shall see them after tea—they're out in the orchard now—they had their teas an hour ago, and they've gone out to play. There's two of them—John and Mary. John's about your own age, and Mary's a year younger.'

'Can't I go out to them?' said Lucian. 'I will, if you will please to excuse me.'

'With pleasure, my dear,' said Mrs. Trippett. 'Go by all means, if you'd like to. Go through the window there—you'll hear them somewhere about, and they'll show you their rabbits and things.'

The boy picked up his hat and went out. Mrs. Trippett followed him with meditative eyes.

'He's not shy, seemingly,' she said, looking at Mr. Pepperdine.

'Not he, ma'am. He's an old-fashioned one, is the lad,' answered Lucian's uncle. 'He's the manners of a man in some things. I reckon, you see, that it's because he's never had other children to play with.'

'He's a handsome boy,' sighed the hostess. 'Like his father as I

8

remember him. He was a fine-looking man, in a foreign way. But he's his mother's eyes—poor Lucy!'

'Yes,' said Mr. Pepperdine. 'He's Lucy's eyes, but all the rest of him's like his father.'

'Were you in time to see his father before he died?' asked Mr. Trippett, who was now attacking the cold beef, after having demolished the greater part of a fowl. 'You didn't think you would be when you went off that morning.'

'Just in time, just in time,' answered Mr. Pepperdine. 'Ay, just in time. He went very sudden and very peaceful. The boy was very brave and very old-fashioned about it—he never says anything now, and I don't mention it.'

'It's best not,' said Mrs. Trippett. 'Poor little fellow!—of course, he'll not remember his mother at all?'

'No,' said Mr. Pepperdine, shaking his head. 'No, he was only two years old when his mother died.'

Mr. Trippett changed the subject, and began to talk of London and what Mr. Pepperdine had seen there. But when the tea-table had been cleared, and Mrs. Trippett had departed to the kitchen regions to bustle amongst her maids, and the two farmers were left in the parlour with the spirit decanters on the table, their tumblers at their elbows and their pipes in their mouths, the host referred to Mr. Pepperdine's recent mission with some curiosity.

'I never rightly heard the story of this nephew of yours,' he said. 'You see, I hadn't come to these parts when your sister was married. The missis says she remembers her, 'cause she used to visit hereabouts in days past. It were a bit of a romance like, eh?'

Mr. Pepperdine took a pull at his glass and shook his head.

'Ah!' said he oracularly. 'It was. A romance like those you read of in the story-books. I remember the beginning of it all as well as if it were yesterday. Lucy—that was the lad's mother, my youngest sister, you know, Trippett—was a girl then, and the prettiest in all these parts: there's nobody'll deny that.'

'I always understood that she was a beauty,' said Mr. Trippett.

'And you understood rightly. There wasn't Lucy's equal for beauty in all the county,' affirmed Mr. Pepperdine. 'The lad has her eyes—eh, dear, I've heard high and low talk of her eyes. But he's naught else of hers—all the rest his father's—Lucy was fair.'

He paused to apply a glowing coal to the tobacco in his long pipe, and he puffed out several thick clouds of smoke before he resumed his story.

'Well, Lucy was nineteen when this Mr. Cyprian Damerel came along. You can ask your missis what like he was—women are better hands at describing a man's looks than a man is. He were a handsome young man, but foreign in appearance, though you wouldn't ha' told it from his tongue. The boy'll be like him some day. He came walking through Simonstower on his way from Scarhaven, and naught would content him but that he must set up his easel and make a picture of the village. He found lodgings at old Mother Grant's, and settled down, and he was one of that sort that makes themselves at home with everybody in five minutes. He'd an open face and an open hand; he'd talk to high and low in just the same way; and he'd a smile for everybody.'

'And naturally all the lasses fell in love with him,' suggested Mr. Trippett, with a hearty laugh. 'I've heard my missis say he'd a way with him that was taking with the wenches—specially them as were inclined that way, like.'

'Undoubtedly he had,' said Mr. Pepperdine. 'Undoubtedly he had. But after he'd seen her, he'd no eyes for any lass but our Lucy. He fell in love with her and she with him as naturally as a duckling takes to water. Ah! I don't think I ever did see two young people quite so badly smitten as they were. It became evident to everybody in the place. But he acted like a man all through—oh yes! My mother was alive then, you know, Trippett,' Mr. Pepperdine continued, with a sigh. 'She was a straight-laced 'un, was my mother, and had no liking for foreigners, and Damerel had a livelyish time with her when he came to th' house and asked her, bold as brass, if he might marry her daughter.'

'I'll lay he wo'd; I'll lay he wo'd,' chuckled Mr. Trippett.

'Ay, and so he had,' continued Mr. Pepperdine. 'She was very stiff and stand-off, was our old lady, and she treated him to some remarks about foreigners and papists, and what not, and gave him to understand that she'd as soon seen her daughter marry a gipsy as a strolling artist, 'cause you see, being old-fashioned, she'd no idea of what an artist, if he's up to his trade, can make. But he was one too many for her, was Damerel. He listened to all she had to say, and then he offered to give her references about himself, and he told her who he was, the son of an Italian gentleman that had come to live in England 'cause of political reasons, and what he earned, and he made it clear enough that Lucy wouldn't want for bread and butter, nor a silk gown neither.'

'Good reasoning,' commented Mr. Trippett. 'Very good reasoning. Love-making's all very well, but it's nowt wi'out a bit o' money at th' back on't.'

'Well, there were no doubt about Damerel's making money,' said Mr. Pepperdine, 'and we'd soon good proof o' that; for as soon as he'd finished his picture of the village he sold it to th' Earl for five hundred pound, and it hangs i' the dining-room at th' castle to this day. I saw it the last time I paid my rent there. Mistress Jones, th' housekeeper, let me have a look at it. And of course, seeing that the young man was able to support a wife, th' old lady had to give way, and they were married. Fifteen year ago that is,' concluded Mr. Pepperdine with a shake of the head. 'Dear-a-me! it seems only like yesterday since that day—they made the handsomest bride and bridegroom I ever saw.'

'She died soon, didn't she?' inquired Mr. Trippett.

'Lived a matter of four years after the marriage,' answered Mr. Pepperdine. 'She wasn't a strong woman, wasn't poor Lucy—there was something wrong with her lungs, and after the boy came she seemed to wear away. He did all that a man could, did her husband—took her off to the south of Europe. Eh, dear, the letters that Keziah and Judith used to have from her, describing the places she saw—they read fair beautiful! But it were no good—she died at Rome, poor lass, when the boy was two years old.'

'Poor thing!' said Mr. Trippett. 'And had all that she wanted, seemingly.'

'Everything,' said Mr. Pepperdine. 'Her life was short but sweet, as you may say.'

'And now he's gone an' all,' said Mr. Trippett.

Mr. Pepperdine nodded.

'Ay,' he said, 'he's gone an' all. I don't think he ever rightly got over his wife's death—anyway, he led a very restless life ever after, first one place and then another, never settling anywhere. Sometimes it was Italy, sometimes Paris, sometimes London—he's seen something, has that boy. Ay, he's dead, is poor Damerel.'

'Leave owt behind him like?' asked Mr. Trippett sententiously.

Mr. Pepperdine polished the end of his nose.

'Well,' he said, 'there'll be a nice little nest-egg for the boy when all's settled up, I dare say. He wasn't a saving sort of man, I should think, but dear-a-me, he must ha' made a lot of money in his time—and spent it, too.'

'Easy come and easy go,' said Mr. Trippett. 'I've heard that's the way with that sort. Will this lad take after his father, then?'

'Nay,' said Mr. Pepperdine, 'I don't think he will. He can't draw a line—doesn't seem to have it in him. Curious thing that, but it is so. No—he's all for reading. I never saw such a lad for books. He's got a great chest full o' books at the station yonder—wouldn't leave London without them.'

'Happen turn out a parson or a lawyer,' suggested Mr. Trippett.

'Nay,' said Mr. Pepperdine. 'It's my impression he'll turn out a

11

poet, or something o' that sort. They tell me there's a good living to be made out o' that nowadays.'

Mr. Trippett lifted the kettle on to the brightest part of the fire, mixed himself another glass of grog, and pushed the decanter towards his friend.

'There were only a poorish market at Oakbro' t'other day,' he said. 'Very low prices, and none so much stuff there, nayther.'

Mr. Pepperdine followed his host's example with respect to the grog, and meditated upon the market news. They plunged into a discussion upon prices. Mrs. Trippett entered the room, took up a basket of stockings, planted herself in her easy-chair, and began to look for holes in toes and heels. The two farmers talked; the grandfather's clock ticked; the fire crackled; the whole atmosphere was peaceful and homelike. At last the talk of prices and produce was interrupted by the entrance of the stout serving-maid.

'If you please'm, there's Jim Wood from the station with two trunks for Mr. Pepperdine, and he says is he to put 'em in Mr. Pepperdine's trap?' she said, gazing at her mistress.

'Tell him to put them in the shed,' said Mr. Pepperdine. 'I'll put 'em in the trap myself. And here, my lass, give him this for his trouble,' he added, diving into his pocket and producing a shilling.

'And give him a pint o' beer and something to eat,' said Mr. Trippett.

'Give him some cold beef and pickles, Mary,' said Mrs. Trippett.

Mary responded 'Yes, sir—Yes'm,' and closed the door. Mr. Pepperdine, gazing at the clock with an air of surprise, remarked that he had no idea it was so late, and he must be departing.

'Nowt o' th' sort!' said Mr. Trippett. 'You're all right for another hour—help yourself, my lad.'

'The little boy's all right,' said Mrs. Trippett softly. 'He's soon made friends with John and Mary—they were as thick as thieves when I left them just now.'

'Then let's be comfortable,' said the host. 'Dang my buttons, there's nowt like comfort by your own fireside. And how were London town looking, then, Mr. Pepperdine?—mucky as ever, I expect.'

Mr. Pepperdine, with a replenished glass and a newly charged pipe, plunged into a description of what he had seen in London. The time slipped away—the old clock struck nine at last, and suddenly reminded him that he had six miles to drive and that his sisters would be expecting his arrival with the boy.

'Time flies fast in good company,' he remarked as he rose with evident reluctance. 'I always enjoy an evening by your hospitable fireside, Mrs. Trippett, ma'am.'

'You're in a great hurry to leave it, anyhow,' said Mr. Trippett, with a broad grin. 'Sit ye down again, man—you'll be home in half an hour with that mare o' yours, and it's only nine o'clock, and ten to one th' owd clock's wrong.'

'Ay, but my watch isn't,' answered Mr. Pepperdine. 'Nay, we must go—Keziah and Judith'll be on the look-out for us, and they'll want to see the boy.'

'Ay, I expect they will,' said Mr. Trippett. 'Well, if you must you must—take another glass and light a cigar.'

Mr. Pepperdine refused neither of these aids to comfort, and lingered a few minutes longer. But at last they all went out into the great kitchen, Mrs. Trippett leading the way with words of regret at her guest's departure. She paused upon the threshold and turned to the two men with a gesture which commanded silence.

The farmhouse kitchen, quaint and picturesque with its old oak furniture, its flitches of bacon and great hams hanging from the ceiling, its bunches of dried herbs and strings of onions depending from hooks in the corners, its wide fireplace and general warmth and cheeriness, formed the background of a group which roused some sense of the artistic in Mrs. Trippett's usually matter-of-fact intellect. On the long settle which stretched on one side of the hearth sat four shock-headed ploughboys, leaning shoulder to shoulder; in an easy-chair opposite sat the red-cheeked maid-servant; close to her, on a low stool, sat a little girl with Mrs. Trippett's features and eyes, whose sunny hair fell in wavy masses over her shoulders; behind her, hands in pockets, sturdy and strong, stood a miniature edition of Mr. Trippett, even to the sandy hair, the breeches, and the gaiters; in the centre of the floor, at a round table on which stood a great oil lamp, sat the porter, busy with a round of beef, a foaming tankard of ale, and a crusty loaf. Of these eight human beings a similar peculiarity was evident. Each one sat with mouth more or less open—the ploughboys' mouths in particular had revolved themselves into round O's, while the porter, struck as it were in the very act of forking a large lump of beef into a cavernous mouth, looked like a man who has suddenly become paralysed and cannot move. The maid-servant's eyes were wider than her mouth; the little girl shrank against the maid's apron as if afraid—it was only the sturdy boy in the rear who showed some symptoms of a faint smile. And the object upon which all eyes were fixed was Lucian, who stood on the hearth, his back to the fire, his face glowing in the lamplight, winding up in a low and thrilling

13

voice the last passages of what appeared to be a particularly blood-curdling narrative.

Mr. Trippett poked Mr. Pepperdine in the ribs.

'Seems to ha' fixed 'em,' he whispered. 'Gow—the lad's gotten the gift o' the gab!—he talks like a book.'

'H'sh,' commanded Mrs. Trippett.

'And so the body hung on the gibbet,' Lucian was saying, 'through all that winter, and the rain, and the hail, and the snow fell upon it, and when the spring came again there remained nothing but the bones of the brigand, and they were bleached as white as the eternal snows; and Giacomo came and took them down and buried them in the little cemetery under the cypress-trees; but the chain still dangles from the gibbet, and you may hear it rattle as you pass that way as it used to rattle when Luigi's bones hung swaying in the wind.'

The spell was broken; the porter sighed deeply, and conveyed the interrupted forkful to his mouth; the ploughboys drew deep breaths, and looked as if they had arisen from a deep sleep; the little girl, catching sight of her mother, ran to her with a cry of 'Is it true? Is it true?' and Mr. Trippett brought everybody back to real life by loud calls for Mr. Pepperdine's horse and trap. Then followed the putting on of overcoats and wraps, and the bestowal of a glass of ginger-wine upon Lucian by Mr. Trippett, in order that the cold might be kept out, and then good-nights and Godspeeds, and he was in the dogcart at Mr. Pepperdine's side, and the mare, very fresh, was speeding over the six miles of highway which separated Mr. Trippett's stable from her own.

CHAPTER III

While Mr. Pepperdine refreshed himself at his friend's house, his sisters awaited the coming of himself and his charge with as much patience as they could summon to their aid. Each knew that patience was not only necessary, but inevitable. It would have been the easiest thing in the world for Mr. Pepperdine to have driven straight home from the station and supped in his own parlour, and that, under the circumstances, would have seemed the most reasonable thing to do. But Mr. Pepperdine made a rule of never

14

passing the gates of the Grange Farm, and his sisters knew that he would tarry there on his homeward journey, accept Mrs. Trippett's invitation to tea, and spend an hour or two afterwards in convivial intercourse with Mr. Trippett. That took place every market-day and every time Mr. Pepperdine had occasion to travel by train; and the Misses Pepperdine knew that it would go on taking place as long as their brother Simpson and his friends at the Grange Farm continued to exist.

At nine o'clock Miss Pepperdine, who had been knitting by the parlour fire since seven, grew somewhat impatient.

'I think Simpson might have come home straight from the station,' she said in sharp, decided tones. 'The child is sure to be tired.'

Miss Judith Pepperdine, engaged on fancy needlework on the opposite side of the hearth, shook her head.

'Simpson never passes the Grange,' she said. 'That night I came with him from Oakborough last winter, I couldn't get him to come home. He coaxed me to go in for just ten minutes, and we had to stop four hours.'

Miss Pepperdine sniffed. Her needles clicked vigorously for a few minutes longer; she laid them down at a quarter past nine, went across the parlour to a cupboard, unlocked it, produced a spirit-case and three glasses, and set them on the table in the middle of the room. At the same moment a tap sounded on the door, and a maid entered bearing a jug of hot water, a dish of lemons, and a bowl of sugar. She was about to leave the room after setting her tray down when Miss Pepperdine stopped her.

'I wonder what the boy had better have, Judith?' she said, looking at her sister. 'He's sure to have had a good tea at the Grange—Sarah Trippett would see to that—but he'll be cold. Some hot milk, I should think. Bring some new milk in the brass pan, Anne, and another glass—I'll heat it myself over this fire.'

Then, without waiting to hear whether Miss Judith approved the notion of hot milk or not, she sat down to her knitting again, and when the maid had brought the brass pan and the glass and withdrawn, the parlour became hushed and silent. It was an old-world room—there was not an article of furniture in it that was less than a hundred years old, and the old silver and old china arranged in the cabinets and on the side-tables were as antiquated as the chairs, the old bureau, and the pictures. Everything was old, good, and substantial; everything smelled of a bygone age and of dried rose-leaves.

The two sisters, facing each other across the hearth, were in thorough keeping with the old-world atmosphere of their parlour.

15

Miss Keziah Pepperdine, senior member of the family, and by no means afraid of admitting that she had attained her fiftieth year, was tall and well-built; a fine figure of a woman, with a handsome face, jet-black hair, and eyes of a decided keenness. There was character and decision in her every movement; in her sharp, incisive speech; in her quick glance; and in the nervous, resolute click of her knitting needles. As she knitted, she kept her lips pursed tightly together and her eyes fixed upon her work: it needed little observation to make sure that whatever Miss Pepperdine did would be done with resolution and thoroughness. She was a woman to be respected rather than loved; feared more than honoured; and there was a flash in her hawk's eyes, and a grimness about her mouth, which indicated a temper that could strike with force and purpose. Further indications of her character were seen in her attire, which was severely simple—a gown of black, unrelieved by any speck of white, hanging in prim, straight folds, and utterly unadorned, but, to a knowing eye, fashioned of most excellent and costly material.

Judith Pepperdine, many years younger than her sister, was dressed in black too, but the sombreness of her attire was relieved by white cuffs and collar, and by a very long thin gold chain, which was festooned twice round her neck ere it sought refuge in the watch-pocket at her waist. She had a slender figure of great elegance, and was proud of it, just as she was proud of the fact that at forty years of age she was still a pretty woman. There was something of the girl still left in her: some dreaminess of eye, a suspicion of coquetry, an innate desire to please the other sex and to be admired by men. Her cheek was still smooth and peach-like; her eyes still bright, and her brown hair glossy; old maid that she undoubtedly was, there were many good-looking girls in the district who had not half her attractions. To her natural good looks Judith Pepperdine added a native refinement and elegance; she knew how to move about a room and walk the village street. Her smile was famous—old Dr. Stubbins, of Normanfold, an authority in such matters, said that for sweetness and charm he would back Judith Pepperdine's smile against the world.

There were many people who wondered why the handsome Miss Pepperdine had never married, but there was scarcely one who knew why she had remained and meant to remain single. Soon after the marriage of her sister Lucy to Cyprian Damerel, Judith developed a love-affair of her own with a dashing cavalry man, a sergeant of the 13th Hussars, then quartered at Oakborough. He was a handsome young man, the son of a local farmer, and his ambition had been for soldiering from boyhood. Coming into the neighbourhood in all his glory, and often meeting Judith at the houses of mutual friends, he had soon laid siege to her and captured her susceptible heart. Their engagement was kept secret, for old Mrs. Pepperdine had almost as great an objection to soldiers as to foreigners, and would have considered a non-commissioned officer beneath her daughter's notice. The sergeant, however, had aspirations—it was his hope to secure a commission in an infantry regiment, and his ambition in this direction seemed likely to be furthered when his regiment was ordered out to India and presently engaged in a frontier campaign. But there his good luck came to an untimely end—he performed a brave action which won him the Victoria Cross, but he was so severely wounded in doing it that he died soon afterwards, and Judith's romance came to a bitter end. She had had many offers of marriage since, and had refused them all—the memory of the handsome Hussar still lived in her sentimental heart, and her most cherished possession was the cross which he had won and had not lived to receive. Time had healed the wound: she no longer experienced the pangs and sorrows of her first grief. Everything had been mellowed down into a soft regret, and the still living affection for the memory of a dead man kept her heart young.

That night Judith for once in a while had no thought of her dead lover—she was thinking of the boy whom Simpson was bringing to them. She remembered Lucy with wondering thoughts, trying to recall her as she was when Cyprian Damerel took her away to London and a new life. None of her own people had ever seen Lucy again—they were stay-at-home folk, and the artist and his wife had spent most of their short married life on the Continent. Now Damerel, too, was dead, and the boy was coming back to his mother's people, and Judith, who was given to dreaming, speculated much concerning him.

'I wonder,' she said, scarcely knowing that she spoke, 'I wonder what Lucian will be like.'

'And I wonder,' said Miss Pepperdine, 'if Damerel has left any money for him.'

'Surely!' exclaimed Judith. 'He earned such large sums by his paintings.'

Miss Pepperdine's needles clicked more sharply than ever.

'He spent large sums too,' she said. 'I've heard of the way in which he lived. He was an extravagant man, like most of his sort. That sort of money is earned easily and spent easily. With his ideas and his tastes, he ought to have been a duke. I hope he has provided for the boy—times are not as good as they might be.'

'You would never begrudge anything to Lucy's child, sister?' said Judith timidly, and with a wistful glance at Miss Pepperdine's

17

stern countenance. 'I'm sure I shouldn't—he is welcome to all I have.'

'Umph!' replied Miss Pepperdine. 'Who talked of begrudging anything to the child? All I say is, I hope his father has provided for him.'

Judith made no answer to this remark, and the silence which followed was suddenly broken by the sound of wheels on the drive outside the house. Both sisters rose to their feet; each showed traces of some emotion. Without a word they passed out of the room into the hall. The maid-servant had already opened the door, and in the light of the hanging lamp they saw their brother helping Lucian out of the dogcart. The sisters moved forward.

'Now, then, here we are!' said Mr. Pepperdine. 'Home again, safe and sound, and no breakages. Lucian, my boy, here's your aunts Keziah and Judith. Take him in, lassies, and warm him—it's a keenish night.'

The boy stepped into the hall, and lifted his hat as he looked up at the two women.

'How do you do?' he said politely.

Miss Pepperdine drew a quick breath. She took the outstretched hand and bent down and kissed the boy's cheek; in the lamplight she had seen her dead sister's eyes look out of the young face, and for the moment she could not trust herself to speak. Judith trembled all over; as the boy turned to her she put both arms round him and drew him into the parlour, and there embraced him warmly. He looked at her somewhat wonderingly and critically, and then responded to her embrace.

'You are my Aunt Judith,' he said. 'Uncle Pepperdine told me about you. You are the handsome one.'

Judith kissed him again. She had fallen in love with him on the spot.

'Yes, I am your Aunt Judith, my dear,' she said. 'And I am very, very glad to see you—we are all glad.'

She still held him in her arms, looking at him long and hungrily. Miss Pepperdine came in, businesslike and bustling; she had lingered in the hall, ostensibly to give an order to the servant, but in reality to get rid of a tear or two.

'Now, then, let me have a look at him,' she said, and drew the boy out of Judith's hands and turned him to the light. 'Your Aunt Judith,' she continued as she scanned him critically, 'is the handsome one, as I heard you say just now—I'm the ugly one. Do you think you'll like me?'

Lucian stared back at her with a glance as keen and searching as her own. He looked her through and through.

18

'Yes,' he said, 'I like you. I think——' He paused and smiled a little.

'You think—what?'

'I think you might be cross sometimes, but you're good,' he said, still staring at her.

Miss Pepperdine laughed. Judith knew that she was conquered.

'Well, you'll find out,' said Miss Pepperdine. 'Now, then, off with your coat—are you hungry?'

'No,' answered Lucian. 'I ate too much at Mrs. Trippett's—English people have such big meals, I think.'

'Give him a drop of something warm,' said Mr. Pepperdine, entering with much rubbing of hands and stamping of feet. ''Tis cold as Christmas, driving through them woods 'twixt here and Wellsby.'

Miss Pepperdine set the brass pan on the fire, and presently handed Lucian a glass of hot milk, and produced an old-fashioned biscuit-box from the cupboard. The boy sat down near Judith, ate and drank, and looked about him, all unconscious that the two women and the man were watching him with all their eyes.

'I like this room better than Mrs. Trippett's,' he said suddenly. 'Hers is a pretty room, but this shows more taste. And all the furniture is Chippendale!'

'Bless his heart!' said Miss Pepperdine, 'so it is. How did you know that, my dear?'

Lucian stared at her.

'I know a lot about old furniture,' he said; 'my father taught me.' He yawned and looked apologetic. 'I think I should like to go to bed,' he added, glancing at Miss Pepperdine. 'I am sleepy—we have been travelling all day.'

Judith rose from her chair with alacrity. She was pining to get the boy all to herself.

'I'll take him to his room,' she said. 'Come along, dear, your room is all ready for you.'

The boy shook hands with Aunt Keziah. She kissed him again and patted his head. He crossed over to Mr. Pepperdine, who was pulling off his boots.

'I'll go riding with you in the morning,' he said. 'After breakfast, I suppose, eh?'

'Ay, after breakfast,' answered Mr. Pepperdine. 'I'll tell John to have the pony ready. Good-night, my lad; your Aunt Judith'll see you're all comfortable.'

Lucian shook hands with his uncle, and went cheerfully away with Judith. Miss Pepperdine sighed as the door closed upon them.

'He's the very image of Cyprian Damerel,' she said; 'but he has Lucy's eyes.'

'He's a fine little lad,' said Mr. Pepperdine. 'An uncommon fine little lad, and quite the gentleman. I'm proud of him.'

He had got into his slippers by this time, and he cast a longing eye at the spirit-case on the table. Miss Pepperdine rose, produced an old-fashioned pewter thimble, measured whisky into it, poured it into a tumbler, added lemon, sugar, and hot water, and handed it to her brother, who received it with an expression of gratitude, and sipped it critically. She measured a less quantity into two other glasses and mixed each with similar ingredients.

'Judith won't be coming down again,' she said. 'I'll take her tumbler up to her room; and I'm going to bed myself—we've had a long day with churning. You'll not want any news to-night, Simpson; it'll keep till to-morrow, and there's little to tell—all's gone on right.'

'That's a blessing,' said Mr. Pepperdine, stretching his legs.

Miss Pepperdine put away her knitting, removed the spirit-case into the cupboard, locked the door and put the key in her pocket, and took up the little tray on which she had placed the tumblers intended for herself and her sister. But on the verge of leaving the room she paused and looked at her brother.

'We were glad you got there in time, Simpson,' she said. 'And you did right to bring the child home—it was the right thing to do. I hope Damerel has made provision for him?'

Mr. Pepperdine was seized with a mighty yawning.

'Oh ay!' he said as soon as he could speak. 'The lad's all right, Keziah—all right. Everything's in my hands—yes, it's all right.'

'You must tell me about it afterwards,' said Miss Pepperdine. 'I'll go now—I just want to see that the boy has all he wants. Good-night, Simpson.'

'Good-night, my lass, good-night,' said the farmer. 'I'll just look round and be off to bed myself.'

Miss Pepperdine left the room and closed the door; her brother heard the ancient staircase creak as she climbed to the sleeping-chambers. He waited a few minutes, and then, rising from his chair, he produced a key from his pocket, walked over to the old bureau, unlocked a small cupboard, and brought forth a bottle of whisky. He drew the cork with a meditative air and added a liberal dose of spirit to that handed to him by his sister. He replaced the bottle and locked up the cupboard, poured a little more hot water into his glass, and sipped the strengthened mixture with approbation. Then he winked solemnly at his reflection in the old mirror above the chimney-piece, and sat down before the fire to enjoy his nightcap in privacy and comfort.

CHAPTER IV

Lucian went to sleep in a chamber smelling of lavender. He was very tired, and passed into a land of gentle dreams as soon as his head touched the pillow. Almost before he realised that he was falling asleep he was wide awake again and it was morning. Broad rays of sunlight flooded the room; he heard the notes of many birds singing outside the window; it was plain that another day was already hastening to noon. He glanced at his watch: it was eight o'clock. Lucian left his bed, drew up the blind, and looked out of the window.

He had seen nothing of Simonstower on the previous evening: it had seemed to him that after leaving Mr. Trippett's farmstead he and Mr. Pepperdine had been swallowed up in deep woods. He had remarked during the course of the journey that the woods smelled like the pine forests of Ravenna, and Mr. Pepperdine had answered that there was a deal of pine thereabouts and likewise fir. Out of the woods they had not emerged until they drove into the lights of a village, clattered across a bridge which spanned a brawling stream, and climbed a winding road that led them into more woods. Then had come the open door, and the new faces, and bed, and now Lucian had his first opportunity of looking about him.

The house stood halfway up a hillside. He saw, on leaning out of the window, that it was stoutly fashioned of great blocks of grey stone and that some of the upper portions were timbered with mighty oak beams. Over the main doorway, a little to the right of his window, a slab of weather-worn stone exhibited a coat of arms, an almost illegible motto or legend, of which he could only make out a few letters, and the initials 'S. P.' over the date 1594. The house, then, was of a respectable antiquity, and he was pleased because of it. He was pleased, too, to find the greater part of its exterior half obscured by ivy, jessamine, climbing rose-trees, honeysuckle, and wistaria, and that the garden which stretched before it was green and shady and old-fashioned. He recognised some features of it— the old, moss-grown sun-dial; the arbour beneath the copper-beech;

the rustic bench beneath the lilac-tree—he had seen one or other of these things in his father's pictures, and now knew what memories had placed them there.

Looking further afield Lucian now saw the village through which they had driven in the darkness. It lay in the valley, half a mile beneath him, a quaint, picturesque place of one long straggling street, in which at that moment he saw many children running about. The houses and cottages were all of grey stone; some were thatched, some roofed with red tiles; each stood amidst gardens and orchards. He now saw the bridge over which Mr. Pepperdine's mare had clattered the night before—a high, single arch spanning a winding river thickly fenced in from the meadows by alder and willow. Near it on rising ground stood the church, square-towered, high of roof and gable, in the midst of a green churchyard which in one corner contained the fallen masonry of some old abbey or priory. On the opposite side of the river, in a small square which seemed to indicate the forum of the village, stood the inn, easily recognisable even at that distance by the pole which stood outside it, bearing aloft a swinging sign, and by the size of the stables surrounding it. This picture, too, was familiar to the boy's eyes—he had seen it in pictures a thousand times.

Over the village, frowning upon it as a lion frowns upon the victim at its feet, hung the grim, gaunt castle which, after all, was the principal feature of the landscape on which Lucian gazed. It stood on a spur of rocky ground which jutted like a promontory from the hills behind it—on three sides at least its situation was impregnable. From Lucian's point of vantage it still wore the aspect of strength and power; the rustic walls were undamaged; the smaller towers and turrets showed little sign of decay; and the great Norman keep rose like a menace in stone above the skyline of the hills. All over the giant mass of the old stronghold hung a drifting cloud of blue smoke, which gradually mingled with the spirals rising from the village chimneys and with the shadowy mists that curled about the pine-clad uplands. And over everything—village, church, river, castle, meadow, and hill, man and beast—shone the spring sun, life-giving and generous. Lucian looked and saw and understood, and made haste to dress in order that he might go out and possess all these things. He had a quick eye for beauty and an unerring taste, and he recognised that in this village of the grey North there was a charm and a romance which nothing could exhaust. His father had recognised its beauty before him and had immortalised it on canvas; Lucian, lacking the power to make a picture of it, had yet a keener æsthetic sense of its appeal and its influence. It was already calling to him with a thousand voices—he was so impatient to revel in it that he grudged the time given to his breakfast. Miss Pepperdine expressed some fears as to the poorness of his appetite; Miss Judith, understanding the boy's eagerness somewhat better, crammed a thick slice of cake into his pocket as he set out. He was in such haste that he had only time to tell Mr. Pepperdine that he would not ride the pony that morning—he was going to explore the village, and the pony might wait. Then he ran off, eager, excited.

He came back at noon, hungry as a ploughman, delighted with his morning's adventures. He had been all over the village, in the church tower, inside the inn, where he had chatted with the landlord and the landlady, he had looked inside the infants' school and praised the red cloaks worn by the girls to an evidently surprised schoolmistress, and he had formed an acquaintance with the blacksmith and the carpenter.

'And I went up to the castle, too,' he said in conclusion, 'and saw the earl, and he showed me the picture which my father painted—it is hanging in the great hall.' Lucian's relatives betrayed various emotions. Mr. Pepperdine's mouth slowly opened until it became cavernous; Miss Pepperdine paused in the act of lifting a potato to her mouth; Miss Judith clapped her hands.

'You went to the castle and saw the earl?' said Miss Pepperdine.

'Yes,' answered Lucian, unaware of the sensation he was causing. 'I saw him and the picture, and other things too. He was very kind—he made his footman give me a glass of wine, but it was home-made and much too sweet.'

Mr. Pepperdine winked at his sisters and cut Lucian another slice of roast-beef.

'And how might you have come to be so hand-in-glove with his lordship, the mighty Earl of Simonstower?' he inquired. 'He's a very nice, affable old gentleman, isn't he, Keziah? Ah—very—specially when he's got the gout.'

'Oh, I went to the castle and rang the bell, and asked if the Earl of Simonstower was at home,' Lucian replied. 'And I told the footman my name, and he went away, and then came back and told me to follow him, and he took me into a big study where there was an old, very cross-looking old gentleman in an old-fashioned coat writing letters. He had very keen eyes....'

'Ah, indeed!' interrupted Mr. Pepperdine. 'Like a hawk's!'

'...and he stared at me,' continued Lucian, 'and I stared at him. And then he said, "Well, my boy, what do you want?" and I said, "Please, if you are the Earl of Simonstower, I want to see the picture you bought from my father some years ago." Then he stared

23

harder than ever, and he said, "Are you Cyprian Damerel's son?" and I said "Yes." He pointed to a chair and told me to sit down, and he talked about my father and his work, and then he took me out to look at the pictures. He wanted to know if I, too, was going to paint, and I had to tell him that I couldn't draw at all, and that I meant to be a poet. Then he showed me his library, or a part of it—I stopped with him a long time, and he shook hands with me when I left, and said I might go again whenever I wished to.'

'Hear, hear!' said Mr. Pepperdine. 'It's very evident there's a soft spot somewhere in the old gentleman's heart.'

'And what did his lordship talk to you about?' asked Miss Pepperdine, who had sufficiently recovered from her surprise to resume her dinner. 'I hope you said "my lord" and "your lordship" when you spoke to him?'

'No, I didn't, because I didn't know,' said Lucian. 'I said "sir," because he was an old man. Oh, we talked about Italy—fancy, he hasn't been in Italy for twenty years!—and he asked me a lot of questions about several things, and he got me to translate a letter for him which he had just received from a professor at Florence—his own Italian, he said, is getting rusty.'

'And could you do it?' asked Miss Pepperdine.

Lucian stared at her with wide-open eyes.

'Why, yes,' he answered. 'It is my native tongue. I know much, much more Italian than English. Sometimes I cannot find the right word in English—it is a difficult language to learn.'

Lucian's adventures of his first morning pleased Mr. Pepperdine greatly. He chuckled to himself as he smoked his after-dinner pipe—the notion of his nephew bearding the grim old earl in his tumble-down castle was vastly gratifying and amusing: it was also pleasing to find Lucian treated with such politeness. As the Earl of Simonstower's tenant Mr. Pepperdine had much respect but little affection for his titled neighbour: the old gentleman was arbitrary and autocratic and totally deaf to whatever might be said to him about bad times. Mr. Pepperdine was glad to get some small change out of the earl through his nephew.

'Did his lordship mention me or your aunties at all?' he said, puffing at his pipe as they all sat round the parlour fire.

'Yes,' answered Lucian, 'he spoke of you.'

'And what did he say like? Something sweet, no doubt,' said Mr. Pepperdine.

Lucian looked at Miss Judith and made no answer.

'Out with it, lad!' said Mr. Pepperdine.

'It was only about Aunt Judith,' answered Lucian. 'He said she was a very pretty woman.'

Mr. Pepperdine exploded in bursts of hearty laughter; Miss Judith blushed like any girl; Miss Pepperdine snorted with indignation. She was about to make some remark on the old nobleman's taste when a diversion was caused by the announcement that Lucian's beloved chest of books had arrived from Wellsby station. Nothing would satisfy the boy but that he must unpack them there and then; he seized Miss Judith by the hand and dragged her away to help him. For the rest of the afternoon the two were arranging the books in an old bookcase which they unearthed from a lumber-room and set up in Lucian's sleeping chamber. Mr. Pepperdine, looking in upon them once or twice and noting their fervour, retired to the parlour or the kitchen with a remark to his elder sister that they were as throng as Throp's wife. Judith, indeed, had some taste in the way of literature—in her own room she treasured a collection of volumes which she had read over and over again. Her taste was chiefly for Lord Byron, Moore, Mrs. Hemans, Miss Landon, and the sentimentalists; she treasured a steel-plate engraving of Byron as if it had been a sacred picture, and gazed with awe upon her nephew when he told her that he had seen the palazzo in which Byron lived during his residence in Pisa, and the house which he had occupied in Venice. Her own romance had given Judith a love of poetry: she told Lucian as she helped him to unpack his books and arrange them that she should expect him to read to her. Modern literature was an unexplored field in her case; her knowledge of letters was essentially early Victorian, and her ideas those of the age in which a poet was most popular when most miserable, and young ladies wore white stockings and low shoes with ankle-straps. She associated fiction with high waists, and essays with full-bottomed wigs, and it seemed the most natural thing to her to shed the tear of sympathy over the Corsair and to sigh with pity for Childe Harold.

CHAPTER V

Lucian settled down in his new surroundings with a readiness and docility that surprised his relatives. He rarely made any allusion to the loss of his father—he appeared to possess a philosophic spirit that enabled him, even at so early an age, to accept the facts of life as they are. He was never backward, however, in talking of the past.

He had been his father's constant companion for six years, and had travelled with him wherever he went, especially in Italy, and he brought out of his memory stores of reminiscences with which to interest and amuse his newly found relatives. He would talk to Mr. Pepperdine of Italian agriculture; to Keziah of Italian domestic life; to Judith of the treasures of Rome and Naples, Pisa and Florence, of the blue skies and sun-kissed groves of his native land. He always insisted on his nationality—the accident of his connection with England on the maternal side seemed to have no meaning for him.

'I am Italian,' he would say when Mr. Pepperdine slyly teased him. 'It does not matter that I was born in England. My real name is Luciano Damerelli, and my father's, if he had used it, was Cypriano.'

Little by little they began to find out the boy's qualities and characteristics. He was strangely old-fashioned, precocious, and unnaturally grave, and cared little for the society of other children, at whom he had a trick of staring as if they had been insects impaled beneath a microscope and he a scientist examining them. He appeared to have two great passions—one for out-door life and nature; the other for reading. He would sit for hours on the bridge watching the river run by, or lie on his back on the lawn in front of the house staring at the drifting clouds. He knew every nook of the ruinous part of the castle and every corner of the old church before he had been at Simonstower many weeks. He made friends with everybody in the village, and if he found out that an old man had some strange legend to tell, he pestered the life out of him until it was told. And every day he did so much reading, always with the stern concentration of the student who means to possess a full mind.

When Lucian had been nearly two months at the farm it was borne in upon Miss Pepperdine's mind that he ought to be sent to school. She was by no means anxious to get rid of him—on the contrary she was glad to have him in the house: she loved to hear him talk, to see him going about, and to watch his various proceedings. But Keziah Pepperdine had been endowed at birth with the desire to manage—she was one of those people who are never happy unless they are controlling, devising, or superintending. Moreover, she possessed a very strict sense of justice—she believed in doing one's duty, especially to those people to whom duty was owing, and who could not extract it for themselves. It seemed to her that it was the plain duty of Lucian's relatives to send Lucian to school. She was full of anxieties for his future. Every attempt which she had made to get her brother to tell her anything about the boy's affairs had resulted in sheer failure—Simpson Pepperdine, celebrated from the North Sea to the

26

Westmoreland border as the easiest-going and best-natured man that ever lived, was a past master in the art of evading direct questions. Keziah could get no information from him, and she was anxious for Lucian's sake. The boy, she said, ought to be fitted out for some walk in life.

She took the vicar into her confidence, seizing the opportunity when he called one day and found no one but herself at home.

'Of course,' she said, 'the boy is a great book-worm. Reading is all that he seems to care about. He brought a quantity of books with him—he has bought others since. He reads in an old-fashioned sort of way—not as you would think a child would. I offered him a child's book one night—it was one that a little boy who once stayed here had left in the house. He took it politely enough, and pretended to look at it, but it was plain to see that he was amused. He is a precocious child, Mr. Chilverstone.'

The vicar agreed. He suggested that he might be better able to judge the situation, and to advise Miss Pepperdine thereon, if he were allowed to inspect Lucian's library, and Keziah accordingly escorted him to the boy's room. Mr. Chilverstone was somewhat taken aback on being confronted by an assemblage of some three or four hundred volumes, arranged with great precision and bearing evidences of constant use. He remarked that the sight was most interesting, and proceeded to make a general inspection. A rapid survey of Lucian's books showed him that the boy had three favourite subjects—history, mediæval romance, and poetry. There were histories of almost every country in Europe, and at least three of the United States of America; there were editions of the ancient chronicles; the great Italian poets were all there in the original; the English poets, ancient and modern, were there too, in editions that bespoke the care of a book-lover. There was nothing of a juvenile, or even a frivolous nature from the top of the old bookcase to the bottom—the nearest approach to anything in the shape of light literature was found in the presence of certain famous historical romances of undoubted verisimilitude, and in much-thumbed copies of Robinson Crusoe and The Pilgrim's Progress.

Mr. Chilverstone was puzzled. As at least one-half of the books before him were in Italian, he concluded that Lucian was as well acquainted with that language as with English, and said so. Miss Pepperdine enlightened him on the point, and gave him a rapid sketch of Lucian's history.

'Just so, just so,' said he. 'No doubt the boy's father formed his taste. It is really most interesting. It is very evident that the child has an uncommon mind—you say that he reads with great attention and concentration?'

'You might let off a cannon at his elbow and he wouldn't take any notice,' said Miss Pepperdine.

'It is evident that he is a born student. This is a capital collection of modern histories,' said Mr. Chilverstone. 'If your nephew has read and digested them all he must be well informed as to the rise and progress of nations. I should like, I think, to have an opportunity of conversing with him.'

Although he did not say so to Miss Pepperdine, the vicar was secretly anxious to find out what had diverted the boy's attention from the usual pursuits of childhood into these paths. He contrived to waylay Lucian and to draw him into conversation, and being a man of some talent and of considerable sympathy, he soon knew all that the boy had to tell. He found that Lucian had never received any education of the ordinary type; had never been to school or known tutor or governess. He could not remember who taught him to read, but cherished a notion that reading and writing had come to him with his speech. As to his choice of books, that had largely had its initiative in his father's recommendation; but there had been a further incentive in the fact that the boy had travelled a great deal, was familiar with many historic scenes and places, and had a natural desire to re-create the past in his own imagination. For six years, in short, he had been receiving an education such as few children are privileged to acquire. He talked of mediæval Italy as if he had lived in its sunny-tinted hours, and of modern Rome as though it lay in the next parish. But Mr. Chilverstone saw that the boy was in no danger of becoming either prig or pedant, and that his mind was as normal as his body was healthy. He was the mere outcome of an exceptional environment. He had lived amongst men who talked and worked and thought but with one object—Art—and their enthusiasm had filled him too. 'I am to be a poet—a great poet,' he said, with serious face and a straight stare from the violet eyes whose beauty brought everybody captive to his feet. 'It is my destiny.'

Mr. Chilverstone had a sheaf of yellow papers locked away in a secret drawer which he had never exhibited to living man or woman—verses written in long dead college days. He was sentimental about them still, and the sentiment inclined him to tenderness with youthful genius. He assured Lucian that he sincerely trusted that he might achieve his heart's desire, and added a word of good advice as to the inadvisability of writing too soon. But he discovered that some one had been beforehand with the boy on that point—the future poet, with a touch of worldly wisdom which sounded as odd as it was quaint, assured the parson that he had a horror of immaturity and had been commanded by his father

28

never to print anything until it had stood the test of cool-headed reflection and twelve months' keeping.

The vicar recognised that here was material which required careful nursing and watchful attention. He soon found that Lucian knew nothing of mathematics, and that his only desire in the way of Greek and Latin was that he might be able to read the poets of those languages in the originals. Of the grammar of the English language he knew absolutely nothing, but as he spoke with an almost too extreme correctness, and in a voice of great refinement, Mr. Chilverstone gave it as his opinion that there was no necessity to trouble him with its complexities. But in presenting his report to Miss Pepperdine the vicar said that it would do the boy good to go to school. He would mix with other boys—he was healthy and normal enough, to be sure, and full of boyish fun in his way, but the society of lads of his own age would be good for him. He recommended Miss Pepperdine to send him to the grammar-school at Saxonstowe, the headmaster of which was a friend of his and would gladly give special attention to any boy whom he recommended. He volunteered, carrying his kindness further, to go over to Saxonstowe and talk to Dr. Babbacombe; for Lucian, he remarked, was no ordinary boy, and needed special attention.

Miss Pepperdine, like most generals who conceive their plans of campaign in secret, found that her troubles commenced as soon as she began to expose her scheme to criticism. Mr. Pepperdine, as a lifelong exponent of the art of letting things alone, wanted to know what she meant by disturbing everything when all was going on as comfortably as it could be. He was sure the boy had as much book-learning as the archbishop himself—besides, if he was sent away to school, he, Simpson Pepperdine, would have nobody to talk to about how they farmed in foreign countries. Judith, half recognising the force of her sister's arguments, was still angry with Keziah for allowing them to occur to her—she knew that the boy had crept so closely into her heart and had so warmed it with new fire that she hated the thought of his leaving her, even though Saxonstowe was only thirty miles away. Consequently Miss Pepperdine fought many pitched battles with her brother and sister, and Simpson and Judith, who knew that she had more brains in her little finger than they possessed in their two heads, took to holding conferences in secret in the vain hope of circumventing her designs.

It came as a vast surprise to these two conspirators that Lucian himself, on whose behalf they basely professed to be fighting, deserted to, or rather openly joined, the enemy as soon as the active campaign began. Miss Pepperdine, like the astute woman she was, gained the boy's ear and had talked him over before either

Simpson or Judith could pervert his mind. He listened to all she had to say, showed that he was impressed, and straightway repaired to the vicarage to seek Mr. Chilverstone's advice. That evening, in the course of a family council, shared in by Mr. Pepperdine with a gloomy face and feelings of silent resentment against Keziah, and by Judith with something of the emotion displayed by a hen who is about to be robbed of her one chicken, Lucian announced that he would go to school, adding, however, that if he found there was nothing to be learnt there he would return to his uncle's roof. Mr. Pepperdine plucked up amazingly after this announcement, for he cherished a secret conviction that his nephew already knew more than any schoolmaster could teach him; but Judith shed tears when she went to bed, and felt ill-disposed towards Keziah for the rest of the week.

Lucian went to Saxonstowe presently with cheerfulness and a businesslike air, and the three middle-aged Pepperdines were miserable. Mr. Pepperdine took to going over to the Grange at Wellsby nearly every night, and Judith was openly rebellious. Miss Pepperdine herself felt that the house was all the duller for the boy's absence, and wondered how they had endured its dumb monotony before he came. There was much of the Spartan in her, however, and she bore up without sign; but the experience taught her that Duty, when actually done, is not so pleasing to the human feelings as it seems to be when viewed from a distance.

No word came from Lucian for two weeks after his departure; then the postman brought a letter addressed to Mr. Pepperdine, which was opened amidst great excitement at the breakfast table. Mr. Pepperdine, however, read it in silence.

'My dear Uncle Simpson Pepperdine,' wrote Lucian, 'I did not wish to write to you until I had been at school quite two weeks, so that I could tell you what I thought of it, and whether it would suit me. It is a very nice school, and all the boys are very nice too, and I like Dr. Babbacombe, and his wife, and the masters. We have very good meals, and I should be quite content in that respect if one could sometimes have a cup of decent coffee, but I believe that is impossible in England. They have a pudding here, sometimes, which the boys call Spotted Dog—it is very satisfying and I do not remember hearing of it before—it has what English people call plums in it, but they are in reality small dried raisins.

'I am perfectly content with my surroundings and my new friends, but I greatly fear that this system of education will not suit me. In some subjects, such as history and general knowledge, I find that I already know much more than Dr. Babbacombe usually teaches to boys. As regards other subjects I find that it is not en règle to permit discussion or argument between master and pupil. I can quite see the reasonableness of that, but it is the only way in which I have ever learnt everything. I am not quick at learning anything—I have to read a thing over and over again before I arrive at the true significance. It may be that I would spend a whole day in accounting to myself why a certain cause produces a certain effect—the system of education in use here, however, requires one to learn many things in quite a short time. It reminds me of the man who taught twelve parrots all at once. In more ways than one it reminds me of this, because I feel that many boys here learn the sound of a word and yet do not know what the word means. That is what I have been counselled to avoid.

'I am anxious to be amenable to your wishes, but I think I shall waste time here. If I could have my own way I should like to have Mr. Chilverstone for a tutor, because he is a man of understanding and patience, and would fully explain everything to me. I am not easy in my mind here, though quite so in my body. Everybody is very kind and the life is comfortable, but I do not think Dr. Babbacombe or his masters are great savants, though they are gracious and estimable gentlemen.

'I send my love to you and my aunts, and to Mr. Chilverstone and Mr. and Mrs. Trippett. I have bought a cricket-bat for John Trippett and a doll for Mary, which I shall send in a box very soon.—And I am your affectionate kinsman,
        'Lucian Damerel.

As the greater part of this remarkable epistle was pure Greek to Mr. Pepperdine, he repaired to the vicarage with it and laid it before Mr. Chilverstone, who, having duly considered it, returned with Lucian's kinsman to the farm and there entered into solemn conclave with him and his sisters. The result of their deliberations was that the boy was soon afterwards taken from the care of the gracious and estimable gentlemen who were not savants, and placed, so far as his education was concerned, under the sole charge of the vicar.

CHAPTER VI

Mr. Chilverstone was one of those men upon whom many sorrows and disappointments are laid. He had set out in life with a choice selection of great ambitions, and at forty-five not one of them had fructified. Ill-health had always weighed him down in one direction; ill-luck in another; the only piece of good fortune which had ever come to him came when the Earl of Simonstower, who had heard of him as an inoffensive man content to serve a parish without going to extremes in either of the objectionable directions, presented him to a living which even in bad times was worth five hundred pounds a year. But just before this preferment came in his way Mr. Chilverstone had the misfortune to lose his wife, and the enjoyment of the fit things of a country living was necessarily limited to him for some time. He was not greatly taxed by his pastoral duties, for his flock, from the earl downwards, loved that type of parson who knows how to keep his place, and only insists on his professional prestige on Sundays and the appointed days, and he had no great inclination to occupy himself in other directions. As the bitterness of his great sorrow slipped away from him he found his life resolving itself into a level—his time was passed in reading, in pottering about his garden, and, as she grew up, in educating his only child, a girl who at the time of her mother's death was little more than an infant. At the time of Lucian's arrival in the village Mr. Chilverstone's daughter was at school in Belgium—the boy's first visits to the vicarage were therefore made to a silent and lonely house, and they proved very welcome to its master.

Lucian's experience at the grammar-school was never repeated under the new régime. The vicar had been somewhat starved in the matter of conversation for more years than he cared to remember, and it was a Godsend to him to have a keen and inquiring mind opposed to his own. His pupil's education began and was continued in an unorthodox fashion; there was no system and very little order in it, but it was good for man and boy. They began to spend much time together, in the field as much as in the study. Mr. Chilverstone, encouraged thereto by Lucian, revived an ancient taste for archæology, and the two made long excursions to the ruined abbeys, priories, castles, and hermitages in their neighbourhood. Miss Pepperdine, to whom Lucian invariably applied for large supplies of sandwiches on these occasions, had an uncomfortable suspicion that the boy would have been better employed with a copy-book or a slate, but she had great faith in the vicar, and acknowledged that her nephew never got into mischief, though he had certainly set his room on fire one night by a bad habit of reading in bed. She had become convinced that Lucian was an odd chicken, who had got into the brood by some freak of fortune, and she fell into the prevalent fashion of the family in regarding him as something uncommon that was not to be judged by ordinary rules of life or interfered with. To Mr. Pepperdine and to Judith he remained a constant source of wonder, interest, and amusement, for his tongue never ceased to wag, and he communicated to them everything that he saw, heard, and thought, with a freedom and generosity that kept them in a perpetual state of mental activity.

Towards the end of June, when Lucian had been three months at Simonstower, he walked into the vicar's study one morning to find him in a state of mild excitement. Mr. Chilverstone nodded his head at a letter which lay open on his desk.

'The day after to-morrow,' he said, 'you will see my daughter. She is coming home from school.'

Lucian made no answer. It seemed to him that this bare announcement wrought some subtle change. He knew nothing whatever of girls—they had never come into his life, and he was doubtful about them. He stared hard at the vicar.

'Will you be glad to see her?' he asked.

'Why, surely!' exclaimed Mr. Chilverstone. 'Yes—I have not seen her for nearly a year, and it is two years since she left home. Yes—Millie is all I have.'

Lucian felt a pang of jealousy. It was part of his nature to fall in love with every new friend he made; in return, he expected each new friend to devote himself to him. He had become very fond of the vicar; they got on together excellently; it was not pleasant to think that a girl was coming between them. Besides, what Mr. Chilverstone said was not true. This Millie was not all he had—he had some of him, Lucian.

'You will like my little girl,' the vicar went on, utterly oblivious of the fact that he was making the boy furiously jealous. 'She is full of life and fun—a real ray of sunshine in a house.' He sighed heavily and looked at a portrait of his wife. 'Yes,' he continued, 'she is quite a lively girl, my little Millie. A sort of tomboy, you know. I call her Sprats; it seems to fit her, somehow.'

Lucian almost choked with rage and grief. All the old, pleasant companionship; all the long talks and walks; all the disputations and scholarly wrangles were to be at an end, and all because of a girl whose father called her Sprats! It was unbelievable. He gazed at the unobservant clergyman with eyes of wonder; he had come to have a great respect for him as a scholar, and could not understand how a man who could make the Greek grammar so interesting could feel

33

any interest in a girl, even though that girl happened to be his own daughter. For women like his aunts, and Mrs. Trippett, and the housekeeper at the castle, Lucian had a great liking; they were all useful in one way or another, either to get good things to eat out of, or to talk to when one wanted to talk; but girls—whatever place had they in the economy of nature! He had never spoken to a girl in his life, except to little Mary Trippett, who was nine, and to whom he sometimes gave sweets and dolls. Would he be expected to talk to this girl whose father called her Sprats? He turned hot and cold at the thought.

His visit to the vicarage that morning was a dead failure. Mr. Chilverstone's behaviour was foolish and ridiculous: he would talk of Sprats. He even went as far as to tell Lucian of some of Sprats's escapades. They were mostly of the practical-joke order, and seemed to afford Mr. Chilverstone huge amusement—Lucian wondered how he could be so silly. He endeavoured to be as polite as possible, but he declined an invitation to stay to lunch. He would cheerfully listen to Mr. Chilverstone on the very dryest points of an irregular verb, but Mr. Chilverstone on Sprats was annoying—he almost descended to futility.

Lucian refused two invitations that afternoon. Mr. Pepperdine offered to take him with him to York, whither he was proceeding on business; Miss Judith asked him if he would like to go with her to the house of a friend in whose grounds was a haunted hermitage. He declined both invitations with great politeness and went out in solitude. Part of the afternoon he spent with an old man who mended the roads. The old man was stone-deaf and needed no conversational effort on the part of a friend, and when he spoke himself he talked of intelligent subjects, such as rheumatism, backache, and the best cure for stone in the bladder. Lucian thought him a highly intelligent man, and presented him with a screw of tobacco purchased at the village shop—it was a tacit thankoffering to the gods that the old man had avoided the subject of girls. His spirits improved after a visit to the shoemaker, who told him a brand-new ghost story for the truth of which he vouched with many solemn asseverations, and he was chatty with his Aunt Keziah when they took tea together. But that night he did not talk so much as usual, and he went to bed early and made no attempt to coax Miss Pepperdine into letting him have the extra light which she had confiscated after he had set his bed on fire.

Next day Lucian hoped to find the vicar in a saner frame of mind, but to his astonishment and disgust Mr. Chilverstone immediately began to talk of Sprats again, and continued to do so until he became unbearable. Lucian was obliged to listen to stories which to him seemed inept, fatuous, and even imbecile. He was told of Sprats's first distinct words; of her first tooth; of her first attempts to walk; of the memorable occasion upon which she placed her pet kitten on the fire in order to warm it. The infatuated father, who had not had an opportunity of retailing these stories for some time, and who believed that he was interesting his listener, continued to pour forth story after story, each more feeble and ridiculous than the last, until Lucian could have shrieked with the agony which was tearing his soul to pieces. He pleaded a bad headache at last and tried to slip away—Mr. Chilverstone detained him in order to give him an anti-headache powder, and accompanied his researches into the medicine cupboard with a highly graphic description of a stomach-ache which Sprats had once contracted from too lavish indulgence in unripe apples, and was cured by himself with some simple drug. The vicar, in short, being a disingenuous and a simple-minded man, had got Sprats on the brain, and he imagined that every word he said was meeting with a responsive thrill in the boy's heart.

Lucian escaped the fatuous father at last. He rushed out into the sunlight, almost choking with rage, grief, and disappointment. He flung the powder into the hedge-bottom, sat down on a stone-heap at the side of the road, and began to swear in Italian. He swore freely and fluently until he had exhausted that eloquent vocabulary which one may pick up in Naples and Venice and in the purlieus of Hatton Garden, and when he had finished he began it all over again and repeated it with as much fervour as one should display, if one is honest, in reciting the Rosary. This saved him from apoplexy, but the blood grew black within him and his soul was scratched. It had been no part of Lucian's plans for the future that Sprats should come between him and his friend.

He slept badly that night, and while he lay awake he said to himself that it was all over. It was a mere repetition of history—a woman always came between men. He had read a hundred instances—this was one more. Of course, the Sprats creature would oust him from his place—nothing would ever be as it had been. All was desolate, and he was alone. He read several pages of the fourth canto of Childe Harold as soon as it was light, and dropped asleep with the firm conviction that life is a grey thing.

All that day and the next Lucian kept away from the vicarage. The domestic deities wondered why he did not go as usual; he invented plausible excuses with facile ingenuity. He neglected his books and betrayed a suspicious interest in Mr. Pepperdine's recent purchases of cattle; he was restless and at times excited, and Miss Keziah looked at his tongue and felt his forehead and made him

35

swallow a dose of a certain home-made medicine by which she set great store. On the third day the suppressed excitement within him reached boiling-point. He went out into the fields mad to work it off, and by good or ill luck lighted upon an honest rustic who was hoeing turnips under a blazing midsummer sun. Lucian looked at the rustic with the eye of a mocking and mischievous devil.

'Boggles,' he said, with a Mephistophelian coaxing, 'would you like to hear some Italian?' Boggles ruminated.

'Why, Master Lucian,' he said, 'I don't know as I ever did hear that language—can't say as I ever did, anyhow.'

'Listen, then,' said Lucian. He treated Boggles to a string of expletives, delivered with native force and energy, making use of his eyes and teeth until the man began to feel frightened.

'Lord sakes, Master Lucian!' he said, 'one 'ud think you was going to murder somebody—you look that fierce. It's a queer sort o' language that, sir—I never heard nowt like it. It flays a body.'

'It is the most delightful language in the world when you want to swear,' said Lucian. 'It....'

'Nonsense! It isn't a patch on German. You wait till I get over the hedge and I'll show you,' cried a ringing and very authoritative voice. 'I can reel off twice as much as that.'

Lucian turned round with an instinctive feeling that a critical moment was at hand. He caught sight of something feminine behind the hedgerow; the next instant a remarkably nimble girl came over a half-made gap. The turnip-hoeing man uttered an exclamation which had much joy in it.

'Lord sakes if it isn't Miss Millie!' he said, touching his cap. 'Glad to see 'ee once again, missie. They did tell me you was coming from them furrineerin' countries, and there you be, growed quite up, as one might say.'

'Not quite, but nearly, Boggles,' answered Miss Chilverstone. 'How's your rheumatics, as one might call 'em? They were pretty bad when I went away, I remember.'

'They're always bad i' th' winter, miss,' said Boggles, leaning on his hoe and evincing a decided desire to talk, 'and a deal better in summer, allus providing the Lord don't send no rain. Fine, dry weather, miss, is what I want—the rain ain't no good to me.'

'A little drop wouldn't hurt the turnips, anyway,' said Miss Chilverstone, looking about her with a knowing air. 'Seem pretty well dried up, don't they?' She looked at Lucian. Their eyes met: the boy stared and blushed; the girl stared and laughed.

'Did it lose its tongue, then?' she said teasingly. 'It seemed to have a very long and very ready one when it was swearing at poor old Boggles. What made him use such bad language to you, Boggles?'

'Lord bless 'ee, missie,' said Boggles hurriedly, 'he didn't mean no harm, didn't Master Lucian—he was telling me how they swear in Eye-talian. Not but what it didn't sound very terrible—but he wouldn't hurt a fly, wouldn't Master Lucian, miss, he wouldn't indeed.'

'Dear little lamb!' she said mockingly, 'I shouldn't think he would.' She turned on the boy with a sudden twist of her shoulders. 'So you are Lucian, are you?' she asked.

'I am Lucian, yes,' he answered.

'Do you know who I am?' she asked, with a flashing look.

Lucian stared back at her, and the shadow of a smile stole into his face.

'I think,' he said musingly, 'I think you must be Sprats.'

Then the two faced each other and stared as only stranger children can stare.

Mr. Boggles, his watery old eyes keenly observant, leaned his chin upon his hoe and stared also, chuckling to himself. Neither saw him; their eyes were all for each other. The girl, without acknowledging it, perhaps without knowing it, recognised the boy's beauty and hated him for it in a healthy fashion. He was too much of a picture; his clothes were too neat; his collar too clean; his hands too white; he was altogether too much of a fine and finicking little gentleman; he ought, she said to herself, to be stuck in a velvet suit, and a point-lace collar, and labelled. The spirit of mischief entered into her at the sight of him.

Lucian examined this strange creature with care. He was relieved to find that she was by no means beautiful. He saw a strong-limbed, active-looking young damsel, rather older and rather taller than himself, whose face was odd, rather than pretty, and chiefly remarkable for a prodigality of freckles and a healthy tan. Her nose was pugnacious and inclined to be of the snub order; her hair sandy and anything but tidy; there was nothing beautiful in her face but a pair of brown eyes of a singularly clear and honest sort. As for her attire, it was not in that order which an exacting governess might have required: she wore a blue serge frock in which she had evidently been climbing trees or scrambling through hedgerows, a battered straw hat wherein she or somebody had stuck the long feathers from a cock's tail; there was a rent in one of her stockings, and her stout shoes looked as if she had tramped through several ploughed fields in them. All over and round her glowed a sort of aureole of rude and vigorous health, of animal spirits, and of a love of mischief—the youthful philosopher confronting her recognised a new influence and a new nature.

'Yes,' she said demurely, 'I'm Sprats, and you've a cheek to call me so—who gave you leave, I'd like to know? What would you think if I told you that you'd look nice if you had a barrel-organ and a monkey on it? Ha! ha! had him there, hadn't I, Boggles? Well, do you know where I am going, monkey-boy?'

Lucian sighed resignedly.

'No,' he answered.

'Going to fetch you,' she said. 'You haven't been to your lessons for two days, and you're to go this instant minute.'

'I don't think I want any lessons to-day,' replied Lucian.

'Hear him!' she said, making a grimace. 'What do they do with little boys who won't go to school, Boggles—eh?'

If Lucian had known more of a world with which he had never, poor child, had much opportunity of making acquaintance, he would have seen that Sprats was meditating mischief. Her eyes began to glitter: she smiled demurely.

'Are you coming peaceably?' she asked.

'But I'm not coming at all,' replied Lucian.

'Aren't you, though? We'll soon settle that, won't we, Boggles?' she exclaimed. 'Now then, monkey—off you go!'

She was on him with a rush before he knew what was about to happen, and had lifted him off his feet and swung him on to her shoulder ere he could escape her. Lucian expostulated and beseeched; Sprats, shouting and laughing, made for a gap in the hedgerow; Boggles, hugely delighted, following in the wake. At the gap a battle royal ensued—Lucian fighting to free himself, the girl clinging on to him with all the strength of her vigorous young arms.

'Let me go, I say!' cried Lucian. 'Let me down!'

'You'd best to go quiet and peaceable, Master Lucian,' counselled Boggles. 'Miss Millie ain't one to be denied of anything.'

'But I won't be carried!' shouted Lucian, half mad with rage. 'I won't....'

He got no further. Sprats, holding on tight to her captive, caught her foot in a branch as she struggled over the gap, and pitched headlong through. There was a steep bank at the other side with a wide ditch of water at its foot: Boggles, staring over the hedge with all his eyes, beheld captor and captive, an inextricable mass of legs and arms, turn a series of hurried somersaults and collapse into the duck-weed and water-lilies with a splash that drowned their mutual screams of rage, indignation, and delight.

CHAPTER VII

It followed as a matter of inevitable consequence that Lucian and Sprats when they emerged from the waters of the wayside ditch had become fast friends for life; from that time forward they were as David and Jonathan, loving much, and having full confidence in each other. They became inseparable, and their lives were spent together from an early hour of the morning until the necessary bedtime. The vicar was to a certain degree shelved: his daughter possessed the charm of youth and high spirits which was wanting in him. He became a species of elder brother, who was useful in teaching one things and good company on occasions. He, like the philosopher which life had made him, accepted the situation. He saw that the devotion which Lucian had been about to pour out at his own feet had by a sudden whim of fate been diverted to his daughter, and he smiled. He took from these two children all that they gave him, and was sometimes gorged to satiety and sometimes kept on short commons, according to their vagaries and moods. Like all young and healthy things, they believed that the world had been made for their own particular benefit, and they absorbed it. Perhaps there had never been such a close companionship as that which sprang up between these two. The trifling fact that one was a boy and the other a girl never seemed to strike them: they were sexless and savage in their freedom. Under Sprats's fostering care Lucian developed a new side of his character: she taught him to play cricket and football, to climb trees and precipices, to fish and to ride, and to be an out-of-door boy in every way. He, on his part, repaid her by filling her mind with much of his own learning: she became as familiar with the scenes of his childhood as if she had lived in them herself.

For three years the vicar, Sprats, and Lucian lived in a world of their own, with the Pepperdines as a closely fitting environment. Miss Pepperdine was accustomed to remark that she did not know whether Lucian really lived at the farm or at the vicarage, but as the vicar often made a similar observation with respect to his daughter, things appeared to be equalised. It was true that the two children treated the houses with equal freedom. If they happened to be at the farm about dinner-time they dined there, but the vicarage would have served them equally well if it had harboured them when the luncheon-bell rang. Mr. Pepperdine was greatly delighted when he found them filling a side of his board: their remarks on things in general, their debates, disputes, and more than all, their quarrels, afforded him much amusement. They were not so well understood by Miss Pepperdine, who considered the young lady from the vicarage to be something of a hoyden, and thought it the vicar's duty to marry again and provide his offspring with a mother.

'And a pretty time she'd have!' remarked Mr. Pepperdine, to whom this sage reflection was offered. 'A nice handful for anybody, is that young Sprats—as full of mischief as an egg is full of meat. But a good ge'l, a good ge'l, Keziah, and with a warm heart, you make no mistake.'

Sprats's kindness of heart, indeed, was famous throughout the village. She was her father's almoner, and tempered charity with discrimination in a way that would have done credit to a professional philanthropist. She made periodical visits through the village, followed by Lucian, who meekly carried a large basket containing toothsome and seasonable doles, which were handed out to this or that old woman in accordance with Sprats's instructions. The instinct of mothering something was strong within her. From the moment of her return from school she had taken her father in hand and had shaken him up and pulled him together. He had contracted bad habits as regards food and was becoming dyspeptic; he was careless about his personal comfort and neglectful of his health—Sprats dragooned him into the paths of rectitude. But she extended her mothering instincts to Lucian even more than to her father. She treated him at times as if he were a child with whom it was unnecessary to reason; there was always an affectionate solicitude in her attitude towards him which was, perhaps, most marked when she bullied him into subjection. Once when he was ill and confined to his room for a week or two she took up her quarters at the farm, summarily dismissed Keziah and Judith from attendance on the invalid, and nursed him back to convalescence. It was useless to argue with her on these occasions. Sprats, as Boggles had truly said, was not one to be denied of anything, and every year made it more manifest that when she had picked Lucian up in the turnip-field and had fallen headlong into the ditch with him, it had been a figure of her future interest in his welfare.

It was in the fourth summer of Lucian's residence at Simonstower, and he was fifteen and Sprats nearly two years older, when the serpent stole into their Paradise. Until the serpent came all had gone well with them. Sprats was growing a fine girl; she was more rudely healthy than ever, and just as sunburned; her freckles had increased rather than decreased; her hair, which was growing deeper in colour, was a perpetual nuisance to her. She had grown a little quieter in manner, but would break out at times; the mere fact that she wore longer skirts did not prevent her from climbing trees

40

or playing cricket. And she and Lucian were still hand-in-glove, still David and Jonathan; she had no friends of her own sex, and he none of his; each was in a happy state of perfect content. But the stage of absolute perfection is by no means assured even in the Arcadia of childhood—it may endure for a time, but sooner or later it must be broken in upon, and not seldom in a rudely sudden way.

The breaking up of the old things began one Sunday morning in summer, in the cool shade of the ancient church. Nothing heralded the momentous event; everything was as placid as it always was. Lucian, sitting in the pew sacred to the family of Pepperdine, looked about him and saw just what he saw every Sunday. Mr. Pepperdine was at the end of the pew in his best clothes; Miss Pepperdine was gorgeous in black silk and bugles; Miss Judith looked very handsome in her pearl-grey. In the vicarage pew, all alone, sat Sprats in solemn state. Her freckled face shone with much polishing; her sailor hat was quite straight; as for the rest of her, she was clothed in a simple blouse and a plain skirt, and there were no tears in either. All the rest was as usual. The vicar's surplice had been newly washed, and Sprats had mended a bit of his hood, which had become frayed by hanging on a nail in the vestry, but otherwise he presented no different appearance to that which always characterised him. There were the same faces, and the same expressions upon them, in every pew, and that surely was the same bee that always buzzed while they waited for the service to begin, and the three bells in the tower droned out. 'Come to church—come to church—come to church!'

It was at this very moment that the serpent stole into Paradise. The vicar had broken the silence with 'When the wicked man turneth away from his wickedness,' and everybody had begun to rustle the leaves of their prayer-books, when the side-door of the chancel opened and the Earl of Simonstower, very tall, and very gaunt, and very irascible in appearance, entered in advance of two ladies, whom he marshalled to the castle pew with as much grace and dignity as his gout would allow. Lucian and Sprats, with a wink to each other which no one else perceived, examined the earl's companions during the recitation of the General Confession, looking through the slits of their hypocritical fingers. The elder lady appeared to be a woman of fashion: she was dressed in a style not often seen at Simonstower, and her attire, her lorgnette, her vinaigrette, her fan, and her airs and graces formed a delightful contrast to the demeanour of the old earl, who was famous for the rustiness of his garments, and stuck like a leech to the fashion of the 'forties.'

But it was neither earl nor simpering madam at which Lucian

41

gazed at surreptitious moments during the rest of the service. The second of the ladies to enter into the pew of the great house was a girl of sixteen, ravishingly pretty, and gay as a peacock in female flaunts and fineries which dazzled Lucian's eyes. She was dark, and her eyes were shaded by exceptionally long lashes which swept a creamy cheek whereon there appeared the bloom of the peach, fresh, original, bewitching; her hair, curling over her shoulders from beneath a white sun-bonnet, artfully designed to communicate an air of innocence to its wearer, was of the same blue-black hue that distinguished Lucian's own curls. It chanced that the boy had just read some extracts from Don Juan: it seemed to him that here was Haidee in the very flesh. A remarkably strange sensation suddenly developed in the near region of his heart—Lucian for the first time in his life had fallen in love. He felt sick and queer and almost stifled; Miss Pepperdine noticed a drawn expression on his face, and passed him a mint lozenge. He put it in his mouth—something nearly choked him, but he had a vague suspicion that the lozenge had nothing to do with it.

Mr. Chilverstone had a trick of being long-winded if he found a text that appealed to him, and when Lucian heard the subject of that morning's discourse he feared that the congregation was in for a sermon of at least half an hour's duration. The presence of the Earl of Simonstower, however, kept the vicar within reasonable bounds, and Lucian was devoutly thankful. He had never wished for anything so much in all his life as he then wished to be out of church and safely hidden in the vicarage, where he always lunched on Sunday, or in some corner of the woods. For the girl in the earl's pew was discomposing, not merely because of her prettiness but because she would stare at him, Lucian. He, temperamentally shy where women were concerned, had only dared to look at her now and then; she, on the contrary, having once seen him looked at nothing else. He knew that she was staring at him all through the sermon. He grew hot and uncomfortable and wriggled, and Miss Judith increased his confusion by asking him if he were not quite well. It was with a great sense of relief that he heard Mr. Chilverstone wind up his sermon and begin the Ascription—he felt that he could not stand the fire of the girl's eyes any longer.

He joined Sprats in the porch and seemed in a great hurry to retreat upon the vicarage. Sprats, however, had other views—she wanted to speak to various old women and to Miss Pepperdine, and Lucian had to remain with her. Fate was cruel—the earl, for some mad reason or other, brought his visitors down the church instead of taking them out by the chancel door; consequently Haidee passed close by Lucian. He looked at her; she raised demure eyelids and

42

looked at him. The soul within him became as water—he was lost. He seemed to float into space; his head burned, his heart turned icy-cold, and he shut his eyes, or thought he did. When he opened them again the girl, a dainty dream of white, was vanishing, and Sprats and Miss Judith were asking him if he didn't feel well. New-born love fostered dissimulation: he complained of a sick headache. The maternal instinct was immediately aroused in Sprats: she conducted him homewards, stretched him on a comfortable sofa in a darkened room, and bathed his forehead with eau-de-cologne. Her care and attention were pleasant, but Lucian's thoughts were of the girl whose eyes had smitten him to the heart.

The sick headache formed an excellent cloak for the shortcomings of the afternoon and evening. He recovered sufficiently to eat some lunch, and he afterwards lay on a rug in the garden and was tended by the faithful Sprats with a fan and more eau-de-cologne. He kept his eyes shut most of the time, and thought of Haidee. Her name, he said to himself, must be Haidee—no other name would fit her eyes, her hair, and her red lips. He trembled when he thought of her lips; Sprats noticed it, and wondered if he was going to have rheumatic fever or ague. She fetched a clinical thermometer out of the house and took his temperature. It was quite normal, and she was reassured, but still a little puzzled. When tea-time came she brought his tea and her own out into the garden—she observed that he ate languidly, and only asked twice for strawberries. She refused to allow him to go to church in the evening, and conducted him to the farm herself. On the way, talking of the events of the day, she asked him if he had noticed the stuck-up doll in the earl's pew. Lucian dissembled, and replied in an indifferent tone—it appeared from his reply that he had chiefly observed the elder lady, and had wondered who she was. Sprats was able to inform him upon this point—she was a Mrs. Brinklow, a connection, cousin, half-cousin, or something, of Lord Simonstower's, and the girl was her daughter, and her name was Haidee.

Lucian knew it—it was Fate, it was Destiny. He had had dreams that some such mate as this was reserved for him in the Pandora's box which was now being opened to him. Haidee! He nearly choked with emotion, and Sprats became certain that he was suffering from indigestion. She had private conversation with Miss Pepperdine at the farm on the subject of Lucian's indisposition, with the result that a cooling draught was administered to him and immediate bed insisted upon. He retired with meek resignation; as a matter of fact solitude was attractive—he wanted to think of Haidee.

43

In the silent watches of the night—disturbed but twice, once by Miss Pepperdine with more medicine, and once by Miss Judith with nothing but solicitude—he realised the entire situation. Haidee had dawned upon him, and the Thing was begun which made all poets mighty. He would be miserable, but he would be great. She was a high-born maiden, who sat in the pews of earls, and he was—he was not exactly sure what he was. She would doubtless look upon him with scorn: well, he would make the world ring with his name and fame; he would die in a cloud of glory, fighting for some oppressed nation, as Byron did, and then she would be sorry, and possibly weep for him. By eleven o'clock he felt as if he had been in love all his life; by midnight he was asleep and dreaming that Haidee was locked up in a castle on the Rhine, and that he had sworn to release her and carry her away to liberty and love. He woke early next morning, and wrote some verses in the metre and style of my Lord Byron's famous address to a maiden of Athens; by breakfast-time he knew them by heart.

It was all in accordance with the decrees of Fate that Lucian and Haidee were quickly brought into each other's company. Two days after the interchange of glances in the church porch the boy rushed into the dining-room at the vicarage one afternoon, and found himself confronted by a group of persons, of whom he for the first bewildering moment recognised but one. When he realised that the earth was not going to open and swallow him, and that he could not escape without shame, he saw that the Earl of Simonstower, Mrs. Brinklow, Mr. Chilverstone, and Sprats were in the room as well as Haidee. It was fortunate that Mrs. Brinklow, who had an eye for masculine beauty and admired pretty boys, took a great fancy to him, and immediately began to pet him in a manner which he bitterly resented. That cooled him, and gave him self-possession. He contrived to extricate himself from her caresses with dignity, and replied to the questions which the earl put to him about his studies with modesty and courage. Sprats conducted Haidee to the garden to inspect her collection of animals; Lucian went with them, and became painfully aware that for every glance which he and Haidee bestowed on rabbits, white mice, piebald rats, and guinea-pigs, they gave two to each other. Each glance acted like an electric thrill—it seemed to Lucian that she was the very spirit of love, made flesh for him to worship. Sprats, however, had an opinion of Miss Brinklow which was diametrically opposed to his own, and she expressed it with great freedom. On any other occasion he would have quarrelled with her: the shame and modesty of love kept him silent; he dared not defend his lady against one of her own sex.

It was in the economy of Lucian's dream that he and Haidee

were to be separated by cruel and inexorable Fate: Haidee, however, had no intention of permitting Fate or anything else to rob her of her just dues. On the afternoon of the very next day Lord Simonstower sent for Lucian to read an Italian magazine to him; Haidee, whose mother loved long siestas on summer days, and was naturally inclined to let her daughter manage her own affairs, contrived to waylay the boy with the beautiful eyes as he left the Castle, and as pretty a piece of comedy ensued as one could wish to see. They met again, and then they met in secret, and Lucian became bold and Haidee alluring, and the woods by the river, and the ruins in the Castle, might have whispered of romantic scenes. And at last Lucian could keep his secret no longer, and there came a day when he poured into Sprats's surprised and sisterly ear the momentous tidings that he and Haidee had plighted their troth for ever and a day, and loved more madly and despairingly than lovers ever had loved since Leander swam to Hero across the Hellespont.

CHAPTER VIII

Sprats was of an eminently practical turn of mind. She wanted to know what was to come of all this. To her astonishment she discovered that Lucian was already full of plans for assuring bread and butter and many other things for himself and his bride, and had arranged their future on a cut-and-dried scheme. He was going to devote himself to his studies more zealously than ever, and to practise himself in the divine art which was his gift. At twenty he would publish his first volume of poems, in English and in Italian; at the same time he would produce a great blank verse tragedy at Milan and in London, and his name would be extolled throughout Europe, and he himself probably crowned with laurel at Rome, or Florence, or somewhere. He would be famous, and also rich, and he would then claim the hand of Haidee, who in the meantime would have waited for him with the fidelity of a Penelope. After that, of course, there would follow eternal bliss—it was not necessary to look further ahead. But he added, with lordly condescension, that he and Haidee would always love Sprats, and she, if she liked, might live with them.

'Did Haidee tell you to tell me so?' asked Sprats, 'because the prospect is not exactly alluring. No, thank you, my dear—I'm not so fond of Haidee as all that. But I will teach her to mend your clothes and darn your socks, if you like—it will be a useful accomplishment.'

Lucian made no reply to this generous offer. He knew that there was no love lost between the two girls, and could not quite understand why, any more than he could realise that they were sisters under their skins. He understood the Sprats of the sisterly, maternal, good-chum side; but Haidee was an ethereal being though possessed of a sound appetite. He wished that Sprats were more sympathetic about his lady-love; she was sympathetic enough about himself, and she listened to his rhapsodies with a certain amount of curiosity which was gratifying to his pride. But when he remarked that she too would have a lover some day, Sprats's rebellious nature rose up and kicked vigorously.

'Thank you!' she said, 'but I don't happen to want anything of that sort. If you could only see what an absolute fool you look when you are anywhere within half a mile of Haidee, you'd soon arrive at the conclusion that spooniness doesn't improve a fellow! I suppose it's all natural, but I never expected it of you, you know, Lucian. I'm sure I've acted like a real pal to you—just look what a stuck-up little monkey you were when I took you in hand!—you couldn't play cricket nor climb a tree, and you used to tog up every day as if you were going to an old maid's muffin-worry. I did get you out of all those bad ways—until the Dolly came along (she is a Dolly, and I don't care!). You didn't mind going about with a hole or two in your trousers and an old straw hat and dirty hands, and since then you've worn your best clothes every day, and greased your hair, and yesterday you'd been putting scent on your handkerchief! Bah!—if lovers are like that, I don't want one—I could get something better out of the nearest lunatic asylum. And I don't think much of men anyhow—they're all more or less babies. You're a baby, and so is his Vicarness' (this was Sprats's original mode of referring to her father), 'and so is your uncle Pepperdine—all babies, hopelessly feeble, and unable to do anything for yourselves. What would any of you do without a woman? No, thank you, I'm not keen about men— they worry one too much. And as for love—well, if it makes you go off your food, and keeps you awake at night, and turns you into a jackass, I don't want any of it—it's too rotten altogether.'

'You don't understand,' said Lucian pityingly, and with a deep sigh.

'Don't want to,' retorted Sprats. 'Oh, my—fancy spending your time in spooning when you might be playing cricket! You have degenerated, Lucian, though I expect you can't help it—it's

46

inevitable, like measles and whooping-cough. I wonder how long you will feel bad?'

Lucian waxed wroth. He and Haidee had sworn eternal love and faithfulness—they had broken a coin in two, and she had promised to wear her half round her neck, and next to the spot where she believed her heart to be, for ever; moreover, she had given him a lock of her hair, and he carried it about, wrapped in tissue paper, and he had promised to buy her a ring with real diamonds in it. Also, Haidee already possessed fifteen sonnets in which her beauty, her soul, and a great many other things pertaining to her were praised, after love's extravagant fashion—it was unreasonable of Sprats to talk as if this were an evanescent fancy that must needs pass. He let her see that he thought so.

'All right, old chap!' said Sprats. 'It's for life, then. Very well; there is, of course, only one thing to be done. You must act on the square, you know—they always do in these cases. If it's such a serious affair, you must play the part of a man of honour, and ask the permission of the young lady's mamma, and of her distinguished relative the Earl of Simonstower—mouldy old ass!—to pay your court to her.'

Lucian seemed disturbed and uneasy.

'Yes—yes—I know!' he answered hurriedly. 'I know that's the right thing to do, but you see, Sprats, Haidee doesn't wish it, at present at any rate. She—she's a great heiress, or something, and she says it wouldn't do. She wishes it to be kept secret until I'm twenty. Everything will be all right then, of course. And it's awfully easy to arrange stolen meetings at present; there are lots of places about the Castle and in the woods where you can hide.'

'Like a housemaid and an under-footman,' remarked Sprats. 'Um—well, I suppose that's inevitable, too. Of course the earl would never look at you, and it's very evident that Mrs. Brinklow would be horrified—she wants the Dolly kid to marry into the peerage, and you're a nobody.'

'I'm not a nobody!' said Lucian, waxing furious. 'I am a gentleman—an Italian gentleman. I am the earl's equal—I have the blood of the Orsini, the Odescalchi, and the Aldobrandini in my veins! The earl?—why, your English noblemen are made out of tradesfolk—pah! It is but yesterday that they gave a baronetcy to a man who cures bacon, and a peerage to a fellow who brews beer. In Italy we should spit upon your English peers—they have no blood. I have the blood of the Cæsars in me!'

'Your mother was the daughter of an English farmer, and your father was a macaroni-eating Italian who painted pictures,' said Sprats, with imperturbable equanimity. 'You yourself ought to go

47

about with a turquoise cap on your pretty curls, and a hurdy-gurdy with a monkey on the top. Tant pis for your rotten old Italy!—anybody can buy a dukedom there for a handful of centesimi!'

Then they fought, and Lucian was worsted, as usual, and came to his senses, and for the rest of the day Sprats was decent to him and even sympathetic. She was always intrusted with his confidence, however much they differed, and during the rest of the time which Haidee spent at the Castle she had to listen to many ravings, and more than once to endure the reading of a sonnet or a canzonet with which Lucian intended to propitiate the dark-eyed nymph whose image was continually before him. Sprats, too, had to console him on those days whereon no sight of Miss Brinklow was vouchsafed. It was no easy task: Lucian, during these enforced abstinences from love's delights and pleasures, was preoccupied, taciturn, and sometimes almost sulky.

'You're like a bear with a sore head,' said Sprats, using a homely simile much in favour with the old women of the village. 'I don't suppose the Dolly kid is nursing her sorrows like that. I saw Dicky Feversham riding up to the Castle on his pony as I came in from taking old Mother Hobbs's rice-pudding.'

Lucian clenched his fists. The demon of jealousy was aroused within him for the first time.

'What do you mean?' he cried.

'Don't mean anything but what I said,' replied Sprats. 'I should think Dickie has gone to spend the afternoon there. He's a nice-looking boy, and as his uncle is a peer of the rel-lum, Mrs. Brinklow doubtless loves him.'

Lucian fell into a fever of rage, despair, and love. To think that Another should have the right of approaching His Very Own!—it was maddening; it made him sick. He hated the unsuspecting Richard Feversham, who in reality was a very inoffensive, fun-loving, up-to-lots-of-larks sort of schoolboy, with a deadly hatred. The thought of his addressing the Object was awful; that he should enjoy her society was unbearable. He might perhaps be alone with her—might sit with her amongst the ruined halls of the Castle, or wander with her through the woods of Simonstower. But Lucian was sure of her—had she not sworn by every deity in the lover's mythology that her heart was his alone, and that no other man should ever have even a cellar-dwelling in it? He became almost lachrymose at the mere thought that Haidee's lofty and pure soul could ever think of another, and before he retired to his sleepless bed he composed a sonnet which began—

48

'Thy dove-like soul is prisoned in my heart
With gold and silver chains that may not break,'

and concluded—

'While e'er the world remaineth, thou shalt be
Queen of my heart as I am king of thine.'

He had an assignation with Haidee for the following afternoon, and was looking forward to it with great eagerness, more especially because he possessed a new suit of grey flannel, a new straw hat, and new brown boots, and he had discovered from experience that the young lady loved her peacock to spread his tail. But, as ill-luck would have it, the earl, with the best intention in the world, spoiled the whole thing. About noon Lucian and Sprats, having gone through several pages of Virgil with the vicar, were sitting on the gate of the vicarage garden, recreating after a fashion peculiar to themselves, when the earl and Haidee, both mounted, came round the corner and drew rein. The earl talked to them for a few minutes, and then asked them up to the Castle that afternoon. He would have the tennis-lawn made ready for them, he said, and they could eat as many strawberries as they pleased, and have tea in the garden. Haidee, from behind the noble relative, made a moue at this; Lucian was obliged to keep a straight face, and thank the earl for his confounded graciousness. Sprats saw that something was wrong.

'What's up?' she inquired, climbing up the gate again when the earl had gone by. 'You look jolly blue.'

Lucian explained the situation. Sprats snorted.

'Well, of all the hardships!' she said. 'Thank the Lord, I'd rather play tennis and eat strawberries and have tea—especially the Castle tea—than go mooning about in the woods! However, I suppose I must contrive something for you, or you'll groan and grumble all the way home. You and the Doll must lose yourselves in the gardens when we go for strawberries. I suppose ten minutes' slobbering over each other behind a hedge or in a corner will put you on, won't it?'

Lucian was overwhelmed at her kindness. He offered to give her a brotherly hug, whereupon she smacked his face, rolled him into the dust in the middle of the road, and retreated into the garden, bidding him turn up with a clean face at half-past two. When that hour arrived she found him awaiting her in the porch; one glance at him showed that he had donned the new suit, the new hat, and the new boots. Sprats shrieked with derision.

'Lord have mercy upon us!' she cried. 'It might be a Bank Holiday! Do you think I am going to walk through the village with a thing like that? Stick a cabbage in your coat—it'll give a finishing touch to your appearance. Oh, you miserable monkey-boy!— wouldn't I like to stick you in the kitchen chimney and shove you up and down in the soot for five minutes!'

Lucian received this badinage in good part—it was merely Sprats's way of showing her contempt for finicking habit. He followed her from the vicarage to the Castle—she walking with her nose in the air, and from time to time commiserating him because of the newness of his boots; he secretly anxious to bask in the sunlight of Haidee's smiles. And at last they arrived, and there, sprawling on the lawn near the basket-chair in which Haidee's lissome figure reposed, was the young gentleman who rejoiced in the name of Richard Feversham. He appeared to be very much at home with his young hostess; the sound of their mingled laughter fell on the ears of the newcomers as they approached. Lucian heard it, and shivered with a curious, undefinable sense of evil; Sprats heard it too, and knew that a moral thunderstorm was brewing.

The afternoon was by no means a success, even in its earlier stages. Mrs. Brinklow had departed to a friend's house some miles away; the earl might be asleep or dead for all that was seen of him. Sprats and Haidee cherished a secret dislike of each other; Lucian was proud, gloomy, and taciturn; only the Feversham boy appeared to have much zest of life left in him. He was a somewhat thick-headed youngster, full of good nature and high spirits; he evidently did not care a straw for public or private opinion, and he made boyish love to Haidee with all the shamelessness of depraved youth. Haidee saw that Lucian was jealous, and encouraged Dickie's attentions—long before tea was brought out to them the materials for a vast explosion were ready and waiting. After tea—and many plates of strawberries and cream—had been consumed, the thick-headed youth became childishly gay. The tea seemed to have mounted to his head—he effervesced. He had much steam to let off: he suggested that they should follow the example of the villagers at the bun-struggles and play kiss-in-the-ring, and he chased Haidee all round the lawn and over the flower-beds in order to illustrate the way of the rustic man with the rustic maid. The chase terminated behind a hedge of laurel, from whence presently proceeded much giggling, screaming, and confused laughter. The festive youngster emerged panting and triumphant; his rather homely face wore a broad grin. Haidee followed with highly becoming blushes, settling her tumbled hair and crushed hat. She remarked with a pout that

50

Dickie was a rough boy; Dickie replied that you don't play country games as if you were made of egg-shell china.

The catastrophe approached consummation with the inevitableness of a Greek tragedy. Lucian waxed gloomier and gloomier; Sprats endeavoured, agonisingly, to put things on a better footing; Haidee, now thoroughly enjoying herself, tried hard to make the other boy also jealous. But the other boy was too full of the joy of life to be jealous of anything; he gambolled about like a young elephant, and nearly as gracefully; it was quite evident that he loved horseplay and believed that girls were as much inclined to it as boys. At any other time Sprats would have fallen in with his mood and frolicked with him to his heart's content; on this occasion she was afraid of Lucian, who now looked more like a young Greek god than ever. The lightning was already playing about his eyes; thunder sat on his brows.

At last the storm burst. Haidee wanted to shoot with bow and arrow at a target; she despatched the two youngsters into the great hall of the Castle to fetch the materials for archery. Dickie went off capering and whistling; Lucian followed in sombre silence. And inside the vaulted hall, mystic with the gloom of the past, and romantic with suits of armour, tattered banners, guns, pikes, bows, and the rest of it, the smouldering fires of Lucian's wrath burst out. Master Richard Feversham found himself confronted by a figure which typified Wrath, and Indignation, and Retribution.

'You are a cad!' said Lucian.

'Cad yourself!' retorted Dickie. 'Who are you talking to?'

'I am talking to you,' answered Lucian, stern and cold as a stone figure of Justice. 'I say you are a cad—a cad! You have grossly insulted a young lady, and I will punish you.'

Dickie's eyes grew round—he wondered if the other fellow had suddenly gone off his head, and if he'd better call for help and a strait waistcoat.

'Grossly insulted—a young lady!' he said, puckering up his face with honest amazement. 'What the dickens do you mean? You must be jolly well dotty!'

'You have insulted Miss Brinklow,' said Lucian. 'You forced your unwelcome attentions upon her all the afternoon, though she showed you plainly that they were distasteful to her, and you were finally rude and brutal to her—beast!'

'Good Lord!' exclaimed Dickie, now thoroughly amazed, 'I never forced any attention on her—we were only larking. Rude? Brutal? Good heavens!—I only kissed her behind the hedge, and I've kissed her many a time before!'

Lucian became insane with wrath.

51

'Liar!' he hissed. 'Liar!'

Master Richard Feversham straightened himself, mentally as well as physically. He bunched up his fists and advanced upon Lucian with an air that was thoroughly British.

'Look here,' he said, 'I don't know who the devil you are, you outrageous ass, but if you call me a liar again, I'll hit you!'

'Liar!' said Lucian, 'Liar!'

Dickie's left fist, clenched very artistically, shot out like a small battering-ram, and landed with a beautiful plunk on Lucian's cheek, between the jaw and the bone. He staggered back.

'I kept off your nose on purpose,' said Dickie, 'but, by the Lord, I'll land you one there and spoil your pretty eyes for you if you don't beg my pardon.'

'Pardon!' Lucian's voice sounded hollow and strange. 'Pardon!' He swore a strange Italian oath that made Dickie creep. 'Pardon!—of you? I will kill you—beast and liar!'

He sprang to the wall as he spoke, tore down a couple of light rapiers which hung there, and threw one at his enemy's feet.

'Defend yourself!' he said. 'I shall kill you.'

Dickie recoiled. He would have faced anybody twice his size with fists as weapons, or advanced on a battery with a smiling face, but he had no taste for encountering an apparent lunatic armed with a weapon of which he himself did not know the use. Besides, there was murder in Lucian's eye—he seemed to mean business.

'Look here, I say, you chap!' exclaimed Dickie, 'put that thing down. One of us'll be getting stuck, you know, if you go dancing about with it like that. I'll fight you as long as you like if you'll put up your fists, but I'm not a fool. Put it down, I say.'

'Coward!' said Lucian. 'Defend yourself!'

He made at Dickie with fierce intent, and the latter was obliged to pick up the other rapier and fall into some sort of a defensive position.

'Of all the silly games,' he said, 'this is——'

But Lucian was already attacking him with set teeth, glaring eyes, and a resolute demeanour. There was a rapid clashing of blades; then Dickie drew in his breath sharply, and his weapon dropped to the ground. He looked at a wound in the back of his hand from which the blood was flowing rather freely.

'I knew you'd go and do it with your silliness!' he said. 'Now there'll be a mess on the carpet and we shall be found out. Here—wipe up that blood with your handkerchief while I tie mine round my hand. We.... Hello, here they all are, of course! Now there will be a row! I say, you chap, swear it was all a lark—do you hear?'

Lucian heard but gave no sign. He still gripped his rapier and stared fixedly at Haidee and Sprats, who had run to the hall on hearing the clash of steel and now stood gazing at the scene with dilated eyes. Behind them, gaunt, grey, and somewhat amused and cynical, stood the earl. He looked from one lad to the other and came forward.

'I heard warlike sounds,' he said, peering at the combatants through glasses balanced on the bridge of the famous Simonstower nose, 'and now I see warlike sights. Blood, eh? And what may this mean?'

'It's all nothing, sir,' said Dickie in suspicious haste, 'absolutely nothing. We were larking about with these two old swords, and the other chap's point scratched my hand, that's all, sir—'pon my word.'

'Does the other chap's version correspond?' inquired the earl, looking keenly at Lucian's flushed face. 'Eh, other chap?'

Lucian faced him boldly.

'No, sir,' he answered; 'what he says is not true, though he means honourably. I meant to punish him—to kill him.'

'A candid admission,' said the earl, toying with his glasses. 'You appear to have effected some part of your purpose. And his offence?'

'He——' Lucian paused. The two girls, fascinated at the sight of the rapiers, the combatants, and the blood, had drawn near and were staring from one boy's face to the other's; Lucian hesitated at sight of them.

'Come!' said the earl sharply. 'His offence?'

'He insulted Miss Brinklow,' said Lucian gravely. 'I told him I should punish him. Then he told lies—about her. I said I would kill him. A man who lies about a woman merits death.'

'A very excellent apothegm,' said the earl. 'Sprats, my dear, draw that chair for me—thank you. Now,' he continued, taking a seat and sticking out his gouty leg, 'let me have a clear notion of this delicate question. Feversham, your version, if you please.'

'I—I—you see, it's all one awfully rotten misunderstanding, sir,' said Dickie, very ill at ease. 'I—I—don't like saying things about anybody, but I think Damerel's got sunstroke or something—he's jolly dotty, or carries on as if he were. You see, he called me a cad, and said I was rude and brutal to Haidee, just because I—well, because I kissed her behind the laurel hedge when we were larking in the garden, and I said it was nothing and I'd kissed her many a time before, and he said I was a liar, and then—well, then I hit him.'

'I see,' said the earl, 'and of course there was then much stainless honour to be satisfied. And how was it that gentlemen of such advanced age resorted to steel instead of fists?'

53

The boys made no reply: Lucian still stared at the earl; Dickie professed to be busy with his impromptu bandage. Sprats went round to him and tied the knot.

'I think I understand,' said the earl. 'Well, I suppose honour is satisfied?'

He looked quizzingly at Lucian. Lucian returned the gaze with another, dark, sombre, and determined.

'He is still a liar!' he said.

'I'm not a liar!' exclaimed Dickie, 'and as sure as eggs are eggs I'll hit you again, and on the nose this time, if you say I am,' and he squared up to his foe utterly regardless of the earl's presence. The earl smiled.

'Why is he a liar?' he asked, looking at Lucian.

'He lies when he says that—that——' Lucian choked and looked, almost entreatingly, at Haidee. She had stolen up to the earl's chair and leaned against its high back, taking in every detail of the scene with eager glances. As Lucian's eyes met hers, she smiled; a dimple showed in the corner of her mouth.

'I understand,' said the earl. He twisted himself round and looked at Haidee. 'I think,' he said, 'this is one of those cases in which one may be excused if one appeals to the lady. It would seem, young lady, that Mr. Feversham, while abstaining, like a gentleman, from boasting of it——'

'Oh, I say, sir!' burst out Dickie; 'I—didn't mean to, you know.'

'I say that Mr. Feversham, like a gentleman, does not boast of it, but pleads that you have indulged him with the privileges of a lover. His word has been questioned—his honour is at stake. Have you so indulged it, may one ask?'

Haidee assumed the airs of the coquette who must fain make admissions.

'I—suppose so,' she breathed, with a smile which included everybody.

'Very good,' said the earl. 'It may be that Mr. Damerel has had reason to believe that he alone was entitled to those privileges. Eh?'

'Boys are so silly!' said Haidee. 'And Lucian is so serious and old-fashioned. And all boys like to kiss me. What a fuss to make about nothing!'

'I quite understand your position and your meaning, my dear,' said the earl. 'I have heard similar sentiments from other ladies.' He turned to Lucian. 'Well?' he said, with a sharp, humorous glance.

Lucian had turned very pale, but a dark flush still clouded his forehead. He put aside his rapier, which until then he had held tightly, and he turned to Dickie.

'I beg your pardon,' he said; 'I was wrong—quite wrong. I offer you my sincere apologies. I have behaved ill—I am sorry.'

Dickie looked uncomfortable and shuffled about.

'Oh, rot!' he said, holding out his bandaged hand. 'It's all right, old chap. I don't mind at all now that you know I'm not a liar. I—I'm awfully sorry, too. I didn't know you were spoons on Haidee, you know—I'm a bit dense about things. Never mind, I shan't think any more of it, and besides, girls aren't worth—at least, I mean—oh, hang it, don't let's say any more about the beastly affair!'

Lucian pressed his hand. He turned, looked at the earl, and made him a low and ceremonious bow. Lord Simonstower rose from his seat and returned it with equal ceremony. Without a glance in Haidee's direction Lucian strode from the hall—he had forgotten Sprats. He had, indeed, forgotten everything—the world had fallen in pieces.

An hour later Sprats, tracking him down with the unerring sagacity of her sex, found him in a haunt sacred to themselves, stretched full length on the grass, with his face buried in his arms. She sat down beside him and put her arm round his neck and drew him to her. He burst into dry, bitter sobs.

'Oh, Sprats!' he said. 'It's all over—all over. I believed in her ... and now I shall never believe in anybody again!'

CHAPTER IX

That night, when the last echoes of the village street had died away, and the purple and grey of the summer twilight was dissolving into the deep blue and gold of night, Sprats knelt at the open window of her bedroom, staring out upon the valley with eyes that saw nothing. She was thinking and wondering, and for the first time in her life she wished that a mother's heart and a mother's arms were at hand—she wanted to hear the beating love of the one and feel the protecting strength of the other.

Something had come to her that afternoon as she strove to comfort Lucian. The episode of the duel; Lucian's white face and burning eyes as he bowed to the cynical, polite old nobleman and strode out of the hall with the dignity and grace of a great prince;

the agony which had exhausted itself in her own arms; the resolution with which he had at last choked everything down, and had risen up and shaken himself as if he were a dog that throws off the last drop of water;—all these things had opened the door into a new world for the girl who had seen them. She had been Lucian's other self; his constant companion, his faithful mentor, for three years; it was not until now that she began to realise him. She saw now that he was no ordinary human being, and that as long as he lived he would never be amenable to ordinary rules. He was now a child in years, and he had the heart of a man; soon he would be a man, and he would still be a child. He would be a child all his life—self-willed, obstinate, proud, generous, wayward; he would sin as a child sins, and suffer as a child suffers; and there would always be something of wonder in him that either sin or suffering should come to him. When she felt his head within her protecting and consoling arm, Sprats recognised the weakness and helplessness which lay in Lucian's soul—he was the child that has fallen and runs to its mother for consolation. She recognised, too, that hers was the stronger nature, the more robust character, and that the strange, mysterious Something that ordains all things, had brought her life and Lucian's together so that she might give help where help was needed. All their lives—all through the strange mystic To Come into which her eyes were trying to look as she stared out into the splendour of the summer night—she and Lucian were to be as they had been that evening; her breast the harbour of his soul. He might drift away; he might suffer shipwreck; but he must come home at last, and whether he came early or late his place must be ready for him.

This was knowledge—this was calm certainty: it changed the child into the woman. She knelt down at the window to say her prayers, still staring out into the night, and now she saw the stars and the deep blue of the sky, and she heard the murmur of the river in the valley. Her prayers took no form of words, and were all the deeper for it; underneath their wordless aspiration ran the solemn undercurrent of the new-born knowledge that she loved Lucian with a love that would last till death.

CHAPTER X

Within twelve months Lucian's recollections of the perfidious Haidee were nebulous and indistinct. He had taken the muse for mistress and wooed her with such constant persistency that he had no time to think of anything else. He used up much manuscript paper and made large demands upon Sprats and his Aunt Judith, the only persons to whom he condescended to show his productions, and he was alike miserable and happy. Whenever he wrote a new poem he was filled with elation, and for at least twenty-four hours glowed with admiration of his own powers; then set in a period of uncertainty, followed by one of doubt and another of gloom—the lines which had sounded so fine that they almost brought tears to his eyes seemed banal and weak, and were not infrequently cast into the fire, where his once-cherished copies of the Haidee sonnets had long since preceded them. Miss Judith nearly shed tears when these sacrifices were made, and more than once implored him tenderly to spare his offspring, but with no result, for no human monster is so savage as the poet who turns against his own fancies. It was due to her, however, that one of Lucian's earliest efforts was spared. Knowing his propensity for tearing and rending his children, she surreptitiously obtained his manuscript upon one occasion and made a fair copy of a sentimental story written in imitation of Lara, which had greatly moved her, and it was not until many years afterwards that Lucian was confronted and put to shame by the sight of it.

At the age of eighteen Lucian celebrated his birthday by burning every manuscript he had, and announcing that he would write no more verses until he was at least twenty-one. But chancing to hear a pathetic story of rural life which appealed powerfully to his imagination, he began to write again; and after a time, during which he was unusually morose and abstracted, he presented himself to Sprats with a bundle of manuscript. He handed it over to her with something of shyness.

'I want you to read it—carefully,' he said.

'Of course,' she answered. 'But is it to share the fate of all the rest, Lucian? You made a clean sweep of everything, didn't you?'

'That stuff!' he said, with fine contempt. 'I should think so! But this——' he paused, plunged his hands into his pockets, and strode up and down the room—'this is—well, it's different. Sprats!— I believe it's good.'

'I wish you'd let my father read it,' she said. 'Do, Lucian.'

'Perhaps,' he answered. 'But you first—I want to know what you think. I can trust you.'

Sprats read the poem that evening, and as she read she marvelled. Lucian had done himself justice at last. The poem was full of the true country life; there was no false ring in it; he had realised the pathos of the story he had to tell; it was a moving performance, full of the spirit of poetry from the first line to the last. She was proud, glad, full of satisfaction. Without waiting to ask Lucian's permission, she placed the manuscript in the vicar's hands and begged him to read it. He carried it away to his study; Sprats sat up later than usual to hear his verdict. She occupied herself with no work, but with thoughts that had a little of the day-dream glamour in them. She was trying to map out Lucian's future for him. He ought to be protected and shielded from the world, wrapped in an environment that would help him to produce the best that was in him; the ordinary cares of life ought never to come near him. He had a gift, and the world would be the richer if the gift were poured out lavishly to his fellow-creatures; but he must be treated tenderly and skilfully if the gift was to be poured out at all. Sprats, country girl though she was, knew something of the harshnesses of life; she knew, too, that Lucian's nature was the sort that would rebel at a crumpled rose-leaf. He was still, and always would be, a child that feels rather than understands.

The vicar came back to her with the manuscript—it was then nearly midnight, but he was too much excited to wonder that Sprats should still be downstairs. He came tapping the manuscript with his fingers—his face wore a delighted and highly important expression.

'My dear,' he said, 'this is a considerable performance. I am amazed, pleased, gratified, proud. The boy is a genius—he will make a great name for himself. Yes—it is good. It is sound work. It is so charmingly free from mere rhetoric—there is a restraint, a chasteness which one does not often find in the work of a young writer. And it is classical in form and style. I am proud of Lucian. You see now the result of only reading and studying the best masters. He is perhaps a little imitative—that is natural; it will wear away. Did you not notice a touch of Wordsworth, eh!—I was reminded of Michael. He will be a new Wordsworth—a Wordsworth with more passion and richer imagery. He has the true eye for nature—I do not know when I have been so pleased as with the bits of colour that I find here. Oh, it is certainly a remarkable performance.'

'Father,' said Sprats, 'don't you think it might be published?'

Mr. Chilverstone considered the proposition gravely.

'I feel sure it would meet with great approbation if it were,' he said. 'I have no doubt whatever that the best critics would recognise its merit and its undoubted promise. I wonder if Lucian would allow the earl to read it?—his lordship is a fine judge of classic poetry, and though I believe he cherishes a contempt for modern verse, he cannot fail to be struck by this poem—the truth of its setting must appeal to him.'

'I will speak to Lucian,' said Sprats.

She persuaded Lucian to submit his work to Lord Simonstower next day;—the old nobleman read, re-read, and was secretly struck by the beauty and strength of the boy's performance. He sent for Lucian and congratulated him warmly. Later on in the day he walked into the vicar's study.

'Chilverstone,' he said, 'what is to be done with that boy Damerel? He will make a great name if due care is taken of him at the critical moment. How old is he now—nearly nineteen? I think he should go to Oxford.'

'That,' said the vicar, 'is precisely my own opinion.'

'It would do him all the good in the world,' continued the earl. 'It is a thing that should be pushed through. I think I have heard that the boy has some money? I knew his father, Cyprian Damerel. He was a man who earned a good deal, but I should say he spent it. Still, I have always understood that he left money in Simpson Pepperdine's hands for the boy.'

Mr. Chilverstone observed that he had always been so informed, though he did not know by whom.

'Simpson Pepperdine should be approached,' said Lord Simonstower. 'I have a good mind to talk to him myself.'

'If your lordship would have the kindness to do so,' said the vicar, 'it would be a most excellent thing. Pepperdine is an estimable man, and very proud indeed of Lucian—I am sure he would be induced to give his consent.'

'I will see him to-morrow,' said the earl.

But before the morrow dawned an event had taken place in the history of the Pepperdine family which involved far-reaching consequences. While the earl and the vicar were in consultation over their friendly plans for Lucian's benefit, Mr. Pepperdine was travelling homewards from Oakborough, whither he had proceeded in the morning in reference to a letter which caused him no little anxiety and perturbation. It was fortunate that he had a compartment all to himself in the train, for he groaned and sighed at frequent intervals, and manifested many signs of great mental distress. When he left Wellsby station he walked with slow and heavy steps along the road to Mr. Trippett's farm, where, as usual, he had left his horse and trap. Mrs. Trippett, chancing to look out of

59

the parlour window, saw him approaching the house and noticed the drag in his step. He walked, she said, discussing the matter later on with her husband, as if he had suddenly become an old man. She hastened to the door to admit him; Mr. Pepperdine gazed at her with a lack-lustre eye.

'Mercy upon us, Mr. Pepperdine!' exclaimed Mrs. Trippett, 'you do look badly. Aren't you feeling well?'

Mr. Pepperdine made an effort to pull himself together. He walked in, sat down in the parlour, and breathed heavily.

'It's a very hot day, ma'am,' he said. 'I'm a bit overdone.'

'You must have a drop of brandy and water,' said Mrs. Trippett, and bustled into the kitchen for water and to the sideboard for brandy. 'Take a taste while it's fresh,' she said, handing him a liberal mixture. 'It'll revive you.'

Mr. Pepperdine sipped at his glass and nodded his head in acknowledgment of her thoughtfulness.

'Thank you kindly,' said he. 'I were feeling a bit badly like. Is the master anywhere about? I would like to see him.'

Mrs. Trippett replied that the master was in the fold, and she would let him know that Mr. Pepperdine was there. She went herself to fetch her husband, and hinted to him that his old friend did not seem at all well—she was sure there was something wrong with him. Mr. Trippett hastened into the house and found Mr. Pepperdine pacing the room and sighing dismally.

'Now then!' said Mr. Trippett, whose face was always cheery even in times of trouble, 'th' owd woman says you don't seem so chirpy like. Is it th' sun, or what?—get another taste o' brandy down your throttle, lad.'

Mr. Pepperdine sat down again and shook his head.

'John,' he said, gazing earnestly at his friend. 'I'm in sore trouble—real bad trouble. I doubt I'm a ruined man.'

'Nay, for sure!' exclaimed Mr. Trippett. 'What's it all about, like?'

'It's all on account of a damned rascal!' answered Mr. Pepperdine, with a burst of indignation. 'Ah!—there's a pretty to-do in Oakborough this day, John. You haven't heard nothing about Bransby?'

'What, the lawyer?'

'Ah, lawyer and rogue and the Lord knows what!' replied Mr. Pepperdine, groaning with wrath and misery. 'He's gone and cleared himself off, and he's naught but a swindler. They do say there that it's a hundred thousand pound job.'

Mr. Trippett whistled.

'I allus understood 'at he were such a well-to-do, upright sort o' man,' he said. 'He'd a gre't reppytation, any road.'

'Ay, and seems to have traded on it!' said Mr. Pepperdine bitterly. 'He's been a smooth-tongued 'un, he has. He's done me, he has so—dang me if I ever trust the likes of him again!'

Then he told his story. The absconded Mr. Bransby, an astute gentleman who had established a reputation for probity by scrupulous observance of the conventionalities dear to the society of a market town and had never missed attendance at his parish church, had suddenly vanished into the Ewigkeit, leaving a few widows and orphans, several tradespeople, and a large number of unsuspecting and confiding clients, to mourn, not his loss, but his knavery. Simpson Pepperdine had been an easy victim. Some years previously he had consented to act as trustee for a neighbour's family—Mr. Bransby was his co-trustee. Simpson had left everything in Mr. Bransby's hands—it now turned out that Mr. Bransby had converted everything to his own uses, leaving his careless coadjutor responsible. But this was not all. Simpson, who had made money by breeding shorthorns, had from time to time placed considerable sums in the lawyer's hands for investment, and had trusted him entirely as to their nature. He had received good interest, and had never troubled either to ask for or inspect the securities. It had now been revealed to him that there had never been any securities—his money had gone into Mr. Bransby's own coffers. Simpson Pepperdine, in short, was a ruined man.

Mr. Trippett was genuinely disturbed by this news. He felt that his good-natured and easy-going friend had been to blame in respect to his laxity and carelessness. But he himself had had some slight dealings with Mr. Bransby, and he knew the plausibility and suaveness of that gentleman's manner.

'It's a fair cropper!' he exclaimed. 'I could ha' trusted that Bransby like the Bank of England. I allus understood he were doing uncommon well.'

'So he were,' answered Mr. Pepperdine, 'uncommon well—out of fools like me.'

'I hope,' said Mr. Trippett, mentioning the subject with some shyness, 'I hope the gals' money isn't lost, an' all?'

'What, Keziah and Judith? Nay, nay,' replied Mr. Pepperdine. 'It isn't. What bit they have—matter of five hundred pound each, may be—is safe enough.'

'Nor the lad's, either,' said Mr. Trippett.

'The lad's?' said Mr. Pepperdine questioningly. 'Oh, Lucian? Oh—ay—of course, he's all right.'

Mr. Trippett went over to the sideboard, produced the whisky decanter, mixed himself a glass, lighted his pipe, and proceeded to think hard.

'Well,' he said, after some time, 'I know what I should do if I were i' your case, Simpson. I should go to his lordship and tell him all about it.'

Mr. Pepperdine started and looked surprised.

'I've never asked a favour of him yet,' he said. 'I don't know—'

'I didn't say aught about asking any favour,' said Mr. Trippett. 'I said—go and tell his lordship all about it. He's the reppytation of being a long-headed 'un, has Lord Simonstower—he'll happen suggest summut.'

Mr. Pepperdine rubbed his chin meditatively.

'He's a sharp-tongued old gentleman,' he said; 'I've always fought a bit shy of him. Him an' me had a bit of a difference twenty years since.'

'Let bygones be bygones,' counselled Mr. Trippett. 'You and your fathers afore you have been on his land and his father's land a bonny stretch o' time.'

'Three hundred and seventy-five year come next spring,' said Mr. Pepperdine.

'And he'll not see you turned off wi'out knowing why,' said Mr. Trippett with conviction. 'Any road, it'll do no harm to tell him how you stand. He'd have to hear on't sooner or later, and he'd best hear it from yourself.'

Turning this sage counsel over in his mind, Mr. Pepperdine journeyed homewards, and as luck would have it he met the earl near the gates of the Castle. Lord Simonstower had just left the vicarage, and Mr. Pepperdine was in his mind. He put up his hand in answer to the farmer's salutation. Mr. Pepperdine drew rein.

'Oh, Pepperdine,' said the earl, 'I want to have some conversation with you about your nephew. I have just been talking with the vicar about him. When can you come up to the Castle?'

'Any time that pleases your lordship,' answered Mr. Pepperdine. 'It so happens that I was going to ask the favour of an interview with your lordship on my own account.'

'Then you had better drive up now and leave your horse and trap in the stables,' said the earl. 'Tell them to take you to the library—I'll join you there presently.'

Closeted with his tenant, Lord Simonstower plunged into his own business first—it was his way, when he took anything in hand, to go through with it with as little delay as possible. He came to the point at once by telling Mr. Pepperdine that his nephew was a gifted youth who would almost certainly make a great name in the world of letters, and that it would be a most excellent thing to send him to

Oxford. He pointed out the great advantages which would accrue to Lucian if this course were adopted, spoke of his own interest in the boy, and promised to help him in every way he could. Mr. Pepperdine listened with respectful and polite attention.

'My lord,' he said, when the earl had explained his views for Lucian, 'I'm greatly obliged to your lordship for your kindness to the lad and your interest in him. I agree with every word your lordship says. I've always known there was something out of the common about Lucian, and I've wanted him to get on in his own way. I never had no doubt about his making a great name for himself—I could see that in him when he were a little lad. Now about this going to Oxford—it would cost a good deal of money, wouldn't it, my lord?'

'It would certainly cost money,' replied the earl. 'But I would put it to you in this way—or, rather, this is the way in which it should be put to the boy himself. I understand he has some money; well, he can make no better investment of a portion of it than by spending it on his education. Two or three years at Oxford will fit him for the life of a man of letters as nothing else would. He need not be extravagant—two hundred pounds a year should suffice him.'

Mr. Pepperdine listened to this with obvious perplexity and unrest. He hesitated a little before making any reply. At last he looked at the earl with the expression of a man who is going to confess something.

'My lord,' he said, 'I'll tell your lordship what nobody else knows—not even my sisters. I'm sure your lordship'll say naught to nobody about it. My lord, the lad hasn't a penny. He never had. Your lordship knows that his father sent for me when he was dying in London—he'd just come back, with the boy, from Italy—and he put Lucian in my care. He'd made a will and I was trustee and executor. He thought that there was sufficient provision made for the boy, but he hadn't been well advised—he'd put all his eggs in one basket—the money was all invested in a building society in Rome, and every penny of it was lost. I did hear,' affirmed Mr. Pepperdine solemnly, 'that the Pope of Rome himself lost a deal of money at the same time and in the same society.'

'That's quite true,' said the earl. 'I remember it very well.

'Well, there it was,' continued Mr. Pepperdine. 'It was gone for ever—there wasn't a penny saved. I never said naught to my sisters, you know, my lord, because I didn't want 'em to know. I never said nothing to the boy, either—and he's the sort of lad that would never ask. He's a bit of a child in money matters—his father (but your lordship'll remember him as well as I do) had always let him have all he wanted, and——'

'And his uncle has followed in his father's lines, eh?' said the earl, with a smile that was neither cynical nor unfriendly. 'Well, then, Pepperdine, I understand that the lad has been at your charges all this time as regards everything—I suppose you've paid Mr. Chilverstone, too?'

Mr. Pepperdine waved his hands.

'There's naught to talk of, my lord,' he said. 'I've no children, and never shall have. I never were a marrying sort, and the lad's been welcome. And if it had been in my power he should have gone to Oxford; but, my lord, there's been that happened within this last day or so that's brought me nigh to ruin. It was that that I wanted to see your lordship about—it's a poor sort of tale for anybody's ears, but your lordship would have to hear it some time or other. You see, my lord'—and Mr. Pepperdine, with praiseworthy directness and simplicity, set forth the story of his woes.

The Earl of Simonstower listened with earnest attention until his tenant had spread out all his ruined hopes at his feet. His face expressed nothing until the regrettable catalogue of foolishness and wrongs came to an end. Then he laughed, rather bitterly.

'Well, Pepperdine,' he said, 'you've been wronged, but you've been a fool into the bargain. And I can't blame you, for, in a smaller way—a matter of a thousand pounds or so—this man Bransby has victimised me. Well, now, what's to be done? There's one thing certain—I don't intend to lose you as a tenant. If nothing else can be done, my solicitors must settle everything for you, and you must pay me back as you can. I understand you've been doing well with your shorthorns, haven't you?'

Mr. Pepperdine could hardly believe his ears. He had always regarded his landlord as a somewhat cold and cynical man, and no thought of such generous help as that indicated by the earl's last words had come into his mind in telling the story of his difficulties. He was a soft-hearted man, and the tears sprang into his eyes and his voice trembled as he tried to frame suitable words.

'My lord!' he said brokenly, 'I—I don't know what to say——'

'Then say nothing, Pepperdine,' said the earl. 'I understand what you would say. It's all right, my friend—we appear to be fellow-passengers in Mr. Bransby's boat, and if I help you it's because I'm not quite as much damaged as you are. And eventually there will be no help about it—you'll have helped yourself. However, we'll discuss that later on; at present I want to talk about your nephew. Pepperdine, I don't want to give up my pet scheme of sending that boy to Oxford. It is the thing that should be done; I think it must be done, and that I must be allowed to do it. With your consent, Pepperdine, I will charge myself with your nephew's expenses for three years from the time he goes up; by the end of the three years he will be in a position to look after himself. Don't try to give me any thanks. I have something of a selfish motive in all this. But now, listen: I do not wish the boy to know that he is owing this to anybody, and least of all to me. We must invent something in the nature of a conspiracy. There must be no one but you, the vicar, and myself in the secret—no one, Pepperdine, and last of all any womankind, so your mouth must be closed as regards your sisters. I will get Mr. Chilverstone to talk to the boy, who will understand that the money is in your hands and that he must look to you. I want you to preach economy to him—economy, mind you, not meanness. I will talk to him in the same way myself, because if he is anything like his father he will develop an open-handedness which will be anything but good for him. Remember that you are the nominal holder of the purse-strings—everything will pass through you. I think that's all I wanted to say, Pepperdine,' concluded the earl. 'You'll remember your part?'

'I shall indeed, my lord,' said Mr. Pepperdine, as he shook the hand which the earl extended; 'and I shall remember a deal more, too, to my dying day. I can't rightly thank your lordship at this moment.'

'No need, Pepperdine, no need!' said Lord Simonstower hastily. 'You'd do the same for me, I'm sure. Good-day to you, good-day; and don't forget the conspiracy—no talking to the women, you know.'

Mr. Pepperdine drove homewards with what country folk call a heart-and-a-half. He was unusually lightsome in mood and garrulous in conversation that evening, but he would only discourse on one topic—the virtues of the British aristocracy. He named no names and condescended to no particulars—the British aristocracy in general served him for the text of a long sermon which amused Miss Judith and Lucian to a high degree, and made Miss Pepperdine wonder how many glasses of whisky Simpson had consumed at the 'White Lion' in Oakborough. It so happened that the good man had been so full of trouble that he had forgotten to take even one—his loquacity that evening was simply due to the fact that while he was preparing to wail De Profundis he had been commanded to sing Te De Laudamus, and his glorification of lords was his version of that pæan of joyfulness.

CHAPTER XI

Lucian received the news which Mr. Chilverstone communicated to him in skilful and diplomatic fashion with an equanimity which seemed natural to him when hearing of anything that appeared to be his just due. He had so far had everything that he desired—always excepting the fidelity of Haidee, which now seemed a matter of no moment and was no longer a sore point—and he took it as a natural consequence of his own existence that he should go to Oxford, the fame of which ancient seat of learning had been familiar to him from boyhood. He made no inquiries as to the cost of this step—anything relating to money had no interest for him, save as regards laying it out on the things he desired. He had been accustomed as a child to see his father receive considerable sums and spend them with royal lavishness, and as he had never known what it was to have to earn money before it could be enjoyed, he troubled himself in nowise as to the source of the supplies which were to keep him at Oxford for three years. He listened attentively to Mr. Pepperdine's solemn admonitions on the subjects of economy and extravagance, and replied at the end thereof that he would always let his uncle have a few days' notice when he wanted a cheque—a remark which made Lord Simonstower's fellow-conspirator think a good deal.

It was impossible at this stage to do anything or say anything to shake Lucian's confidence in his destiny. He meant to work hard and to do great things, and without being conceited he was sure of success—it seemed to him to be his rightful due. Thanks to the influence of his father in childhood and to that of Mr. Chilverstone at a later stage, he had formed a fine taste and was already an accomplished scholar. He had never read any trash in his life, and it was now extremely unlikely that he ever would, for he had developed an almost womanish dislike of the unlovely, the mean, and the sordid, and a delicate contempt for anything in literature that was not based on good models. Mr. Chilverstone had every confidence in him, and every hope of his future; it filled him with pride to know that he was sending so promising a man to his own university; but he was cast down when he found that Lord Simonstower insisted on Lucian's entrance at St. Benedict's, instead of at St. Perpetua's, his own old college.

The only person who was full of fears was Sprats. She had been Lucian's other self for six years, and she, more than any one else, knew his need of constant help and friendship. He was full of simplicity; he credited everybody with the possession of qualities and sympathies which few people possess; he lived in a world of dreams rather than of stern facts. He was obstinate, wayward, impulsive; much too affectionate, and much too lovable; he lived for the moment, and only regarded the future as one continual procession of rosy hours. Sprats, with feminine intuition, feared the moment when he would come into collision with stern experience of the world and the worldly—she longed to be with him when that moment came, as she had been with him when the frailty and coquetry of the Dolly kid nearly broke his child's heart. And so during the last few days of his stay at Simonstower she hovered about him as a faithful mother does about a sailor son, and she gave him much excellent advice and many counsels of perfection.

'You know you are a baby,' she said, when Lucian laughed at her. 'You have been so coddled all your life that you will cry if a pin pricks you. And there will be no Sprats to tie a rag round the wound.'

'It would certainly be better if Sprats were going too,' he said thoughtfully, and his face clouded. 'But then,' he continued, flashing into a smile, 'after all, Oxford is only two hundred miles from Simonstower, and there are trains which carry one over two hundred miles in a very short time. If I should chance to fall and bump my nose I shall take a ticket by the next train and come to Sprats to be patched up.'

'I shall keep a stock of ointments and lotions and bandages in perpetual readiness,' she said. 'But it must be distinctly understood, Lucian, that I have the monopoly of curing you—I have a sort of notion, you know, that it is my chief mission in life to be your nurse.'

'The concession is yours,' he answered, with mock gravity.

It was with this understanding that they parted. There came a day when all the good-byes had been said, the blessings and admonitions received, and Lucian departed from the village with a pocket full of money (largely placed there through the foolish feminine indulgence of Miss Pepperdine and Miss Judith, who had womanly fears as to the horrible situations in which he might be placed if he were bereft of ready cash) and a light and a sanguine heart. Mr. Chilverstone went with him to Oxford to see his protégé settled and have a brief holiday of his own; on their departure Sprats drove them to the station at Wellsby. She waved her handkerchief until the train had disappeared; she was conscious when she turned away that her heart had gone with Lucian.

CHAPTER XII

About the middle of a May afternoon, seven years later, a young man turned out of the Strand into a quiet street in the neighbourhood of Covent Garden and began looking about him as if endeavouring to locate the whereabouts of some particular place. Catching sight of the name William Robertson on a neighbouring window, with the word Publisher underneath it, he turned into the door of the establishment thus designated, and encountering an office-boy who was busily engaged in reading a comic journal inside a small pen labelled 'Inquiries,' he asked with great politeness if Mr. Robertson was at that moment disengaged. The office-boy in his own good time condescended to examine the personal appearance of the inquirer, and having assured himself that the gentleman was worthy his attention he asked in sharp tones if he had an appointment with Mr. Robertson. To this the stranger replied that he believed he was expected by Mr. Robertson during the afternoon, but not at any particular hour, and produced a card from which the office-boy learned that he was confronting the Viscount Saxonstowe. He forthwith disappeared into some inner region and came back a moment later with a young gentleman who cultivated long hair and an æsthetic style of necktie, and bowed Lord Saxonstowe through various doors into a pleasant ante-room, where he accommodated his lordship with a chair and the Times, and informed him that Mr. Robertson would be at liberty in a few moments. Lord Saxonstowe remarked that he was in no hurry at all, and would wait Mr. Robertson's convenience. The young gentleman with the luxuriant locks replied politely that he was quite sure Mr. Robertson would not keep his lordship waiting long, and added that they were experiencing quite summer-like weather. Lord Saxonstowe agreed to this proposition, and opened the Times. His host or keeper for the time being seated himself at a desk, one half of which was shared by a lady typist who had affected great interest in her work since Lord Saxonstowe's entrance, and who now stole surreptitious glances at him as he scanned the newspaper. The clerk scribbled a line or two on a scrap of paper and passed it across to her. She untwisted it and read: 'This is the chap that did that tremendous exploration in the North of Asia: a real live lord, you know.' She scribbled an answering line: 'Of course I know—do you think I didn't recognise the name?' and passed it over with a show of indignation. The clerk indited another epistle: 'Don't look as if he'd seen much of anything, does he?' The girl perused this, scribbled back: 'His eyes and moustache are real jam!' and fell to work at her machine again. The clerk sighed, caressed a few sprouts on his top-lip, and remarking to his own soul that these toffs always catch the girls' eyes, fell to doing nothing in a practised way.

Viscount Saxonstowe, quite unconscious of the interest he was exciting, stared about him after a time and began to wonder if the two young people at the desk usually worked with closed windows. The atmosphere was heavy, and there was a concentrated smell of paper, and ink, and paste. He thought of the wind-swept plains and steppes on which he had spent long months—he had gone through some stiff experiences there, but he confessed to himself that he would prefer a bitter cold night in winter in similar solitudes to a summer's day in that ante-room. His own healthy tan and the clearness of his eyes, his alert look and the easy swing with which he walked, would never have been developed amidst such surroundings, and the consciousness of his own rude health made him feel sorry for the two white slaves before him. He felt that if he could have his own way he would cut the young gentleman's hair, put him into a flannel shirt and trot him round; as for the young lady, he would certainly send her into the country for a holiday. And while he thus indulged his fancies a door opened and he heard voices, and two men stepped into the ante-room.

He instinctively recognised one as the publisher whom he had come to see; at the other, a much younger man, he found himself staring with some sense of recognition which was as yet vague and unformed. He felt sure that he had met him before, and under some unusual circumstances, but he could not remember the occasion, nor assure his mind that the face on which he looked was really familiar—it was more suggestive of something that had been familiar than familiar in itself. He concluded that he must have seen a photograph of it in some illustrated paper; the man was in all likelihood a popular author. Saxonstowe carefully looked him over as he stood exchanging a last word with the publisher on the threshold of the latter's room. He noted the gracefulness of the slim figure in the perfectly fashioned clothes, and again he became conscious that his memory was being stirred. The man under observation was swinging a light walking-cane as he chatted; he made a sudden movement with it to emphasise a point, and Saxonstowe's memory cleared itself. His thoughts flew back ten years: he saw two boys, one the very image of incarnate Wrath, the other an equally faithful impersonation of Amazement, facing each other in an antique hall, with rapiers in hand and a sense of battle writ large upon their faces and figures.

69

'And I can't remember the chap's name!' he thought. 'But this is he.'

He looked at his old antagonist more closely, and with a keener interest. Lucian was now twenty-five; he had developed into a tall, well-knit man of graceful and sinuous figure; he was dressed with great care and with strict attention to the height of the prevalent fashion, but with a close study of his own particular requirements; his appearance was distinguished and notable, and Saxonstowe, little given to sentiment as regards manly beauty, confessed to himself that the face on which he looked might have been moulded by Nature from a canvas or marble of the Renaissance. It was a face for which some women would forget everything,—Saxonstowe, with this thought half-formed in his mind, caught sight of the anæemic typist, who, oblivious of anything else in the room, had fixed all her attention on Lucian. Her hands rested, motionless, on the keys of the machine before her; her head was slightly tilted back, her eyes shone, her lips were slightly parted; a faint flush of colour had stolen into her cheeks, and for the moment she was a pretty girl. Saxonstowe smiled—it seemed to him that he had been privileged to peep into the secret chamber of a girlish soul. 'She would give something to kiss his hand,' he thought.

Lucian turned away from the publisher with a nod; his eye caught Saxonstowe's and held it. A puzzled look came into his face; he paused and involuntarily stretched out his hand, staring at Saxonstowe searchingly. Saxonstowe smiled and gave his hand in return.

'We have met somewhere,' said Lucian wonderingly, 'I cannot think where.'

'Nor can I remember your name,' answered Saxonstowe. 'But—we met in the Stone Hall at Simonstower.'

Lucian's face lighted with the smile which had become famous for its sweetness.

'And with rapiers!' he exclaimed. 'I remember—I remember! You are Dickie—Dickie Feversham.' He began to laugh. 'How quaint that scene was!' he said. 'I have often thought that it had the very essence of the dramatic in it. Let me see—what did we fight about? Was it Haidee? How amusing—because Haidee and I are married.'

'That,' said Saxonstowe, 'seems a happy ending to the affair. But I think it ended happily at the time. And even yet I cannot remember your name.'

Mr. Robertson stepped forward before Lucian could reply. He introduced the young men to each other in due form. Then Saxonstowe knew that his old enemy was one of the great literary lions of the day; and Lucian recognised Saxonstowe as the mighty traveller of whose deeds most people were talking. They looked at each other with interest, and Mr. Robertson felt a glow of pride when he remembered that his was the only imprint which had ever appeared on a title-page of Lucian Damerel's, and that he was shortly to publish the two massive volumes in which Viscount Saxonstowe had given to the world an account of his wondrous wanderings. He rubbed his hands as he regarded these two splendid young men; it did him good to be near them.

Lucian was worshipping Saxonstowe with the guileless adoration of a child that looks on a man who has seen great things and done great things. It was a trick of his: he had once been known to stand motionless for an hour, gazing in silence at a man who had performed a deed of desperate valour, had suffered the loss of his legs in doing it, and had been obliged to exhibit himself with a placard round his neck in order to scrape a living together. Lucian was now conjuring up a vision of the steppes and plains over which Saxonstowe had travelled with his life in his hands.

'When will you dine with us?' he said, suddenly bursting into speech. 'To-night—to-morrow?—the day after—when? Come before everybody snaps you up—you will have no peace for your soul or rest for your body after your book is out.'

'Then I shall run away to certain regions where one can easily find both,' answered Saxonstowe laughingly. 'I assure you I have no intention of wasting either body or soul in London.'

Then they arranged that the new lion was to dine with Mr. and Mrs. Lucian Damerel on the following day, and Lucian departed, while Saxonstowe followed Mr. Robertson into his private room.

'Your lordship has met Mr. Damerel before?' said the publisher, who had something of a liking for gossip about his pet authors.

'Once,' answered Saxonstowe. 'We were boys at the time. I had no idea that he was the poet of whose work I have heard so much since coming home.'

'He has had an extraordinarily successful career,' said Mr. Robertson, glancing complacently at a little row of thin volumes bound in dark green cloth which figured in a miniature book-case above his desk. 'I have published all his work—he leaped into fame with his first book, which I produced when he was at Oxford, and since then he has held a recognised place. Yes, one may say that Damerel is one of fortune's spoiled darlings—everything that he has done has turned out a great success. He has the grand manner in poetry. I don't know whether your lordship has read his great

71

tragedy, Domitia, which was staged so magnificently at the Athenæum, and proved the sensation of the year?'

'I am afraid,' replied Saxonstowe, 'that I have had few opportunities of reading anything at all for the past five years. I think Mr. Damerel's first volume had just appeared when I left England, and books, you know, are not easily obtainable in the wilds of Central Asia. Now that I have better chances, I must not neglect them.'

'You have a great treat in store, my lord,' said the publisher. He nodded his head several times, as if to emphasise the remark. 'Yes,' he continued, 'Damerel has certainly been favoured by fortune. Everything has conspired to increase the sum of his fame. His romantic marriage, of course, was a great advertisement.'

'An advertisement!'

'I mean, of course, from my standpoint,' said Mr. Robertson hastily. 'He ran away with a very beautiful girl who was on the very eve of contracting a most advantageous marriage from a worldly point of view, and the affair was much talked about. There was a great rush on Damerel's books during the next few weeks—it is wonderful how a little sensation like that helps the sale of a book. I remember that Lord Pintleford published a novel with me some years ago which we could not sell at all. He shot his coachman in a fit of anger—that sold the book like hot cakes.'

'I trust the unfortunate coachman was not seriously injured,' said Saxonstowe, who was much amused by these revelations. 'It is, I confess, an unusual method of advertising a book, and one which I should not care to adopt.'

'Oh, we can spare your lordship the trouble!' said Mr. Robertson. 'There'll be no need to employ any unusual methods in making your lordship's book known. I have already subscribed two large editions of it.'

With this gratifying announcement Mr. Robertson plunged into the business which had brought Lord Saxonstowe to his office, and for that time no more was said of Lucian Damerel and his great fame. But that night Saxonstowe dined with his aunt, Lady Firmanence, a childless widow who lived on past scandals and present gossip, and chancing to remark that he had encountered Lucian and renewed a very small acquaintance with him, was greeted with a sniff which plainly indicated that Lady Firmanence had something to say.

'And where, pray, did you meet Lucian Damerel at any time?' she inquired. 'He was unknown, or just beginning to be known, when you left England.'

'It is ten years since I met him,' answered Saxonstowe. 'It was when I was staying at Saxonstowe with my uncle. I met Damerel at Simonstower, and the circumstances were rather amusing.'

He gave an account of the duel, which afforded Lady Firmanence much amusement, and he showed her the scar on his hand, and laughed as he related the story of Lucian's terrible earnestness.

'But I have never forgotten,' he concluded, 'how readily and sincerely he asked my forgiveness when he found that he had been in the wrong—it rather knocked me over, you know, because I didn't quite understand that he really felt the thing—we were both such boys, and the girl was a child.'

'Oh, Lucian Damerel has good feeling,' said Lady Firmanence. 'You wouldn't understand the Italian strain in him. But it is amusing that you should have fought over Haidee Brinklow, who is now Mrs. Lucian. I'm glad he married her, and that you didn't.'

'Considering that I am to dine with Mr. and Mrs. Lucian Damerel to-morrow,' said Saxonstowe, 'it is a bit odd that I don't know any more of them than this. She, I remember, was some connection of Lord Simonstower's; but who is he?'

'Lucian Damerel? Oh, he was the son of Cyprian Damerel, an Italian artist who married the daughter of one of Simonstower's tenants. Simonstower was at all times greatly interested in him, and it has always been my firm impression that it was he who sent the boy to Oxford. At any rate, when he died, which was just before Lucian Damerel came of age, Simonstower left him ten thousand pounds.'

'That was good,' said Saxonstowe.

'I don't know,' said Lady Firmanence. 'It has always seemed to me from what I have seen of him—and I keep my eyes open on most things—that it would have been far better for that young man if fortune had dealt him a few sound kicks instead of so many halfpence. Depend upon it, Saxonstowe, it's a bad thing for a man, and especially for a man of that temperament, to be pampered too much. Now, Lucian Damerel has been pampered all his life—I know a good deal about him, because I was constantly down at Saxonstowe during the last two or three years of your uncle's life, and Saxonstowe, as you may remember, is close to Simonstower. I know how Lucian was petted and pampered by his own people, and by the parson and his daughter, and by the old lord. His way has always been made smooth for him—it would have done him good to find a few rough places here and there. He had far too much flattery poured upon him when his success came, and he has got used to expecting it, though indeed,' concluded the old lady, laughing, 'Heaven knows I'm wrong in saying "got used," for Damerel's one of

73

the sort who take all the riches and luxuries of the world as their just due.'

'He seemed to me to be very simple and unaffected,' said Saxonstowe.

Lady Firmanence nodded the ribbons of her cap.

'Yes,' she said, 'he's sadly too simple, and I wish—for I can't help liking him—that he was as affected as some of those young upstarts who cultivate long hair and velvet coats on the strength of a slim volume printed on one side of the paper only. No—Lucian Damerel hasn't a scrap of affectation about him, and he isn't a poseur. I wish he were affected and that he would pose—I do indeed, for his own sake.'

Saxonstowe knew that his aunt was a clever woman. He held his tongue, asking her by his eyes to explain this desire of hers, which seemed so much at variance with her well-known love of humbug and cant.

'Oh, of course I know you're wondering at that!' she said. 'Well, the explanation is simple enough. I wish Lucian Damerel were a poseur, I wish he were affected, even to the insufferable stage, for the simple reason that if he were these things it would show that he was alive to the practical and business side of the matter. What is he? A writer. He'll have to live by writing—at the rate he and Haidee live they'll soon exhaust their resources—and he ought to be alive to the £ s. d. of his trade, for it is a trade. As things are, he isn't alive. The difference between Lucian Damerel and some other men of equal eminence in his own craft is just this: they are for ever in an attitude, crying out, "Look at me—is it not wonderful that I am so clever?" Lucian, on the other hand, seems to suggest an attitude and air of "Wouldn't it be curious if I weren't?"'

'I think,' said Saxonstowe, 'that there may be some affectation in that.'

'Affectation,' said Lady Firmanence, 'depends upon two things if it is to be successful: the power to deceive cleverly, and the ability to deceive for ever. Lucian Damerel couldn't deceive anybody—he's a child, the child who believes the world to be an illimitable nursery crammed with inexhaustible toys.'

'You mean that he plays at life?'

'I mean that he plays in life,' said Lady Firmanence. 'He's still sporting on his mother's breast, and he'll go on sporting until somebody picks him up, smacks him soundly, and throws him into a corner. Then, of course, he will be vastly surprised to find that such treatment could be meted out to him.'

'Then let us hope that he will be able to live in his world of dreams for ever,' said Saxonstowe.

'So he might, if the State were to establish an asylum for folk of his sort,' said Lady Firmanence. 'But he happens to be married, and married to Haidee Brinklow.'

'My publisher,' remarked Saxonstowe, 'gloated over the romantic circumstances of the marriage, and appeared to think that that sort of thing was good for trade—made books sell, you know.'

'I have no doubt that Damerel's marriage made his books sell, and kept Domitia running at the Athenæum for at least three months longer,' replied Lady Firmanence.

'Were the circumstances, then, so very romantic?'

'I dare say they appealed to the sensations, emotions, feelings, and notions of the British public,' said the old lady. 'Haidee Brinklow, after a campaign of two seasons, was about to marry a middle-aged person who had made much money in something or other, and was prepared to execute handsome settlements. It was all arranged when Lucian burst upon the scene, blazing with triumph, youth, and good looks. He was the comet of that season, and Haidee was attracted by the glitter of his tail. I suppose he and she were madly in love with each other for quite a month—unfortunately, during that month they committed the indiscretion of marriage.'

'A runaway marriage, was it not?'

'Under the very noses of the mamma and the bridegroom-elect. There was one happy result of the affair,' said Lady Firmanence musingly; 'it drove Mrs. Brinklow off to somewhere or other on the Continent, and there she has since remained—she took her defeat badly. Now the jilted gentleman took it in good part—it is said that he is quite a sort of grandpapa in the establishment, and has realised that there are compensations even in being jilted.'

Saxonstowe meditated upon these things in silence.

'Mrs. Damerel was a pretty girl,' he said, after a time.

'Mrs. Damerel is a nice little doll,' said Lady Firmanence, 'a very pretty toy indeed. Give her plenty of pretty things to wear and sweets to eat, and all the honey of life to sip at, and she'll do well and go far; but don't ask her to draw cheques against a mental balance which she never had, or you'll get them back—dishonoured.'

'Are there any children?' Saxonstowe asked.

'Only themselves,' replied his aunt, 'and quite plenty too, in one house. If it were not for Millie Chilverstone, I don't know what they would do—she descends upon them now and then, straightens them up as far as she can, and sets the wheels working once more. She is good to them.'

'And who is she? I have some sort of recollection of her name,' said Saxonstowe.

'She is the daughter of the parson at Simonstower—the man who tutored Lucian Damerel.'

'Ah, I remember—she was the girl who came with him to the Castle that day, and he called her Sprats. A lively, good-humoured girl, with a heap of freckles in a very bright face,' said Saxonstowe.

'She is little altered,' remarked Lady Firmanence. 'Now, that was the girl for Lucian Damerel! She would have taken care of his money, darned his socks, given him plain dinners, seen that the rent was paid, and made a man of him.'

'Admirable qualifications,' laughed Saxonstowe. 'But one might reasonably suppose that a poet of Damerel's quality needs others—some intellectual gifts, for example, in his helpmeet.'

'Stuff and nonsense!' retorted Lady Firmanence. 'He wants a good managing housekeeper with a keen eye for the butcher's bill and a genius for economy. As for intellect—pray, Saxonstowe, don't foster the foolish notion that poets are intellectual. Don't you know that all genius is lopsided? Your poet has all his brain-power in one little cell—there may be a gold-mine there, but the rest of him is usually weak even to childishness. And the great need of the weak man is the strong woman.'

Saxonstowe's silence was a delicate and flattering compliment to Lady Firmanence's perspicacity.

CHAPTER XIII

Lady Firmanence's observations upon the family history of Mr. and Mrs. Lucian Damerel sent Lord Saxonstowe to their house at seven o'clock the following evening with feelings of pleasant curiosity. He had been out of the world—as that phrase is known by people whose chief idea of life is to live in social ant-heaps—long enough to enjoy a renewed acquaintance with it, and since his return to England had found a hitherto untasted pleasure in studying the manners and customs of his fellow-subjects. He remembered little about them as they had presented themselves to him before his departure for the East, for he was then young and unlicked: the five years of comparative solitude which he had spent in the deserts and waste places of the earth, only enlivened by the doubtful company of Kirghese, Tartars, and children of nature, had lifted him upon an eminence from whence he might view civilised humanity with a critical eye. So far everything had amused him—it seemed to him that never had life seemed so small and ignoble, so mean and trifling, as here where the men and women were as puppets pulled by strings which fate had attached to most capricious fingers. Like all the men who come back from the deserts and the mountains, he gazed on the whirling life around him with a feeling that was half pity, half contempt. The antics of the puppets made him wonder, and in the wonder he found amusement.

Mr. and Mrs. Lucian Damerel, as befitted young people untroubled by considerations of economy, resided in one of those smaller streets in Mayfair wherein one may find a house large enough to turn round in without more than an occasional collision with the walls. Such a house is not so comfortable as a suburban residence at one-tenth the rent, but it has the advantage of being in the middle of the known world, and if its frontage to the street is only one of six yards, its exterior may be made pretty and even taking by a judicious use of flowering plants, bright paint, and a quaint knocker. The interior is usually suggestive of playing at doll's house; but the absence of even one baby makes a great difference, and in Lucian's establishment there were no children. Small as it was, the house was a veritable nest of comfort—Lucian and Haidee had the instinct of settling themselves amongst soft things, and surrounding their souls with an atmosphere of æsthetic delight, and one of them at least had the artist's eye for colour, and the true collector's contempt for the cheap and obvious. There was scarcely a chair or table in the rooms sacred to the householders and their friends which had not a history and a distinction: every picture was an education in art; the books were masterpieces of the binder's craft; the old china and old things generally were the despair of many people who could have afforded to buy a warehouse full of the like had they only known where to find it. Lucian knew, and when he came into possession of Lord Simonstower's legacy he began to surround himself with the fruits of money and knowledge, and as riches came rolling in from royalties, he went on indulging his tastes until the house was full, and would hold no more examples of anything. But by that time it was a nest of luxury wherein even the light, real and artificial, was graduated to a fine shade, where nothing crude in shape or colour interfered with the delicate susceptibilities of a poetic temperament.

When Lord Saxonstowe was shown into the small drawing-room of this small house he marvelled at the cleverness and delicacy of the taste which could make so much use of limited dimensions. It was the daintiest and prettiest room he had ever seen, and though he himself had small inclinations to ease and luxury of any sort, he drank in the pleasantness of his surroundings with a distinct sense of personal gratification. The room was empty of human life when he entered it, but the marks of a personality were all over it, and the personality was neither masculine nor feminine—it was the personality of a neuter thing, and Saxonstowe dimly recognised that it meant Art. He began to understand something of Lucian as he looked about him, and to conceive him as a mind which dominated its enveloping body to a love of beauty that might easily degenerate into a slavedom to luxury. He began to wonder if Lucian's study or library, or wherever he worked, were similarly devoted to the worship of form and colour.

He was turning over the leaves of an Italian work, a book sumptuous in form and wonderful in its vellum binding and gold scroll-work, when a rustle of skirts aroused him from the first stages of a reverie. He turned, expecting to see his hostess—instead he saw a young lady whom he instinctively recognised as Miss Chilverstone, the girl of the merry eyes and the innumerable freckles of ten years earlier. He looked at her closely as she approached him, and he saw that the merry eyes had lost some of their roguery, but were still frank, clear, and kindly; some of the freckles had gone, but a good many were still there, adding piquancy to a face that had no pretensions to beauty, but many to the charms which spring from the possession of a kindly heart and a purposeful temperament. Good temper and good health appeared to radiate from Miss Chilverstone; the active girl of sixteen had developed into a splendid woman, and Lord Saxonstowe, as she moved towards him, admired her with a sudden recognition of her feminine strength—she was just the woman, he said to himself, who ought to be the mate of a strong man, a man of action and purpose and determination.

She held out her hand to him with a frank smile.

'Do you remember me?' she said. 'It is quite ten years since that fateful afternoon at Simonstower.'

'Was it fateful?' he answered. 'Yes, I remember quite well. In those days you were called Sprats.'

'I am still Sprats,' she answered, with a laugh. 'I shall always be Sprats. I am Sprats to Lucian and Haidee, and even to my children.'

'To your children?' he said wonderingly.

'I have twenty-five,' she replied, smiling at his questioning look. 'But of course you do not know. I have a private orphanage, all of my own, in Bayswater—it is my hobby. If you are interested in babies and children, do come to see me there, and I will introduce you to all my charges.'

78

'I will certainly do that,' he said. 'Isn't it hard work?'

'Isn't everything hard work that is worth doing?' she answered. 'Yes, I suppose it is hard work, but I like it. I have a natural genius for mothering helpless things—that is why I occasionally condescend to put on fine clothes and dine with children like Lucian and Haidee when they entertain great travellers who are also peers of the realm.'

'Do they require mothering?' he asked.

'Very much so sometimes—they are very particular babies. I come to them every now and then to scold them, smack them, straighten them up, and see that they are in no danger of falling into the fire or upsetting anything. Afterwards I dine with them in order to cheer them up after the rough time they have had.'

Saxonstowe smiled. He had been watching her closely all the time.

'I see,' he said, 'that you are still Sprats. Has the time been very rough to-day?'

'Somewhat rough on poor Haidee, perhaps,' answered Sprats. 'Lucian has wisely kept out of the way until he can find safety in numbers. But please sit down and tell me about your travels until our hostess appears—it seems quite funny to see you all in one piece after such adventures. Didn't they torture you in some Thibetan town?' she inquired, with a sudden change from gaiety to womanly concern.

'They certainly were rather inhospitable,' he answered. 'I shouldn't call it torture, I think—it was merely a sort of gentle hint as to what they would do if I intruded upon them again.'

'But I want to know what they did,' she insisted. 'You look so nice and comfortable sitting there, with no other sign of discomfort about you than the usual I-want-my-dinner look, that one would never dream you had gone through hardships.'

Saxonstowe was not much given to conversation—his nomadic life had communicated the gift of silence to him, but he recognised the sympathetic note in Miss Chilverstone's voice, and he began to tell her about his travels in a somewhat boyish fashion that amused her. As he talked she examined him closely and decided that he was almost as young as on the afternoon when he occasioned such mad jealousy in Lucian's breast. His method of expressing himself was simple and direct and schoolboyish in language, but the exuberance of spirits which she remembered had disappeared and given place to a staid, old-fashioned manner.

'I wonder what did it?' she said, unconsciously uttering her thought.

'Did what?' he asked.

'I was thinking aloud,' she answered. 'I wondered what had made you so very staid in a curiously young way—you were a rough-and-tumble sort of boy that afternoon at Simonstower.'

Saxonstowe blushed. He had recollections of his youthfulness.

'I believe I was an irrepressible sort of youngster,' he said. 'I think that gets knocked out of you though, when you spend a lot of time alone—you get no end of time for thinking, you know, out in the deserts.'

'I should think so,' she said. 'And I suppose that even this solitude becomes companionable in a way that only those who have experienced it can understand?'

He looked at her with some surprise and with a new interest and strange sense of kinship.

'Yes,' he replied. 'That's it—that is it exactly. How did you know?'

'It isn't necessary to go into the deserts and steppes to feel a bit lonely now and then, is it?' she said, with a laugh. 'I suppose most of us get some sort of notion of solitude at some time or other.'

At that juncture Haidee entered, and Saxonstowe turned to her with a good deal of curiosity. He was somewhat surprised to find that ten years of added age had made little difference in her. She was now a woman, it was true, and her girlish prettiness had changed into a somewhat luxurious style of beauty—there was no denying the loveliness of face and figure, of charm and colour, he said to himself, but he was quick to observe that Haidee's beauty depended entirely upon surface qualities. She fell, without effort or consciousness, into poses which other women vainly tried to emulate; it was impossible to her to walk across a room, sit upon an unaccommodating chair, or loll upon a much becushioned sofa in anything but a graceful way; it was equally impossible, so long as nothing occurred to ruffle her, to keep from her lips a perpetual smile, or inviting glances from her dark eyes. She reminded Saxonstowe of a fluffy, silky-coated kitten which he had seen playing on Lady Firmanence's hearthrug, and he was not surprised to find, when she began to talk to him, that her voice had something of the feline purr in it. Within five minutes of her entrance he had determined that Mrs. Damerel was a pretty doll. She showed to the greatest advantage amidst the luxury of her surroundings, but her mouth dropped no pearls, and her pretty face showed no sign of intellect, or of wit, or of any strong mental quality. It was evident that conversation was not Mrs. Damerel's strong point—she indicated in an instinctive fashion that men were expected to amuse and admire her without drawing upon her intellectual resources, and Saxonstowe soon formed the opinion that a judicious use of monosyllables would carry her a long way in uncongenial company. Her beauty had something of sleepiness about it—there was neither vivacity nor animation in her manner, but she was beautifully gowned and daintily perfect, and as a picture deserved worship and recognition.

Saxonstowe was presently presented to another guest, Mrs. Berenson, a lady who had achieved great distinction on the stage, and who claimed a part proprietorship in Lucian Damerel because she had created the part of the heroine in his tragedy, and almost worn herself to skin and bone in playing it in strenuous fashion for nearly three hundred nights. She was now resting from these labours, and employing her leisure in an attempt to induce Lucian to write a play around herself, and the project was so much in her mind that she began to talk volubly of it as soon as she entered his wife's drawing-room. Saxonstowe inspected her with curiosity and amusement. He had seen her described as an embodiment of sinuous grace; she seemed to him an angular, scraggy woman, whose joints were too much in evidence, and who would have been the better for some addition to her adipose tissue. From behind the footlights Mrs. Berenson displayed many charms and qualities of beauty—Saxonstowe soon came to the conclusion that they must be largely due to artificial aids and the power of histrionic art, for she presented none of them on the dull stage of private life. Her hair, arranged on the principle of artful carelessness, was of a washed-out colour; her complexion was mottled and her skin rough; she had an unfortunately prominent nose which evinced a decided partiality to be bulbous, and her mouth, framed in harsh lines and drooping wrinkles, was so large that it seemed to stretch from one corner of an elongated jaw to the other. She was noticeable, but not pleasant to look upon, and in spite of a natural indifference to such things, Saxonstowe wished that her attire had been either less eccentric or better suited to her. Mrs. Berenson, being very tall and very thin, wore a gown of the eighteenth-century-rustic-maiden style, made very high at the waist, low at the neck, and short in the sleeves—she thus looked like a lamp-post, or a bean-stalk, topped with a mask and a flaxen wig. She was one of those women who wear innumerable chains, and at least half-a-dozen rings on each hand, and she had an annoying trick of clasping her hands in front of her and twisting the chains round her fingers, which were very long and very white, and apt to get on other people's nerves. It was also to be observed that she never ceased talking, and that her one subject of conversation was herself.

As Saxonstowe was beginning to wish that his host would appear, Mr. Eustace Darlington was announced, and he found

81

himself diverted from Mrs. Berenson by a new object of interest, in the shape of the man whom Mrs. Damerel had jilted in order to run away with Lucian. Mr. Darlington was a man of apparently forty years of age; a clean-shaven, keen-eyed individual, who communicated an immediate impression of shrewd hard-headedness. He was very quiet and very self-possessed in manner, and it required little knowledge of human nature to predict of him that he would never do anything in a hurry, or in a perfunctory manner—a single glance of his eye at the clock as eight struck served to indicate at least one principal trait of his character.

'It is utterly useless to look at the clock,' said Haidee, catching Mr. Darlington's glance. 'That won't bring Lucian any sooner—he has probably quite forgotten that he has guests, and gone off to dine at his club or something of that sort. He gets more erratic every day. I wish you'd talk seriously to him, Sprats. He never pays the least attention to me. Last week he asked two men to dine—utter strangers to me—and at eight o'clock came a wire from Oxford saying he had gone down there to see a friend and was staying the night.'

'I think that must be delightful in the man to whom you are married,' said Mrs. Berenson. 'I should hate to live with a man who always did the right thing at the right moment—so dull, you know.'

'There is much to be said on both sides,' said Darlington dryly. 'In husbands, as in theology, a happy medium would appear to be found in the via media. I presume, Mrs. Berenson, that you would like your husband to wear his waistcoat outside his coat and dine at five o'clock in the morning?'

'I would prefer even that to a husband who lived on clock-work principles,' Mrs. Berenson replied. 'Eccentricity is the surest proof of strong character.'

'I should imagine,' said Sprats, with a glance at Saxonstowe which seemed to convey to him that the actress was amusing. 'I should imagine that Lord Saxonstowe and Mr. Darlington are men of clock-work principles.'

Mrs. Berenson put up her pince-nez and favoured the two men with a long, steady stare. She dropped the pince-nez with a deep sigh.

'They do look like it, don't they?' she said despairingly. 'There's something in the way they wear their clothes and hold their hands that suggests it. Do you always rise at a certain hour?' she went on, turning to Saxonstowe. 'My husband had a habit of getting up at six in summer and seven in winter—it brought on an extraordinary form of nervous disease in me, and the doctors warned him that they would not be responsible for my life if he persisted. I believe he tried to break the habit off, poor fellow, but he died, and so of course there was an end of it.'

Ere Saxonstowe could decide whether he was expected to reply to the lady's question as to his own habits, the sound of a rapidly driven and sharply pulled-up cab was heard outside, followed by loudly delivered instructions in Lucian's voice. A minute later he rushed into the drawing-room. He had evidently come straight out of the cab, for he wore his hat and forgot to take it off— excitement and concern were written in large letters all over him. He began to gesticulate, addressing everybody, and talking very quickly and almost breathlessly. He was awfully sorry to have kept them waiting, and even now he must hurry away again immediately. He had heard late that afternoon of an old college friend who had fallen on evil days after an heroic endeavour to make a fortune out of literature, and had gone to him to find that the poor fellow, his wife, and two young children were all in the last stages of poverty, and confronting a cold and careless world from the insecure bastion of a cheap lodging in an unknown quarter of the town named Ball's Pond. He described their plight and surroundings in a few graphic sentences, looking from one to the other with quick eager glances, as if appealing to them for comprehension, or sympathy, or assent.

'And of course I must see to the poor chap and his family,' he said. 'They want food, and money, and lots of things. And the two children—Sprats, you must come back with me just now. I am keeping the cab—you must come and take those children away to your hospital. And where is Hoskins? I want food and wine for them; he must put it on top of the hansom.'

'Are we all to go without dinner?' asked Mrs. Damerel.

'By no means, by no means!' said Lucian. 'Pray do not wait longer—indeed I don't know when I shall return, there will be lots to do, and——'

'But Sprats, if she goes with you, will go hungry,' Mrs. Damerel urged.

Lucian stared at Sprats, and frowned, as if some deep mental problem had presented itself to him.

'You can't be very hungry, Sprats, you know,' he said, with visible impatience. 'You must have had tea during the afternoon— can't you wait an hour or two and we'll get something later on? Those two children must be brought away—my God! you should see the place—you must come, of course.'

'Oh, I'm going with you!' answered Sprats. 'Don't bother about us, you other people—angels of mercy are not very pleasant things at the moment you're starving for dinner—go and dine and leave Lucian to me; I'll put a cloak or something over my one swell gown

83

and go with him. Now, Lucian, quick with your commissariat arrangements.'

'Yes, yes, I'll be quick,' answered Lucian. 'You see,' he continued, turning to Saxonstowe with the air of a child who has asked another child to play with it, and at the last moment prefers an alternative amusement; 'it's an awful pity, isn't it, but you do quite understand? The poor chap's starving and friendless, you know, and I don't know when I shall get back, but——'

'Please don't bother about me,' said Saxonstowe; 'I quite understand.'

Lucian sighed—a sigh of relief. He looked round; Sprats had disappeared, but Hoskins, a staid and solemn butler, lingered at the door. Lucian appealed to him with the pathetic insistence of the man who wants very much to do something, and is not quite sure how to do it.

'Oh, I say, Hoskins, I want—some food, you know, and wine, and——'

'Yes, sir,' said Hoskins. 'Miss Chilverstone has just given me instructions, sir.'

'Oh, then we can go!' exclaimed Lucian. 'I say, you really mustn't mind—oh! I am forgetting that I must take some money,' he said, and hurriedly left the room. His wife sighed and looked at Darlington.

'I suppose we may now go to dinner,' she said. 'Lucian will sup on a sandwich somewhere about midnight.'

In the hall they found Sprats enveloped in an ulster which completely covered her dinner-gown; Lucian was cramming a handful of money, obviously taken at random from a receptacle where paper-currency and gold and silver coins were all mingled together, into a pocket; a footman was carrying a case of food and wine out to the cab. Mrs. Berenson insisted on seeing the two apostles of charity depart—the entire episode had put her into a good temper, and she enlivened the next hour with artless descriptions of her various states of feeling. Her chatter amused Saxonstowe; Darlington and Mrs. Damerel appeared to have heard much of it on previous occasions, and received it with equanimity. As soon as dinner was over she announced that if Lucian had been at home she had meant to spend the rest of the evening in expounding her ideas on the subject of the wished-for drama to him, but as things were she would go round to the Empire for an hour—she would just be in time, she said, to see a turn in which the performer, a contortionist, could tie himself into a complicated knot, dislocate every joint in his body, and assume the most grotesque positions, all without breaking himself in pieces.

'It is the grimmest performance,' she said to Saxonstowe; 'it makes me dream, and I wake screaming; and the sensation of finding that the dream is a dream, and not a reality, is so exquisite that I treat myself to it at least once a week. I think that all great artists should cultivate sensations—don't you?'

Upon this point Saxonstowe was unable to give a satisfactory answer, but he replied very politely that he trusted Mrs. Berenson would enjoy her treat. Soon after her departure he made his own adieu, leaving Mrs. Damerel to entertain Darlington and two or three other men who had dropped in after dinner, and who seemed in nowise surprised to find Lucian not at home.

CHAPTER XIV

Lucian swooped down upon the humble dwelling in which his less fortunate fellow resided, like an angel who came to destroy rather than to save. He took everything into his own hands, as soon as the field of operations lay open to him, and it was quite ten minutes before Sprats, by delicate finesse, managed to shut him up in one room with the invalid, while she and the wife talked practical matters in another. At the end of an hour she got him safely away from the house. He was in a pleasurable state of mind; the situation had been full of charm to him, and he walked out into the street gloating over the fact that the sick man and his wife and children were now fed and warmed and made generally comfortable, and had money in the purse wherewith to keep the wolf from the door for many days. His imagination had seized upon the misery which the unlucky couple must have endured before help came in their way: he conjured up the empty pocket, the empty cupboard, the blank despair that comes from lack of help and sympathy, the heart sickness which springs from the powerlessness to hope any longer. He had read of these things but had never seen them: he only realised what they meant when he looked at the faces of the sick man and his wife as he and Sprats left them. Striding away at Sprats's side, his head drooping towards his chest and his hands plunged in his pockets, Lucian ruminated upon these things and became so keenly impressed by them that he suddenly paused and uttered a sharp exclamation.

'By George, Sprats!' he said, standing still and staring at her as if he had never seen her before, 'what an awful thing poverty must be! Did that ever strike you?'

'Often,' answered Sprats, with laconic alacrity, 'as it might have struck you, too, if you'd kept your eyes open.'

'I am supposed to have excellent powers of observation,' he said musingly, 'but somehow I don't think I ever quite realised what poverty meant until to-night. I wonder what it would be like to try it for a while—to go without money and food and have no hope?—but, of course, one couldn't do it—one would always know that one could go back to one's usual habits, and so on. It would only be playing at being poor. I wonder, now, where the exact line would be drawn between the end of hope and the beginning of despair?—that's an awfully interesting subject, and one that I should like to follow up. Don't you think——'

'Lucian,' said Sprats, interrupting him without ceremony, 'are we going to stand here at the street corner all night while you moon about abstract questions? Because if you are, I'm not.'

Lucian came out of his reverie and examined his surroundings. He had come to a halt at a point where the Essex Road is transected by the New North Road, and he gazed about him with the expression of a traveller who has wandered into strange regions.

'This is a quarter of the town which I do not know,' he said. 'Not very attractive, is it? Let us walk on to those lights—I suppose we can find a hansom there, and then we can get back to civilisation.'

They walked forward in the direction of Islington High Street: round about the Angel there was life and animation and a plenitude of bright light; Lucian grew interested, and finally asked a policeman what part of the town he found himself in. On hearing that that was Islington he was immediately reminded of the 'Bailiff's Daughter' and began to recall lines of it. But Islington and old ballads were suddenly driven quite out of his thoughts by an object which had no apparent connection with poetry.

Sprats, keeping her eyes open for a hansom, suddenly missed Lucian from her side, and turned to find him gazing at the windows of a little café-restaurant with an Italian name over its door and a suspicion of Continental cookery about it. She turned back to him: he looked at her as a boy might look whose elder sister catches him gazing into the pastry-cook's window.

'I say, Sprats,' he said coaxingly, 'let's go in there and have supper. It's clean, and I've suddenly turned faint—I've had nothing since lunch. Dinner will be all over now at home, and besides, we're miles away. I've been in these places before—they're all right, really, something like the ristoranti in Italy, you know.'

Sprats was hungry too. She glanced at the little café—it appeared to be clean enough to warrant one in eating, at any rate, a chop in it.

'I think I should like some food,' she said.

'Come on, then,' said Lucian gaily. 'Let's see what sort of place it is.'

He pushed open the swinging doors and entered. It was a small place, newly established, and the proprietor and his wife, two Italians, and their Swiss waiter were glad to see customers who looked as if they would need something more than a cup of coffee and a roll and butter. The proprietor bowed himself double and ushered them to the most comfortable corner in his establishment: he produced a lengthy menu and handed it to Lucian with great empressement; the waiter stood near, deeply interested; the proprietor's wife, gracious of figure and round of face, leaned over the counter thinking of the coins which she would eventually deposit in her cash drawer. Lucian addressed the proprietor in Italian and discussed the menu with him; while they talked, Sprats looked about her, wondering at the red plush seats, the great mirrors in their gilded frames, and the jars of various fruits and conserves arranged on the counter. Every table was adorned with a flowering plant fashioned out of crinkled paper; the ceiling was picked out in white and gold; the Swiss waiter's apron and napkin were very stiffly starched; the proprietor wore a frock coat, which fitted very tightly at the waist, and his wife's gown was of a great smartness. Sprats decided that they were early customers in the history of the establishment—besides themselves there were only three people in the place: an old gentleman with a napkin tucked into his neckband, who was eating his dinner and reading a newspaper propped up against a bottle, and a pair of obvious lovers who were drinking café-au-lait in a quiet corner to the accompaniment of their own murmurs.

'I had no idea that I was so hungry,' said Lucian when he and the proprietor had finally settled upon what was best to eat and drink. 'I am glad I saw this place: it reminds me in some ways of Italy. I say, I don't believe those poor people had had much to eat to-day, Sprats—it is a most fortunate thing that I happened to hear of them. My God! I wouldn't like to get down to that stage—it must be dreadful, especially when there are children.'

Sprats leaned her elbows on the little table, propped her chin in her hands, and looked at him with a curious expression which he did not understand. A half-dreamy, half-speculative look came into her eyes.

'I wonder what you would do if you did get down to that stage?' she said, with a rather quizzical smile.

Lucian stared at her.

'I? Why, what do you mean?' he said. 'I suppose I should do as other men do.'

'It would be for the first time in your life, then,' she answered. 'I fancy seeing you do as other men do in any circumstances.'

'But I don't think I could conceive myself at such a low ebb as that,' he said.

Sprats still stared at him with a speculative expression.

'Lucian,' she said suddenly, 'do you ever think about the future? Everything has been made easy for you so far; does it ever strike you that fortune is in very truth a fickle jade, and that she might desert you?'

He looked at her as a child looks who is requested to face an unpleasant contingency.

'I don't think of unpleasant things,' he answered. 'What's the good? And why imagine possibilities which aren't probabilities? There is no indication that fortune is going to desert me.'

'No,' said Sprats, 'but she might, and very suddenly too. Look here, Lucian; I've the right to play grandmother always, haven't I, and there's something I want to put before you plainly. Don't you think you are living rather carelessly and extravagantly?'

Lucian knitted his brows and stared at her.

'Explain,' he said.

'Well,' she continued, 'I don't think it wants much explanation. You don't bother much about money matters, do you?'

He looked at her somewhat pityingly.

'How can I do that and attend to my work?' he asked. 'I could not possibly be pestered with things of that sort.'

'Very well,' said Sprats, 'and Haidee doesn't bother about them either. Therefore, no one bothers. I know your plan, Lucian— it's charmingly simple. When Lord Simonstower left you that ten thousand pounds you paid it into a bank, didn't you, and to it you afterwards added Haidee's two thousand when you were married. Twice a year Mr. Robertson pays your royalties into your account, and the royalties from your tragedy go to swell it as well. That's one side of the ledger. On the other side you and Haidee each have a cheque-book, and you draw cheques as you please and for what you please. That's all so, isn't it?'

'Yes,' answered Lucian, regarding her with amazement, 'of course it is; but just think what a very simple arrangement it is.'

88

'Admirably simple,' Sprats replied, laughing, 'so long as there is an inexhaustible fund to draw upon. But seriously, Lucian, haven't you been drawing on your capital? Do you know, at this moment, what you are worth?—do you know how you stand?'

'I don't suppose that I do,' he answered. 'But why all this questioning? I know that Robertson pays a good deal into my account twice a year, and the royalties from the tragedy were big, you know.'

'But still, Lucian, you've drawn off your capital,' she urged. 'You have spent just what you pleased ever since you left Oxford, and Haidee spends what she pleases. You must have spent a lot on your Italian tour last year, and you are continually running over to Paris. You keep up an expensive establishment; you indulge expensive tastes; you were born, my dear Lucian, with the instincts of an epicure in everything.'

'And yet I am enjoying a supper in an obscure little café!' he exclaimed laughingly. 'There's not much extravagance here.'

'You may gratify epicurean tastes by a sudden whim to be Spartan-like,' answered Sprats. 'I say that you have the instincts of an epicure, and you have so far gratified them. You've never known what it was, Lucian, to be refused anything, have you? No: well, that naturally inclines you to the opinion that everything will always be made easy for you. Now supposing you lost your vogue as a poet— oh, there's nothing impossible about it, my dear boy!—the public are as fickle as fortune herself—and supposing your next tragedy does not catch the popular taste—ah, and that's not impossible either— what are you going to do? Because, Lucian, you must have dipped pretty heavily into your capital, and if you want some plain truths from your faithful Sprats, you spend a great deal more than you earn. Now give me another potato, and tell me plainly if you know how much your royalties amounted to last year and how much you and Haidee spent.'

'I don't know,' answered Lucian. 'I could tell by asking my bankers. Of course I have spent a good deal of money in travel, and in books, and in pictures, and in furnishing a house—could I have laid out Lord Simonstower's legacy in better fashion? And I do earn large sums—I had a small fortune out of Domitia, you know.'

'There is no doubt,' she replied, 'that you have had enough money to last you for all the rest of your life if it had been wisely invested.'

'Do you mean to say that I have no investments?' he said, half angrily. 'Why, I have thousands of pounds invested in pictures, books, furniture, and china—my china alone is worth two thousand.'

'Dear boy, I don't doubt it,' she answered soothingly, 'but you

89

know it doesn't produce any interest. I like you to have pretty things about you, but you have precious little modesty in your mighty brain, and you sometimes indulge tastes which only a millionaire ought to possess.'

'Well,' he said, sighing, 'I suppose there's a moral at the end of the sermon. What is it, Sprats? You are a brick, of course—in your way there's nobody like you, but when you are like this you make me think of mustard-plaisters.'

'The moral is this,' she answered: 'come down from the clouds and cultivate a commercial mind for ten minutes. Find out exactly what you have in the way of income, and keep within it. Tell Haidee exactly how much she has to spend.'

'You forget,' he said, 'that Haidee has two thousand pounds of her own. It's a very small fortune, but it's hers.'

'Had, you mean, not has,' replied Sprats. 'Haidee must have spent her small fortune twice over, if not thrice over.'

'It would be an unkind thing to be mean with her,' said Lucian, with an air of wise reflection. 'If Haidee had married Darlington she would have had unlimited wealth at her disposal; as she preferred to throw it all aside and marry me, I can't find it in me to deny her anything. No, Sprats—poor little Haidee must have her simple pleasures even if I have to deny myself of my own.'

'Oh, did you ever hear such utter rot!' Sprats exclaimed. 'Catch you denying yourself of anything! Dear boy, don't be an ass— it's bad form. And Haidee's pleasures are not simple.'

'They are simple in comparison with what they might have been if she had married Darlington,' he said.

'Then why didn't she marry Darlington?' inquired Sprats.

'Because she married me,' answered Lucian. 'She gave up the millionaire for the struggling poet, as you might put it if you were writing a penny-dreadful. No; seriously, Sprats, I think there's a good deal due to Haidee in that respect. I think she is really easily contented. When you come to think of it, we are not extravagant— we like pretty things and comfortable surroundings, but when you think of what some people do——'

'Oh, you're hopeless, Lucian!' she said. 'I wish you'd been sent out to earn your living at fifteen. Honour bright—you're living in a world of dreams, and you'll have a nasty awakening some day.'

'I have given the outer world something of value from my world of dreams,' he said, smiling at her.

'You have written some very beautiful poetry, and you are a marvellously gifted man who ought to feel the responsibility of your gifts,' she said gravely. 'And all I want is to keep you, if I can, from the rocks on which you might come to grief. I'm sure that if you took

90

my advice about business matters you would avoid trouble in the future. You're too cock-sure, too easy-going, too thoughtless, Lucian, and this is a hard and a cruel world.'

'It's been a very pleasant world to me so far,' he said. 'I've never had a care or a trouble; I've heaps of friends, and I've always got everything that I wanted. Why, it's a very pleasant world! You, Sprats, have found it so, too.'

'Yes,' she said, 'I have found it pleasant, but it is hard and cruel nevertheless, and one realises it sometimes when one least expects to. One may wake out of a dream to a very cruel reality.'

'You speak as of a personal experience,' he said smiling. 'And yet I swear you never had one.'

'I don't want you to have one,' she answered.

'Is sermonising a cruel reality?' he asked with a mock grimace.

'No, it's a necessary thing; and that reminds me that I have not quite finished mine. Look here, Lucian, here's a straight question to you. Do you think it a good thing to be so very friendly with Mr. Darlington?'

Lucian dropped his knife and fork and stared at her in amazement.

'Why on earth not?' he said. 'Darlington is an awfully good fellow. Of course, I know that he must have felt it when Haidee ran away with me, but he has been most kind to both of us—we have had jolly times on his yacht and at his Scotch place; and you know, Sprats, when you can't afford things yourself it's rather nice to have friends who can give them to you.'

'Lucian, that's a piece of worldliness that's unworthy of you,' she said. 'Well, I can't say anything against Mr. Darlington. He seems kind, and he is certainly generous and hospitable, but it is well known that he was very, very much in love with Haidee, and that he felt her loss a good deal.'

'Yes, it was awfully hard on him,' said Lucian, stroking his chin with a thoughtful air; 'and of course that's just why one feels that one ought to be nice to him. He and Haidee are great friends, and that's far better than that he should cherish any bitter feelings against her because she preferred me to him.'

Sprats looked at him with the half-curious, half-speculative expression which had filled her eyes in the earlier stages of their conversation. They had now finished their repast, and she drew on her gloves.

'I want to go home to my children,' she said. 'One of the babies has croup, and it was rather bad when I left. Pay the bill, Lucian, and get them to call a hansom.'

91

Lucian put his hands in his pockets, and uttered a sudden exclamation of dismay.

'I haven't any money,' he said. 'I left it all with poor Watson. Have you any?'

'No,' she answered, 'of course I haven't. You dragged me away in my dinner-dress, and it hasn't even a pocket in it. What are you going to do?'

'What an awkward predicament!' said Lucian, searching every pocket. 'I don't know what to do—I haven't a penny.'

'Well, you must walk back to Mr. Watson's and get some money there,' said Sprats. 'You will be back in ten minutes.'

'What! borrow money from a man to whom I have just given it?' he cried. 'Oh, I couldn't do that!'

Sprats uttered an impatient exclamation.

'Well, do something!' she said. 'We can't sit here all night.'

Lucian summoned the proprietor and explained the predicament. The situation ended in a procession of two hansom cabs, in one of which rode Sprats and Lucian, in the other the Swiss waiter, who enjoyed a long drive westward and finally returned to the heights of Islington with the amount of the bill and a substantial gratuity in his pocket. As Sprats pointed out with force and unction, Lucian's foolish pride in not returning to the Watsons and borrowing half a sovereign had increased the cost of their supper fourfold. But Lucian only laughed, and Sprats knew that the shillings thrown away were to him as things of no importance.

CHAPTER XV

There had been a moment in Sprats's life when she had faced things—it was when she heard that Lucian and Haidee had made a runaway marriage. This escapade had been effected very suddenly; no one had known that these two young people were contemplating so remarkable a step. It was supposed that Miss Brinklow was fully alive to the blessings and advantages attendant upon a marriage with Mr. Eustace Darlington, who, as head of a private banking firm which carried out financial operations of vast magnitude, was a prize of much consequence in the matrimonial market: no one ever imagined that she would throw away such a chance for mere sentiment. But Haidee, shallow as she was, had a certain vein of romance in her composition; and when Lucian, in all the first flush of manhood and the joyous confidence of youth, burst upon her, she fell in love with him in a fashion calculated to last for at least a fortnight. He, too, fell madly in love with the girl's physical charms: as to her mental qualities, he never gave them a thought. She was Aphrodite, warm, rosy-tinted, and enticing; he neither ate, slept, nor drank until she was in his arms. He was a masterful lover; his passion swept Haidee out of herself, and before either knew what was really happening, they were married. They lived on each other's hearts for at least a week, but their appetites were normal again within the month, and there being no lack of money and each having a keen perception of the joie de vivre, they settled down very comfortably.

Sprats had never heard of Haidee from the time of the latter's visit to Simonstower until she received the news of her marriage to Lucian. The tidings came to her with a curious heaviness. She had never disguised from herself the fact that she herself loved Lucian: now that she knew he was married to another woman she set herself the task of distinguishing between the love that she might have given him and the love which she could give him. Upon one thing she decided at once: since Lucian had elected Haidee as his life's partner, Haidee must be Sprats's friend too, even if the friendship were all on one side. She would love Haidee—for Lucian's sake, primarily: for her own if possible. But when events brought the three together in London, Sprats was somewhat puzzled. Lucian as a husband was the must curious and whimsical of men. He appeared to be absolutely incapable of jealousy, and would watch his wife flirting under his eyes with appreciative amusement. He himself made love to every girl who aroused any interest or curiosity in him—to women who bored him he was cold as ice, and indifferent to the verge of rudeness. He let Haidee do exactly as she pleased; with his own liberty in anything, and under any circumstances, he never permitted interference. Sprats was never able to decide upon his precise feelings for his wife or his attitude towards her—they got on very smoothly, but each went his or her own way. And after a time Haidee's way appeared to run in parallel lines with the way of her jilted lover, Eustace Darlington.

Mr. Darlington had taken his pill with equanimity, and had not even made a wry face over it. He had gone so far as to send the bride a wedding present, and had let people see that he was kindly disposed to her. When the runaways came back to town and Lucian began the meteor-like career which brought his name so

93

prominently before the world, Darlington saw no reason why he should keep aloof. He soon made Lucian's acquaintance, became his friend, and visited the house at regular intervals. Some people, who knew the financier rather well, marvelled at the kindness which he showed to these young people—he entertained them on his yacht and at his place in Scotland, and Mrs. Damerel was seen constantly, sometimes attended by Lucian and sometimes not, in his box at the opera. At the end of two years Darlington was regarded as Haidee's particular cavalier, and one half their world said unkind things which, naturally, never reached Lucian's ears. He was too fond of smoothness in life to say No to anything, and so long as he himself could tread the primrose path unchecked and untroubled, he did not care to interfere in anybody's arrangements—not even in Haidee's. It seemed to him quite an ordinary thing, an everyday occurrence, that he and she and Darlington should be close friends, and he went in and out of Darlington's house just as Darlington went in and out of his.

Lucian, all unconsciously, had developed into an egoist. He watched himself playing his part in life with as much interest as the lover of dramatic art will show in studying the performance of a great actor. He seemed to his own thinking a bright and sunny figure, and he arranged everything on his own stage so that it formed a background against which that figure moved or stood with striking force. He was young; he was a success; people loved to have him in their houses; his photograph sold by the thousands in the shop windows; a stroll along Bond Street or Piccadilly was in the nature of a triumphal procession; hostesses almost went down on their knees to get him to their various functions; he might have dined out every night, if he had liked. He very often did like—popularity and admiration and flattery and homage were as incense to his nostrils, and he accepted every gift poured at his shrine as if nothing could be too good for him. And yet no one could call him conceited, or vain, or unduly exalted: he was transparently simple, ingenuous, and childlike; he took everything as a handsome child takes the gifts showered upon him by admiring seniors. He had a rare gift of making himself attractive to everybody—he would be frivolous and gay with the young, old-fashioned and grave with the elderly. He was a butterfly and a man of fashion; there was no better dressed man in town, nor a handsomer; but he was also a scholar and a student, and in whatever idle fashion he spent most of his time, there were so many hours in each day which he devoted to hard, systematic reading and to his own work. It was the only matter in which he was practical; in all other moods he was a gaily painted, light-winged thing that danced and fluttered in the sunbeams. He was careless, thoughtless, light-hearted, sanguine, and he never stopped to think of consequences or results. But through everything that critical part of him kept an interested and often amused eye on the other parts.

Sprats at this stage watched him carefully. She had soon discovered that he and Haidee were mere children in many things, and wholly incapable of management or forethought. It had been their ill-fortune to have all they wanted all their lives, and they lived as if heaven had made a contract with them to furnish their table with manna and their wardrobes with fine linen, and keep no account of the supply. She was of a practical mind, and had old-fashioned country notions about saving up in view of contingencies, and she expounded them at certain seasons with force and vigour to both Lucian and Haidee. But as Lucian cherished an ineradicable belief in his own star, and had never been obliged to earn his dinner before he could eat it, there was no impression to be made upon him; and Haidee, having always lived in the softest corner of luxury's lap, could conceive of no other state of being, and was mercifully spared the power of imagining one.

CHAPTER XVI

In spite of Sprats's sermon in the little café-restaurant, Lucian made no effort to follow her advice. He was at work on a new tragedy which was to be produced at the Athenæum in the following autumn, and had therefore no time to give to considerations of economy, and when he was not at work he was at play, and play with Lucian was a matter of as much importance, so far as strenuous devotion to it was concerned, as work was. But there came a morning and an occurrence which for an hour at least made him recall Sprats's counsel and ponder rather deeply on certain things which he had never pondered before.

It was ten o'clock, and Lucian and Haidee were breakfasting. They invariably spent a good hour over this meal, for both were possessed of hearty appetites, and Lucian always read his letters and his newspapers while he ate and drank. He was alternately devoting himself to his plate and to a leading article in the Times, when the footman entered and announced that Mr. Pepperdine wished to see him. Lucian choked down a mouthful, uttered a joyous exclamation, and rushed into the hall. Mr. Pepperdine, in all the glories of a particularly horsy suit of clothes, was gazing about him as if he had got into a museum. He had visited Lucian's house before, and always went about in it with his mouth wide open and an air of expectancy—there was usually something fresh to see, and he never quite knew where he might come across it.

'My dear uncle!' cried Lucian, seizing him in his arms and dragging him into the dining-room, 'why didn't you let me know you were coming? Have you breakfasted? Have some more, any way—get into that chair.'

Mr. Pepperdine solemnly shook hands with Haidee, who liked him because he betrayed such ardent and whole-souled admiration of her and had once bought her a pair of wonderful ponies, assured himself by a careful inspection that she was as pretty as ever, and took a chair, but not at the table. He had breakfasted, he said, at his hotel, two hours earlier.

'Then have a drink,' said Lucian, and rang the bell for whisky and soda. 'How is everybody at Simonstower?'

'All well,' answered Mr. Pepperdine, 'very well indeed, except that Keziah has begun to suffer a good deal from rheumatism. It's a family complaint. I'm glad to see you both well and hearty—you keep the roses in your cheeks, ma'am, and the light in your eyes, something wonderful, considering that you are a townbird, as one may say. There are country maidens with less colour and brightness, so there are!'

'You said that so prettily that I shall allow you to smoke a cigar, if you like,' said Haidee. 'Lucian, your case.'

Mr. Pepperdine shook his head knowingly as he lighted a cigar and sipped his whisky and soda. He knew a pretty woman when he saw her, he said to himself, and it was his opinion that Mrs. Lucian Damerel was uncommonly pretty. Whenever he came to see her he could never look at her enough, and Haidee, who accepted admiration on principle, used to smile at him and air her best behaviour. She was sufficiently woman of the world to overlook the fact that Mr. Pepperdine was a tenant-farmer and used the language of the people—he was a handsome man and a dandy in his way, and he was by no means backward, in spite of his confirmed bachelorhood, of letting a pretty woman see that he had an eye for beauty. So she made herself very agreeable to Mr. Pepperdine and told him stories of the ponies, and Lucian chatted of various things, and Mr. Pepperdine, taking in the general air of comfort and luxury which surrounded these young people, felt that his nephew had begun life in fine style and was uncommonly clever.

They went into Lucian's study when breakfast was over, and Lucian lighted a pipe and began to chat carelessly of Simonstower and old times there. Mr. Pepperdine, however, changed the subject somewhat abruptly.

'Lucian, my boy,' he said, 'I'll tell you what's brought me here: I want you to lend me a thousand pounds for a twelvemonth. Will you do that?'

'Why, of course!' exclaimed Lucian. 'I shall be only too pleased—for as long as ever you like.'

'A year will do for me,' answered Mr. Pepperdine. 'I'll explain matters,' and he went on to tell Lucian the story of the Bransby defalcations, and his own loss, and of the late Lord Simonstower's generosity. 'He was very good about it, was the old lord,' he said: 'it made things easy for me while he lived, but now he's dead, and I can't expect the new lord to be as considerate. I've had a tightish time lately, Lucian, my boy, and money's been scarce; but you can have your thousand pounds back at the twelvemonth end—I'm a man of my word in all matters.'

'My dear uncle!' exclaimed Lucian, 'there must be no talk of that sort between us. Of course you shall have the money at once— that is as soon as we can get to the bank. Or will a cheque do?'

'Aught that's of the value of a thousand pounds'll do for me,' replied Mr. Pepperdine. 'I want to complete a certain transaction with the money this afternoon, and if you give me a cheque I can call in at your bank.'

Lucian produced his cheque-book and wrote out a cheque for the amount which his uncle wished to borrow. Mr. Pepperdine insisted upon drawing up a formal memorandum of its receipt, and admonished his nephew to put it carefully away with his other business papers. But Lucian never kept any business papers—his usual practice was to tear everything up that looked like a business document and throw the fragments into the waste-paper basket. He would treasure the most obscure second-hand bookseller's catalogue as if it had been a gilt-edged security, but bills and receipts and business letters annoyed him, and Mr. Pepperdine's carefully scrawled sheet of notepaper went into the usual receptacle as soon as its writer had left the room. And as he crumpled it up and threw it into the basket, laughing at the old-fashioned habits of his uncle, Lucian also threw off all recollection of the incident and became absorbed in his new tragedy.

Coming in from the theatre that night he found a little pile of letters waiting for him on the hall table, and he took them into his study and opened them carelessly. There was a long epistle from Mrs. Berenson—he read half of it and threw that and the remaining sheets away with an exclamation of impatience. There was a note from the great actor-manager who was going to produce the new tragedy—he laid that open on his desk and put a paper-weight upon it. The rest of his letters were invitations, requests for autographs, gushing epistles from admiring readers, and so on—he soon bundled them all together and laid them aside. But there was one which he had kept to the last—a formal-looking affair with the name of his bank engraved on the flap of the envelope, and he opened it with some curiosity. The letter which it enclosed was short and formal, but when Lucian had read it he recognised in some vague and not very definite fashion that it constituted an epoch. He read it again and yet again, with knitted brows and puzzled eyes, and then he put it on his desk and sat staring at it as if he did not understand the news which it was meant to convey to him.

It was a very commonplace communication this, but Lucian had never seen anything of its sort before. It was just a brief, politely worded note from his bankers, informing him that they had that day paid a cheque for one thousand pounds, drawn by him in favour of Simpson Pepperdine, Esquire, and that his account was now overdrawn by the sum of £187, 10s. 0d. That was all—there was not even a delicately expressed request to him to put the account in credit.

Lucian could not quite realise what this letter meant; he said nothing to Haidee of it, but after breakfast next morning he drove to the bank and asked to see the manager. Once closeted with that gentleman in his private room he drew out the letter and laid it on the desk at which the manager sat.

'I don't quite understand this letter,' he said. 'Would you mind explaining it to me?'

The manager smiled.

'It seems quite plain, I think,' he said pleasantly. 'It means that your account is overdrawn to the amount of £187, 10s. 0d.'

Lucian sat down and stared at him.

'Does that mean that I have exhausted all the money I placed in your hands, and have drawn on you for £187, 10s. 0d. in addition?' he asked.

'Precisely, Mr. Damerel,' answered the manager. 'Your balance yesterday morning was about £820, and you drew a cheque in favour of Mr. Pepperdine for £1000. That, of course, puts you in our debt.'

Lucian stared harder than ever.

'You're quite sure there is no mistake?' he said.

The manager smiled.

'Quite sure!' he replied. 'But surely you have had your pass-book?'

Lucian had dim notions that a small book bound in parchment had upon occasions been handed to him over the counter of the bank, and on others had been posted by him to the bank at some clerk's request; he also remembered that he had once opened it and found it full of figures, at the sight of which he had hastily closed it again.

'I suppose I have,' he answered.

'I believe it is in our possession just now,' said the manager. 'If you will excuse me one moment I will fetch it.'

He came back with the pass-book in his hand and offered it to Lucian.

'It is posted up to date,' he said.

Lucian took the book and turned its pages over.

'Yes, but—' he said. 'I—do I understand that all the money that has been paid in to my account here is now spent? You have received royalties on my behalf from Mr. Robertson and from Mr. Harcourt of the Athenæum?'

'You will find them all specified in the pass-book, Mr. Damerel,' said the manager. 'There will, I presume, be further payments to come from the same sources?'

'Of course there will be the royalties from Mr. Robertson every half-year,' answered Lucian, turning the pages of his pass-book. 'And Mr. Harcourt produces my new tragedy at the Athenæum in December.'

'That,' said the manager, with a polite bow, 'is sure to be successful.'

'But,' said Lucian, with a childlike candour, 'what am I to do if you have no money of mine left? I can't go on without money.'

The manager laughed.

'We shall be pleased to allow you an overdraft,' he said. 'Give us some security, or get a friend of stability to act as guarantor for you—that's all that's necessary. I suppose the new tragedy will bring you a small fortune? You did very well out of your first play, if I remember rightly.'

'I can easily procure a guarantor,' answered Lucian. His thoughts had immediately flown to Darlington. 'Yes,' he continued, 'I think we shall have a long run—longer, perhaps, than before.'

Then he went away, announcing that he would make the necessary arrangements. When he had gone, the manager, to satisfy a momentary curiosity of his own, made a brief inspection of Lucian's account. He smiled a little as he totalled it up. Mr. and Mrs.

Lucian Damerel had gone through seventeen thousand pounds in four years, and of that amount twelve thousand represented capital.

Lucian carried the mystifying pass-book to his club and began to study the rows of figures. They made his head ache and his eyes burn, and the only conclusion he came to was that a few thousands of pounds are soon spent, and that Haidee of late had been pretty prodigal with her cheques. One fact was absolutely certain: his ten thousand, and her two thousand, and the five thousand which he had earned, were all gone, never to return. He felt somewhat depressed at this thought, but recovered his spirits when he remembered the value of his pictures, his books, and his other possessions, and the prospects of increased royalties in the golden days to be. He went off to seek out Darlington in the city as joyously as if he had been embarking on a voyage to the Hesperides.

Darlington was somewhat surprised to see Lucian in Lombard Street. He knew all the details of Lucian's business within ten minutes, and had made up his mind within two more.

'Of course, I'll do it with pleasure, old chap,' he said, with great heartiness. 'But I think I can suggest something far preferable. These people don't seem to have given you any particular advantages, and there was no need for them to bother you with a letter reminding you that you owed them a miserable couple of hundred. Look here: you had better open two accounts with us; one for yourself and one for Mrs. Damerel, and keep them distinct—after all, you know, women rather mix things up. Give Robertson and Harcourt instructions to pay your royalties into your own account here, and pay your household expenses and bills out of it. Mrs. Damerel's account won't be a serious matter—mere pinmoney, you know—and we can balance it out of yours at periodic intervals. That's a much more convenient and far simpler thing than giving the other people a guarantee for an overdraft.'

'It seems to be so, certainly,' said Lucian. 'Thanks, very many. And what am I to do in arranging this?'

'At present,' answered Darlington, 'you are to run away as quickly as possible, for I'm over the ears in work. Come in this afternoon at three o'clock, and we will settle the whole thing.'

Lucian went out into the crowded streets, light-hearted and joyous as ever. The slight depression of the morning had worn off; all the world was gold again. A whim seized him: he would spend the three hours between twelve and three in wandering about the city—it was an almost unknown region to him. He had read much of it, but rarely seen it, and the prospect of an acquaintance with it was alluring. So he wandered hither and thither, his taste for the antique leading him into many a quaint old court and quiet alley, and he was fortunate enough to find an old-fashioned tavern and an old-world waiter, and there he lunched and enjoyed himself and went back to Darlington's office in excellent spirits and ready to do anything.

There was little to do. Lucian left the private banking establishment of Darlington and Darlington a few minutes after he had entered it, and he then carried with him two cheque-books, one for himself and one for Haidee, and a request that Mrs. Damerel should call at the office and append her signature to the book wherein the autographs of customers were preserved. He went home and found Haidee just returned from lunching with Lady Firmanence: Lucian conducted her into his study with some importance.

'Look here, Haidee,' he said, 'I've been making some new business arrangements. We're going to bank at Darlington's in future—it's much the wiser plan; and you are to have a separate account. That's your cheque-book. I say—we've rather gone it lately, you know. Don't you think we might economise a little?'

Haidee stared, grew perplexed, and frowned.

'I think I'm awfully careful,' she said. 'If you think——'

Lucian saw signs of trouble and hastened to dispel them.

'Yes, yes,' he said hurriedly, 'I know, of course, that you are. We've had such a lot of absolutely necessary expense, haven't we? Well, there's your cheque-book, and the account is your own, you know.'

Haidee asked no questions, and carried the cheque-book away. When she had gone, Lucian wrote out a cheque for £187, 10s. and forwarded it to his former bankers, with a covering letter in which he explained that it was intended to balance his account and that he wished to close the latter. That done, he put all thoughts of money out of his mind with a mighty sigh of relief. In his own opinion he had accomplished a hard day's work and acquitted himself with great credit. Everything, he thought, had been quite simple, quite easy. And in thinking so he was right—nothing simpler, nothing easier, could be imagined than the operation which had put Lucian and Haidee in funds once more. It had simply consisted of a brief order, given by Eustace Darlington to his manager, to the effect that all cheques bearing the signatures of Mr. and Mrs. Damerel were to be honoured on presentation, and that there was to be no limit to their credit.

CHAPTER XVII

In spite of the amusing defection of his host, Saxonstowe had fully enjoyed the short time he had spent under the Damerels' roof. Mrs. Berenson had amused him almost as much as if she had been a professional comedian brought there to divert the company; Darlington had interested him as a specimen of the rather reserved, purposeful sort of man who might possibly do things; and Haidee had made him wonder how it is that some women possess great beauty and very little mind. But the recollection which remained most firmly fixed in him was of Sprats, and on the first afternoon he had at liberty he set out to find the Children's Hospital which she had invited him to visit.

He found the hospital with ease—an ordinary house in Bayswater Square, with nothing to distinguish it from its neighbours but a large brass plate on the door, which announced that it was a Private Nursing Home for Children. A trim maid-servant, who stared at him with reverent awe after she had glanced at his card, showed him into a small waiting-room adorned with steel engravings of Biblical subjects, and there Sprats shortly discovered him inspecting a representation of the animals leaving the ark. It struck him as he shook hands with her that she looked better in her nurse's uniform than in the dinner-gown which she had worn a few nights earlier—there was something businesslike and strong about her in her cap and cuffs and apron and streamers: it was like seeing a soldier in fighting trim.

'I am glad that you have come just now,' she said. 'I have a whole hour to spare, and I can show you all over the place. But first come into my parlour and have some tea.'

She led him into another room, where Biblical prints were not in evidence—if they had ever decorated the walls they were now replaced by Sprats's own possessions. He recognised several water-colour drawings of Simonstower, and one of his own house and park at Saxonstowe.

'These are the work of Cyprian Damerel—Lucian's father, you know,' said Sprats, as he uttered an exclamation of pleasure at the sight of familiar things. 'Lucian gave them to me. I like that one of Saxonstowe Park—I have so often seen that curious atmospheric effect amongst the trees in early autumn. I am very fond of my pictures and my household gods—they bring Simonstower closer to me.'

'But why, if you are so fond of it, did you leave it?' he asked, as he took the chair which she pointed out to him.

102

'Oh, because I wanted to work very hard!' she said, busying herself with the tea-cups. 'You see, my father married Lucian Damerel's aunt—a very dear, nice, pretty woman—and I knew she would take such great care of him that I could be spared. So I went in for nursing, having a natural bent that way, and after three or four years of it I came here; and here I am, absolute she-dragon of the establishment.'

'Is it very hard work?' he asked, as he took a cup of tea from her hands.

'Well, it doesn't seem to affect me very much, does it?' she answered. 'Oh yes, sometimes it is, but that's good for one. You must have worked hard yourself, Lord Saxonstowe.'

Saxonstowe blushed under his tan.

'I look all right too, don't I?' he said, laughing. 'I agree with you that it's good for one, though. I've thought since I came back that—— ' He paused and did not finish the sentence.

'That it would do a lot of people whom you've met a lot of good if they had a little hardship and privation to go through,' she said, finishing it for him. 'That's it, isn't it?'

'I wouldn't let them off with a little,' he said. 'I'd give them—some of them, at any rate—a good deal. Perhaps I'm not quite used to it, but I can't stand this sort of life—I should go all soft and queer under it.'

'Well, you're not obliged to endure it at all,' said Sprats. 'You can clear out of town whenever you please and go to Saxonstowe—it is lovely in summer.'

'Yes,' he answered, 'I'm going there soon. I—I don't think town life quite appeals to me.'

'I suppose that you will go off to some waste place of the earth again, sooner or later, won't you?' she said. 'I should think that if one once tastes that sort of thing one can't very well resist the temptation. What made you wish to explore?'

'Oh, I don't know,' he answered. 'I always wanted to travel when I was a boy, but I never got any chance. Then the title came to me rather unexpectedly, you know, and when I found that I could indulge my tastes—well, I indulged them.'

'And you prefer the desert to the drawing-room?' she said, watching him.

'Lots!' he said fervently. 'Lots!'

Sprats smiled.

'I should advise you,' she said, 'to cut London the day your book appears. You'll be a lion, you know.'

'Oh, but!' he exclaimed, 'you don't quite recognise what sort of book it is. It's not an exciting narrative—no bears, or Indians, or

103

scalpings, you know. It's—well, it's a bit dry—scientific stuff, and so on.'

Sprats smiled the smile of the wise woman and shook her head.

'It doesn't matter what it is—dry or delicious, dull or enlivening,' she remarked sagely, 'the people who'll lionise you won't read it, though they'll swear to your face that they sat up all night with it. You'll see it lying about, with the pages all cut and a book-marker sticking out, but most of the people who'll rave to your face about it wouldn't be able to answer any question that you asked them concerning it. Lionising is an amusing feature of social life in England—if you don't like the prospect of it, run away.'

'I shall certainly run,' he answered. 'I will go soon. I think, perhaps, that you exaggerate my importance, but I don't want to incur any risk—it isn't pleasant to be stared at, and pointed out, and all that sort of—of——'

'Of rot!' she said. 'No—it isn't, to some people. To other people it seems quite a natural thing. It never seemed to bother Lucian Damerel, for example. You cannot realise the adulation which was showered upon him when he first flashed into the literary heavens. All the women were in love with him; all the girls love-sick because of his dark face and wondrous hair; he was stared at wherever he went; and he might have breakfasted, lunched, and dined at somebody else's expense every day.'

'And he liked—that?' asked Saxonstowe.

'It's a bit difficult,' answered Sprats, 'to know what Lucian does like. He plays lion to perfection. Have you ever been to the Zoo and seen a real first-class, AI diamond-of-the-first-water sort of lion in his cage?—especially when he is filled with meat? Well, you'll have noticed that he gazes with solemn eyes above your head—he never sees you at all—you aren't worth it. If he should happen to look at you, he just wonders why the devil you stand there staring at him, and his eyes show a sort of cynical, idle contempt, and become solemn and ever-so-far-away again. Lucian plays lion in that way beautifully. He looks out of his cage with eyes that scorn the miserable wondering things gathered open-mouthed before him.'

'Does he live in a cage?' asked Saxonstowe.

'We all live in cages,' answered Sprats. 'You had better hang up a curtain in front of yours if you don't wish the crowd to stare at you. And now come—I will show you my children.'

Saxonstowe followed her all over the house with exemplary obedience, secretly admiring her mastery of detail, her quickness of perception, and the motherly fashion in which she treated her charges. He had never been in a children's hospital before, and he saw some sights that sent him back to Sprats's parlour a somewhat sad man.

'I dare say you get used to it,' he said, 'but the sight of all that pain must be depressing. And the poor little mites seem to bear it well—bravely, at any rate.'

Sprats looked at him with the speculative expression which always came into her face when she was endeavouring to get at some other person's real self.

'So you, too, are fond of children?' she said, and responded cordially to his suggestion that he might perhaps be permitted to come again. He went away with a cheering consciousness that he had had a glimpse into a little world wherein good work was being done—it had seemed a far preferable world to that other world of fashion and small things which seethed all around it.

On the following day Saxonstowe spent the better part of the morning in a toy-shop. He proved a good customer, but a most particular one. He had counted heads at the children's hospital: there were twenty-seven in all, and he wanted twenty-seven toys for them. He insisted on a minute inspection of every one, even to the details of the dolls' clothing and the attainments of the mechanical frogs, and the young lady who attended upon him decided that he was a nice gentleman and free-handed, but terribly exacting. His bill, however, yielded her a handsome commission, and when he gave her the address of the hospital she felt sure that she had spent two hours in conversation—on the merits of toys—with a young duke, and for the rest of the day she entertained her shopmates with reminiscences of the supposed ducal remarks, none of which, according to her, had been of a very profound nature.

Saxonstowe wondered how soon he might call at the hospital again—at the end of a week he found himself kicking his heels once more in the room wherein Noah, his family, and his animals trooped gaily down the slopes of Mount Ararat. When Sprats came in she greeted him with an abrupt question.

'Was it you who sent a small cart-load of toys here last week?' she asked.

'I certainly did send some toys for the children,' he answered.

'I thought it must be your handiwork,' she said. 'Thank you. You will now receive a beautifully written, politely worded letter of thanks, inscribed on thick, glossy paper by the secretary—do you mind?'

'Yes, I do mind!' he exclaimed. 'Please don't tell the secretary—what has he or she to do with it?'

'Very well, I won't,' she said. 'But I will give you a practical tip: when you feel impelled to buy toys for children in hospital, buy

105

something breakable and cheap—it pleases the child just as much as an expensive plaything. There was one toy too many,' she continued, laughing, 'so I annexed that for myself—a mechanical spider. I play with it in my room sometimes. I am not above being amused by small things.'

After this Saxonstowe became a regular visitor—he was accepted by some of the patients as a friend and admitted to their confidences. They knew him as 'the Lord,' and announced that 'the Lord' had said this, or done that, in a fashion which made other visitors, not in the secret, wonder if the children were delirious and had dreams of divine communications. He sent these new friends books, and fruit, and flowers, and the house was gayer and brighter that summer than it had ever been since the brass plate was placed on its door.

One afternoon Saxonstowe arrived with a weighty-looking parcel under his arm. Once within Sprats's parlour he laid it down on the table and began to untie the string. She shook her head.

'You have been spending money on one or other of my children again,' she said. 'I shall have to stop it.'

'No,' he said, with a very shy smile. 'This—is—for you.'

'For me?' Her eyes opened with something like incredulous wonder. 'What an event!' she said; 'I so seldom have anything given to me. What is it?—quick, let me see—it looks like an enormous box of chocolate.'

'It's—it's the book,' he answered, shamefaced as a schoolboy producing his first verses. 'There! that's it,' and he placed two formidable-looking volumes, very new and very redolent of the bookbinder's establishment, in her hands. 'That's the very first copy,' he added. 'I wanted you to have it.'

Sprats sat down and turned the books over. He had written her name on the fly-leaf of the first volume, and his own underneath it. She glanced at the maps, the engravings, the diagrams, the scientific tables, and a sudden flush came across her face. She looked up at him.

'I should be proud if I had written a book like this!' she said. 'It means—such a lot of—well, of manliness, somehow. Thank you. And it is really published at last?'

'It is not supposed to be published until next Monday,' he answered. 'The reviewers' copies have gone out to-day, but I insisted on having a copy supplied to me before any one handled another—I wanted you to have the very first.'

'Why?' she asked.

'Because I think you'll understand it,' he said; 'and you'll read it.'

'Yes,' she answered, 'I shall read it, and I think I shall understand. And now all the lionising will begin.'

Saxonstowe shrugged his shoulders.

'If the people who really know about these things think I have done well, I shall be satisfied,' he said. 'I don't care a scrap about the reviews in the popular papers—I am looking forward with great anxiety to the criticisms of two or three scientific periodicals.'

'You were going to run away from the lionising business,' she said. 'When are you going?—there is nothing to keep you, now that the book is out.'

Saxonstowe looked at her. He was standing at the edge of the table on which she had placed the two volumes of his book; she was sitting in a low chair at its side. She looked up at him; she saw his face grow very grave.

'I didn't think anything would keep me,' he said, 'but I find that something is keeping me. It is you. Do you know that I love you?'

The colour rose in her cheeks, and her eyes left his for an instant; then she faced him.

'I did not know it until just now,' she answered, laying her hand on one of the volumes at her side. 'I knew it then, because you wished me to have the first-fruits of your labour. I was wondering about it—as we talked.'

'Well?' he said.

'Will you let me be perfectly frank with you?' she said. 'Are you sure about yourself in this?'

'I am sure,' he answered. 'I love you, and I shall never love any other woman. Don't think that I say that in the way in which I dare say it's been said a million times—I mean it.'

'Yes,' she said; 'I understand. You wouldn't say anything that you didn't mean. And I am going to be equally truthful with you. I don't think it's wrong of me to tell you that I have a feeling for you which I have not, and never had, for any other man that I have known. I could depend on you—I could go to you for help and advice, and I should rely on your strength. I have felt that since we met, as man and woman, a few weeks ago.'

'Then——' he began.

'Stop a bit,' she said, 'let me finish. I want to be brutally plain-spoken—it's really best to be so. I want you to know me as I am. I have loved Lucian Damerel ever since he and I were boy and girl. It is, perhaps, a curious love—you might say that there is very much more of a mother's, or a sister's, love in it than a wife's. Well, I don't know. I do know that it nearly broke my heart when I heard of his marriage to Haidee. I cannot tell—I have never been able to tell—in what exact way it was that I wanted him, but I did not want her to have him. Perhaps all that, or most of that, feeling has gone. I have tried hard, by working for others, to put all thought of another woman's husband out of my mind. But the thought of Lucian is still there—it may, perhaps, always be there. While it is—even in the least, the very least degree—you understand, do you not?' she said, with a sudden note of eager appeal breaking into her voice.

'Yes,' he answered, 'I understand.'

She rose to her feet and held out her hand to him.

'Then don't let us try to put into words what we can feel much better,' she said, smiling. 'We are friends—always. And you are going away.'

The children found out that for some time at any rate there would be no more visits from the Lord. But the toys and the books, the fruit and flowers, came as regularly as ever, and the Lord was not forgotten.

CHAPTER XVIII

During the greater part of that summer Lucian had been working steadily on two things: the tragedy which Mr. Harcourt was to produce at the Athenæum in December, and a new poem which Mr. Robertson intended to publish about the middle of the autumn season. Lucian was flying at high game in respect of both. The tragedy was intended to introduce something of the spirit and dignity of Greek art to the nineteenth-century stage—there was to be nothing common or mean in connection with its production; it was to be a gorgeous spectacle, but one of high distinction, and Lucian's direct intention in writing it was to set English dramatic art on an elevation to which it had never yet been lifted. The poem was an equally ambitious attempt to revive the epic; its subject, the Norman Conquest, had filled Lucian's mind since boyhood, and from his tenth year onwards he had read every book and document procurable which treated of that fascinating period. He had begun the work during his Oxford days; the greater part of it was now in type, and Mr. Robertson was incurring vast expense in the shape of author's corrections. Lucian polished and rewrote in a fashion that was exasperating; his publisher, never suspecting that so many alterations would be made, had said nothing about them in drawing up a formal agreement, and he was daily obliged to witness a disappearance of profits.

'What a pity that you did not make all your alterations and corrections before sending the manuscript to press!' he exclaimed one day, when Lucian called with a bundle of proofs which had been hacked about in such a fashion as to need complete resetting. 'It would have saved a lot of trouble—and expense.'

Lucian stared at him with the eyes of a young owl, round and wondering.

'How on earth can you see what a thing looks like until it's in print?' he said irritably. 'What are printers for?'

'Just so—just so!' responded the publisher. 'But really, you know, this book is being twice set—every sheet has had to be pulled to pieces, and it adds to the expense.'

Lucian's eyes grew rounder than ever.

'I don't know anything about that,' he answered. 'That is your province—don't bother me about it.'

Robertson laughed. He was beginning to find out, after some experience, that Lucian was imperturbable on certain points.

'Very well,' he said. 'By the bye, how much more copy is there—or if copy is too vulgar a word for your mightiness, how many more lines or verses?'

'About four hundred and fifty lines,' answered Lucian.

'Say another twenty-four pages,' said Robertson. 'Well, it runs now to three hundred and fifty—that means that it's going to be a book of close upon four hundred pages.'

'Well?' questioned Lucian.

'I was merely thinking that it is a long time since the public was asked to buy a volume containing four hundred pages of blank verse,' remarked the publisher. 'I hope this won't frighten anybody.'

'You make some very extraordinary remarks,' said Lucian, with unmistakable signs of annoyance. 'What do you mean?'

'Oh, nothing, nothing!' answered Robertson, who was on sufficient terms of intimacy with Lucian to be able to chaff him a little. 'I was merely thinking of trade considerations.'

'You appear to be always "merely thinking" of something extraordinary,' said Lucian. 'What can trade considerations have to do with the length of my poem?'

'What indeed?' said the publisher, and began to talk of something else. But when Lucian had gone he looked rather doubtfully at the pile of interlineated proof, and glanced from it to the thin octavo with which the new poet had won all hearts nearly five years before. 'I wish it had been just a handful of gold like that!'

he said to himself. 'Four hundred pages of blank verse all at one go!—it's asking a good deal, unless it catches on with the old maids and the dowagers, like the Course of Time and the Epic of Hades. Well, we shall see; but I'd rather have some of your earlier lyrics than this weighty performance, Lucian, my boy—I would indeed!'

Lucian finished his epic before the middle of July, and fell to work on the final stages of his tragedy. He had promised to read it to the Athenæum company on the first day of the coming October, and there was still much to do in shaping and revising it. He began to feel impatient and irritable; the sight of his desk annoyed him, and he took to running out of town into the country whenever the wish for the shade of woods and the peacefulness of the lanes came upon him. Before the end of the month he felt unable to work, and he repaired to Sprats for counsel and comfort.

'I don't know how or why it is,' he said, telling her his troubles, 'but I don't feel as if I had a bit of work left in me. I haven't any power of concentration left—I'm always wanting to be doing something else. And yet I haven't worked very hard this year, and we have been away a great deal. It's nearly time for going away again, too—I believe Haidee has already made some arrangement.'

'Lucian,' said Sprats, 'why don't you go down to Simonstower? They would be so glad to have you at the vicarage—there's heaps of room. And just think how jolly it is there in August and September— I wish I could go!'

Lucian's face lighted up—some memory of the old days had suddenly fired his soul. He saw the familiar scenes once more under the golden sunlight—the grey castle and its Norman keep, the winding river, the shelving woods, and, framing all, the gold and purple of the moorlands.

'Simonstower!' he exclaimed. 'Yes, of course—it's Simonstower that I want. We'll go at once. Sprats, why can't you come too?'

Sprats shook her head.

'I can't,' she answered. 'I shall have a holiday in September, but I can't take a single day before. I'm sure it will do you good if you go to Simonstower, Lucian—the north-country air will brighten you up. You haven't been there for four years, and the sight of the old faces and places will act like a tonic.'

'I'll arrange it at once,' said Lucian, delighted at the idea, and he went off to announce his projects to Haidee. Haidee looked at him incredulously.

'Whatever are you thinking of, Lucian?' she said. 'Don't you remember that we're cramful of engagements from the beginning of August to the end of September?' She recited a list of arrangements already entered into, which included a three-weeks' sojourn on Eustace Darlington's steam-yacht, and a fortnight's stay at his shooting-box in the Highlands. 'Had you forgotten?' she asked.

'I believe I had!' he replied; 'we seem to have so many engagements. Look here: do you know, I think I'll back out. I must have this tragedy finished for Harcourt and his people by October, and I can't do it if I go rushing about from one place to another. I think I shall go down to Simonstower and have a quiet time and finish my work there—I'll explain it all to Darlington.'

'As you please,' she answered. 'Of course, I shall keep my engagements.'

'Oh, of course,' he said. 'You won't miss me, you know. I suppose there are lots of other people going?'

'I suppose so,' she replied carelessly, and there was an end of the conversation. Lucian explained to Darlington that night that he would not be able to keep his engagement, and set forth the reasons with a fine air of devotion to business. Darlington sympathised, and applauded Lucian's determination—he knew, he said, what a lot depended upon the success of the new play, and he'd no doubt Lucian wouldn't feel quite easy until it was all in order. After that he must have a long rest—it would be rather good fun to winter in Egypt. Lucian agreed, and next day made his preparations for a descent upon Simonstower. At heart he was rather more than glad to escape the yacht, the Highland shooting-box, and the people whom he would have met. He cared little for the sea, and hated any form of sport which involved the slaying of animals or birds; the thought of Simonstower in the last weeks of summer was grateful to him, and all that he now wanted was to find himself in a Great Northern express gliding out of King's Cross, bound for the moorlands.

He went round to the hospital on the morning of his departure, and told Sprats with the glee of a schoolboy who is going home for the holidays, that he was off that very afternoon. He was rattling on as to his joy when Sprats stopped him.

'And Haidee?' she asked. 'Does she like it?'

'Haidee?' he said. 'But Haidee is not going. She's joining a party on Darlington's yacht, and they're going round the coast to his place in the Highlands. I was to have gone, you know, but really I couldn't have worked, and I must work—it's absolutely necessary that the play should be finished by the end of September.'

Sprats looked anxious and troubled.

'Look here, Lucian,' she said, 'do you think it's quite right to leave Haidee like that?—isn't it rather neglecting your duties?'

'But why?' he asked, with such sincerity that it became plain

111

to Sprats that the question had never even entered his mind. 'Haidee's all right. It would be beastly selfish on my part if I dragged her down to Simonstower for nearly two months—you know, she doesn't care a bit for the country, and there would be no society for her. She needs sea air, and three weeks on Darlington's yacht will do her a lot of good.'

'Who are the other people?' asked Sprats.

'Oh, I don't know,' Lucian replied. 'The usual Darlington lot, I suppose. Between you and me, Sprats, I'm glad I'm not going. I get rather sick of that sort of thing—it's too much of a hot-house existence. And I don't care about the people one meets, either.'

'And yet you let Haidee meet them!' Sprats exclaimed. 'Really, Lucian, you grow more and more paradoxical.'

'But Haidee likes them,' he insisted. 'That's just the sort of thing she does like. And if she likes it, why shouldn't she have it?'

'You are a curious couple,' said Sprats.

'I think we are to be praised for our common-sense view of things,' he said. 'I am often told that I am a dreamer—you've said so yourself, you know—but in real, sober truth, I'm an awfully matter-of-fact sort of person. I don't live on illusions and ideals and things—I worship the God of the Things that Are!'

Sprats gazed at him as a mother might gaze at a child who boasts of having performed an impossible task.

'Oh, you absolute baby!' she said. 'Is your pretty head stuffed with wool or with feathers? Paragon of Common-Sense! Compendium of all the Practical Qualities! I wonder I don't shrivel in your presence like a bit of bacon before an Afric sun. Do you think you'll catch your train?'

'Not if I stay here listening to abuse. Seriously, Sprats, it's all right—about Haidee, I mean,' he said appealingly.

'If you were glissading down a precipice at a hundred miles a minute, Lucian, everything would be all right with you until your head broke off or you snapped in two,' she answered. 'You're the Man who Never Stops to Think. Go away and be quiet at Simonstower—you're mad to get there, and you'll probably leave it within a week.'

In making this calculation, however, Sprats was wrong. Lucian went down to Simonstower and stayed there three weeks. He divided his time between the vicarage and the farm; he renewed his acquaintance with the villagers, and had forgotten nothing of anything relating to them; he spent the greater part of the day in the open air, lived plainly and slept soundly, and during the second week of his stay he finished his tragedy. Mr. Chilverstone read it and the revised proofs of the epic; as he had a great liking for blank

112

verse, rounded periods, and the grand manner, he prophesied success for both. Lucian drank in his applause with eagerness—he had a great belief in his old tutor's critical powers, and felt that whatever he stamped with the seal of his admiration must be good. He had left London in somewhat depressed and irritable spirits because of his inability to work; now that the work was completed and praised by a critic in whom he had good reason to repose the fullest confidence, his spirits became as light and joyous as ever.

Lucian would probably have remained longer at Simonstower but for a chance meeting with Lord Saxonstowe, who had got a little weary of the ancestral hall and had conceived a notion of going across to Norway and taking a long walking tour in a district well out of the tourist track. He mentioned this to Lucian, and—why, he could scarcely explain to himself at the moment—asked him to go with him. Lucian's imagination was fired at the mere notion of exploring a country which he had never seen before, and he accepted the invitation with fervour. A week later they sailed from Newcastle, and for a whole month they spent nights and days side by side amidst comparative solitudes. Each began to understand the other, and when, just before the end of September, they returned to England, they had become firm friends, and were gainers by their pilgrimage in more ways than one.

CHAPTER XIX

When Lucian went back to town Haidee was winding up a short round of visits in the North; she rejoined him a week later in high spirits and excellent health. Everything had been delightful; everybody had been nice to her; no end of people had talked about Lucian and his new play—she was dreaming already of the glories of the first night and of the radiance which would centre about herself as the wife of the brilliant young author. Lucian had returned from Norway in equally good health and spirits; he was confident about the tragedy and the epic: he and his wife therefore settled down to confront an immediate prospect of success and pleasure. Haidee resumed her usual round of social gaieties; Lucian was much busied with rehearsals at the theatre and long discussions with Harcourt; neither had a care nor an anxiety, and the wheels of their little world moved smoothly.

113

Saxonstowe, who had come back to town for a few weeks before going abroad again, took to calling a good deal at the little house in Mayfair. He had come to understand and to like Lucian, and though they were as dissimilar in character as men of different temperament can possibly be, a curious bond of friendship, expressed in tacit acquiescence rather than in open avowal, sprang up between them. Each had a respect for the other's world—a respect which was amusing to Sprats, who, watching them closely, knew that each admired the other in a somewhat sheepish, schoolboy fashion. Lucian, being the less reserved of the two, made no secret of his admiration of the man who had done things the doing of which necessitated bravery, endurance, and self-denial. He was a fervent worshipper—almost to a pathetic extreme—of men of action: the sight of soldiers marching made his toes tingle and his eyes fill with the moisture of enthusiasm; he had been so fascinated by the mere sight of a great Arctic explorer that he had followed him from one town to another during a lecturing tour, simply to stare at him and conjure up for himself the scenes and adventures through which the man had passed. He delighted in hearing Saxonstowe talk about his life in the deserts, and enjoyed it all the more because Saxonstowe had small gift of language and told his tale with the blushes of a schoolboy who hates making a fuss about anything that he has done. Saxonstowe, on his part, had a sneaking liking, amounting almost to worship, for men who live in a world of dreams—he had no desire to live in such a world himself, but he cherished an immense respect for men who, like Lucian, could create. Sometimes he would read a page of the new epic and wonder how on earth it all came into Lucian's head; Lucian at the same moment was probably turning over the leaves of Saxonstowe's book and wondering how a man could go through all that that laconic young gentleman had gone through and yet come back with a stiff upper lip and a smile.

'You and Lucian Damerel appear to have become something of friends,' Lady Firmanence remarked to her nephew when he called upon her one day. 'I don't know that there's much in common between you.'

'Perhaps that is why we are friends,' said Saxonstowe. 'You generally do get on with people who are a bit different to yourself, don't you?'

Lady Firmanence made no direct answer to this question.

'I've no doubt Lucian is easy enough to get on with,' she said dryly. 'The mischief in him, Saxonstowe, is that he's too easy-going about everything. I suppose you know, as you're a sort of friend of the family, that a good deal is being said about Mrs. Damerel and Eustace Darlington?'

'No,' said Saxonstowe; 'I'm not in the way to hear that sort of thing.'

'I don't know that you're any the better for being out of the way. I am in the way. There's a good deal being said,' Lady Firmanence retorted with some asperity. 'I believe some of you young men think it a positive crime to listen to the smallest scrap of gossip—it's nothing of the sort. If you live in the world you must learn all you can about the people who make up the world.'

Saxonstowe nodded. His eyes fixed themselves on a toy dog which snored and snuffled at Lady Firmanence's feet.

'And in this particular case?' he said.

'Why was Lucian Damerel so foolish as to go off in one direction while his wife went in another with the man she originally meant to marry?' inquired Lady Firmanence. 'Come now, Saxonstowe, would you have done that?'

'No,' he said hesitatingly, 'I don't think I should; but then, you see, Damerel looks at things differently. I don't think he would ever give the foolishness of it a thought, and he would certainly think no evil—he's as guileless as a child.'

'Well,' remarked Lady Firmanence, 'I don't admire him any the more for that. I'm a bit out of love with grown-up children. If Lucian Damerel marries a wife he should take care of her. Why, she was three weeks on Darlington's yacht, and three weeks at his place in Scotland (of course there were lots of other people there too, but even then it was foolish), and he was with her at two or three country houses in Northumberland later on—I met them at one myself.'

'Lucian and his wife,' said Saxonstowe, 'are very fond of having their own way.'

Lady Firmanence looked at her nephew out of her eye-corners.

'Oh!' she said, with a caustic irony, 'you think so, do you? Well, you know, young people who like to have their own way generally come to grief. To my mind, your new friends seem to be qualifying for trouble.'

Saxonstowe studied the pattern of the carpet and traced bits of it out with his stick.

'Do you think men like Damerel have the power of reckoning things up?' he said, suddenly looking at his aunt with a quick, appealing glance. 'I don't quite understand these things, but he always seems to me to be a bit impatient of anything that has to do with everyday life, and yet he's keen enough about it in one way.

115

He's a real good chap, you know—kindly natured and open-hearted and all that. You soon find that in him. And I don't believe he ever had a wrong thought of anybody—he's a sort of confiding trust in other people that's a bit amusing, even to me, and I haven't seen such an awful lot of the world. But——' He came to a sudden pause and shook his head. Lady Firmanence laughed.

'Yes, but,' she repeated. 'That "but" makes all the difference. But this is Lucian Damerel—he is a child who sits in a gaily caparisoned, comfortably appointed boat which has been launched on a wide river that runs through a mighty valley. He has neither sail nor rudder, and he is so intent on the beauty of the scenery through which he is swept that he does not recognise their necessity. His eyes are fixed on the rose-flushed peak of a far-off mountain, the glitter of the sunshine on a dancing wave, or on the basket of provisions which thoughtful hands have put in the boat. It may be that the boat will glide to its destination in safety, and land him on the edge of a field of velvety grass wherein he can lie down in peace to dream as long as he pleases. But it also may be that it will run on a rock in mid-stream and knock his fool's paradise into a cocked hat—and what's going to happen then?' asked Lady Firmanence.

'Lots of things might happen,' said Saxonstowe, smiling triumphantly at the thought of beating his clever relative at her own game. 'He might be able to swim, for example. He might right the boat, get into it again, and learn by experience that one shouldn't go fooling about without a rudder. Some other chap might come along and give him a hand. Or the river might be so shallow that he could walk ashore with no more discomfort than he would get from wet feet.'

Lady Firmanence pursed her lips and regarded her nephew with a fixed stare which lasted until the smile died out of his face.

'Or there might be a crocodile, or an alligator, at hand, which he could saddle and bridle, and convert into a park hack,' she said. 'There are indeed many things which might happen; what I'm chiefly concerned about is, what would happen if Lucian's little boat did upset? I confess that I should know Lucian Damerel much more thoroughly, and have a more accurate conception of him, if I knew exactly what he would say and do when the upsetting happened. There is no moment in life, Saxonstowe, wherein a man's real self, real character, real quality, is so severely tested and laid bare as that unexpected one in which Fortune seizes him by the scruff of his neck and bundles him into the horsepond of adversity—it's what he says and does when he comes up spluttering that stamps him as a man or a mouse.'

116

Saxonstowe felt tolerably certain of what any man would say under the circumstances alluded to by Lady Firmanence, but as she seemed highly delighted with her similes and her epigrams, he said nothing of his convictions, and soon afterwards took his departure.

CHAPTER XX

On a certain Monday morning in the following November, Lucian's great epic was published to the trade and the world, and the leading newspapers devoted a good deal of their space to remarking upon its merits, its demerits, and its exact relation to literature. Lucian found a pile of the London morning dailies of the superior sort awaiting his attention when he descended to his breakfast-room, and he went through them systematically. When he had made an end of them he looked across the table at Haidee, and he smiled in what she thought a rather queer way.

'I say, Haidee!' he exclaimed, 'these reviews are—well, they're not very flattering. There are six mighty voices of the press here,— Times, Telegraph, Post, News, Chronicle, and Standard—and there appears to be a strange unanimity of opinion in their pronunciations. The epic poem seems to be at something of a discount.'

The reviews, in fact, were not couched in an enthusiastic vein—taking them as a whole they were cold. There was a ring of disappointment in them. One reviewer, daring to be bold, plain, and somewhat brutal, said there was more genuine poetry in any one page of any of Mr. Damerel's previous volumes than in the whole four hundred of his new one. Another openly declared his belief that the poem was the result of long years of careful, scholarly labour, of constant polishing, resetting, and rewriting; it smelled strongly of the lamp, but the smell of the lamp was not in evidence in the fresh, free, passionate work which they had previously had from the same pen. Mr. Damerel's history, said a third, was as accurate as his lines were polished; one learned almost as much of the Norman Conquest from his poem as from the pages of Freeman, but the spontaneity of his earliest work appeared to be wanting in his latest. Each of the six reviewers seemed to be indulging a sentimental sorrow for the Mr. Damerel of the earlier days; their criticisms had an undercurrent of regret that Lucian had chosen to explore another path than that which he had hitherto trodden in triumph. The consensus of opinion, as represented by the critics of the six morning newspapers lying on Lucian's breakfast-table, amounted to this: that Mr. Damerel's new work, unmistakably the production of a true poet though it was, did not possess the qualities of power and charm which had distinguished his previous volumes. And to show his exact meaning and make out a good case for himself, each critic hit upon the exasperating trick of reprinting those of Lucian's earlier lines which made perpetual music in their own particular souls, pointing to them with a proud finger as something great and glorious, and hinting that they were samples of goods which they would have wished Mr. Damerel to supply for ever.

Lucian was disappointed and gratified; amused and annoyed. It was disappointing to find that the incense to which he had become accustomed was not offered up to him in the usual lavish fashion; but it was pleasing to hear the nice things said of what he had done and of what the critics believed him capable of doing. He was amused at the disappointment of the gentlemen who preferred Lucian the earlier to Lucian the later—and, after all, it was annoying to find one's great effort somewhat looked askance at.

'I've given them too much,' he said, turning to considerations of breakfast with a certain amount of pity for himself. 'I ought to have remembered that the stomach of this generation is a weak one—Tennyson was wise in giving his public the Idylls of the King in fragments—if he'd given his most fervent admirers the whole lot all at once they'd have had a surfeit. I should have followed his example, but I wanted to present the thing as a whole. And it is good, however they may damn it with faint praise.'

'Does this mean that the book won't sell?' asked Haidee, who had gathered up the papers, and was glancing through the columns at the head of which Lucian's name stood out in bold letters.

'Sell? Why, I don't think reviews make much difference to the sales of a book,' answered Lucian. 'I really don't know—I suppose the people who bought all my other volumes will buy this.'

But as he ate his chop and drank his coffee he began to wonder what would happen if the new volume did not sell. He knew exactly how many copies of his other volumes had been sold up to the end of the previous half-year: it was no business instinct that made him carry the figures in his mind, but rather the instinct of the general who counts his prisoners, his captured eagles, and his dead enemies after a victory, and of the sportsman who knows that the magnitude of the winnings of a great racehorse is a tribute to the quality of its blood and bone and muscle. He recalled the figures of the last statement of account rendered to him by his publisher, and their comfortable rotundity cheered him. Whatever the critics might say, he had a public, and a public of considerable size. And after all, this was the first time the critics had not burned incense at his shrine—he forgave them with generous readiness, and ere he rose from the breakfast table was as full as ever of confident optimism. He felt as regards those particular reviewers as a man might feel who bids all and sundry to a great feast, and finds that the first-comers are taken aback by the grand proportions of the banquet—he pitied them for their lack of appetite, but he had no doubt of the verdict of the vast majority of later comers.

But if Lucian had heard some of the things that were said of him and his beloved epic in those holes and corners of literary life wherein one may hear much trenchant criticism plainly voiced, he would have felt less cock-sure about it and himself. It was the general opinion amongst a certain class of critics, who exercised a certain influence upon public thought, that there was too much of the workshop in his magnum opus. It was a magnificent block of marble that he had handled, but he had handled it too much, and the result would have been greater if he had not perpetually hovered about it with a hungry chisel and an itching mallet. It was perfect in form and language and proportion, but it wanted life and fire and rude strength.

'It reminds me,' said one man, discussing it in a club corner where coffee cups, liqueur glasses, and cigarettes were greatly in evidence, 'of the statue of Galatea, flawless, immaculate, but neuter,—yes, neuter—as it appeared at the very moment ere Pygmalion's love breathed into it the very flush, the palpitating, forceful tremor of life.'

This man was young and newly come to town—the others looked at him with shy eyes and tender sympathy, for they knew what it was that he meant to say, and they also knew, being older, how difficult it is to express oneself in words.

'How very differently one sees things!' sighed one of them. 'Damerel's new poem, now, reminds me of a copy of the Pink 'Un, carefully edited by a committee of old maids for the use of mixed classes in infant schools.'

The young man who used mellifluous words manifested signs of astonishment. He looked at the last speaker with inquiring eyes.

'You mean——' he began.

'Ssh!' whispered a voice at his elbow, 'don't ask him what he means at any time. He means that the thing's lacking in virility.'

It may have been the man who likened Lucian's epic to an emasculated and expurgated Pink 'Un to whom was due a subsequent article in the Porthole, wherein, under the heading Lucian the Ladylike, much sympathy was expressed with William the Conqueror at his sad fate in being sung by a nineteenth-century bard. There was much good-humoured satire in that article, but a good many of its points were sharply barbed, and Lucian winced under them. He was beginning to find by that time that his epic was not being greeted with the enthusiasm which he had anticipated for it; the great literary papers, the influential journals of the provinces, and the critics who wrote of it in two or three of the monthly reviews, all concurred that it was very fine as a literary exercise, but each deplored the absence of a certain something which had been very conspicuous indeed in his earlier volumes.

Lucian began to think things over. He remembered how his earlier work had been written—he recalled the free, joyous flush of thought, the impulse to write, the fertility and fecundity which had been his in those days, and he contrasted it all with the infinite pains which he had taken in polishing and revising the epic. It must have been the process of revision, he thought, which had sifted the fire and life out of the poem. He read and re-read passages of it—in spite of all that the critics said, they pleased him. He remembered the labour he had gone through, and valued the results by it. And finally, he put the whole affair away from him, feeling that he and his world were not in accord, and that he had better wrap himself in his cloak for a while. He spoke of the epic no more. But unfortunately for Lucian, there were monetary considerations at the back of the new volume, and when he discovered at the end of a month that the sales were small and already at a standstill, he felt a sudden, strange sinking at the heart. He looked at Mr. Robertson, who communicated this news to him, in a fashion which showed the publisher that he did not quite understand this apparently capricious neglect on the part of the public. Mr. Robertson endeavoured to explain matters to him.

'After all,' he said, 'there is such a thing as a vogue, and the best man may lose it. I don't say that you have lost yours, but here's the fact that the book is at a standstill. The faithful bought as a religious duty as soon as we published; those of the outer courts won't buy. For one thing, your poem is not quite in the fashion— what people are buying just now in poetry is patriotism up-to-date, with extension of the Empire, and Maxim-guns, and deification of the soldier and sailor, and so on.'

'You talk as if there were fashions in poetry as there are in clothes,' said Lucian, with some show of scornful indignation.

'So there are, my dear sir!' replied the publisher. 'If you lived less in the clouds and more in the world of plain fact you would know it. You, for instance, would think it strange, if you had ever read it, to find Pollok's poem, The Course of Time, selling to the extent of thousands and tens of thousands, or of Tupper's Proverbial Philosophy making almost as prominent a figure in the middle-class household as the Bible itself. Of course there's a fashion in poetry, as there is in everything else. Byron was once the fashion; Mrs. Hemans was once the fashion; even Robert Montgomery was once fashionable. You yourself were very fashionable for three years—you see, if you'll pardon me for speaking plainly, you were an interesting young man. You had a beautiful face; you were what the women call "interesting"; you aroused all the town by your romantic marriage—you became a personality. I think you've had a big run of it,' concluded Mr. Robertson. 'Why, lots of men come up and go down within two years—you've had four already.'

Lucian regarded him with grave eyes.

'Do you think of me as of a rocket or a comet?' he said. 'If things are what you say they are, I wish I had never published anything. But I think you are wrong,' and he went away to consider all that had been said to him. He decided, after some thought and reflection, that his publisher was not arguing on sound lines, and he assured himself for the hundredth time that the production of the tragedy would put everything right.

It was now very near to the day on which the tragedy was to be produced at the Athenæum, and both Lucian and Mr. Harcourt had been worried to the point of death by pressmen who wanted to know all about it. Chiefly owing to their persistency the public were now in possession of a considerable amount of information as to what it might expect to hear and see. It was to witness—that portion of it, at any rate, which was lucky enough to secure seats for the first night—an attempt to revive tragedy on the lines of pure Greek art. As this attempt was being made at the close of the nineteenth century, it was quite in accordance with everything that vast sums of money should be laid out on costumes, scenery, and accessories, and it was well known to the readers of the halfpenny newspapers that the production involved the employment of so many hundreds of supernumeraries, that so many thousands of pounds had been spent on the scenery, that certain realistic effects had been worked up at enormous cost, and that the whole affair, to put it in plain language, was a gigantic business speculation—nothing more nor less, indeed, than the provision of a gorgeous spectacular drama, full of life and colour and modern stage effects, which should be enthralling and commanding enough to attract the public until a handsome profit had been made on the outlay. But the words 'an

121

attempt to revive Tragedy on the lines of pure Greek Art' looked well in print, and had a highly respectable sound, and the production of Lucian's second tribute to the tragic muse was looked forward to with much interest by many people who ignored the fact that many thousands of pounds were being expended in placing it upon the stage.

CHAPTER XXI

At twelve o'clock on the night that witnessed the production of the tragedy, Lucian found himself one of a group of six men which had gathered together in Harcourt's dressing-room. There was a blue haze of cigarette smoke all over the room; a decanter of whisky with syphons and glasses stood on a table in the centre; most of the men had already helped themselves to a drink. Lucian found a glass in his own hand, and sipped the mixture in it he recognised the taste of soda, and remembered in a vague fashion that he much preferred Apollinaris, but he said to himself, or something said to him, that it didn't matter. His brain was whirling with the events of the night; he still saw, as in a dream, the misty auditorium as he had seen it from a box; the stage as he had seen it during a momentary excursion to the back of the dress-circle; the busy world behind the scenes where stage-carpenters sweated and swore, and the dust made one's throat tickle. He recalled particular faces and heard particular voices; all the world and his wife had been there, and all the first-nighters, and all his friends, and he had spoken to a great many people. They all seemed to swim before him as in a dream, and the sound of their voices came, as it were, from the cylinder of a phonograph. He remembered seeing Mr. Chilverstone and his wife in the stalls—their faces were rapt and eloquent; in the stalls, too, he had seen Sprats and Lord Saxonstowe and Mrs. Berenson; he himself had spent some of the time with Haidee and Darlington and other people of their set in a box, but he had also wandered in and out of Harcourt's dressing-room a good deal, and had sometimes spoken to Harcourt, and sometimes to his business manager. He had a vague recollection that he had faced the house himself at the end of everything, and had bowed several times in response to cheering which was still buzzing in his ears. The night was over.

He took another drink from the glass in his hand and looked about him; there was a curious feeling in his brain that he himself was not there, that he had gone away, or been left behind somewhere in the world's mad rush, and that he was something else, watching a semblance of himself and the semblance's surroundings. The scene interested and amused whatever it was that was looking on from his brain. Harcourt, free of his Greek draperies, now appeared in a shirt and trousers; he stood before the mirror on his dressing-table, brushing his hair—Lucian wondered where he bought his braces, which, looked at closely, revealed a peculiarly dainty pattern worked by hand. All the time that he was manipulating the brushes he was talking in disconnected sentences. Lucian caught some of them: 'Little cutting here and there—that bit dragged—I'm told that was a fine effect—very favourable indeed— we shall see, we shall see!'—and he wondered what Harcourt was talking about. Near the actor-manager, in an easy-chair, sat an old gentleman of benevolent aspect, white-bearded, white-moustached, who wore a fur-lined cloak over his evening-dress. He was sucking at a cigar, and his hand, very fat and very white, held a glass at which he kept looking from time to time as if he were not quite certain what to do with it. He was reported to be at the back of Harcourt in financial matters, and he blinked and nodded at every sentence rapidly spoken by the actor-manager, but said nothing. Near him stood two men in cloaks and opera-hats, also holding glasses in their hands and smoking cigarettes—one of them Lucian recognised as a great critic, the other as a famous actor. At his own side, talking very rapidly, was the sixth man, Harcourt's business-manager. Lucian suddenly realised that he was nodding his head at this man as if in intelligent comprehension of what he was saying, whereas he had not understood one word. He shook himself together as a man does who throws drowsiness aside.

'I'm sorry,' he said. 'I—I don't think I was paying attention. I don't know why, but I feel half-asleep.'

'It's the reaction,' said Harcourt, hastily getting into his waistcoat and coat. 'I feel tired out—if I had my way there should be no such thing as a first night—it's a most wearing occasion.'

The famous critic turned with a smile.

'Think of being able to lie in bed to-morrow with a sheaf of newspapers on your counterpane!' he said pleasantly.

Then somehow, chatting disjointedly, they got out of the theatre. Harcourt and Lucian drove off in a hansom together—they were near neighbours.

'What do you think?' asked Lucian, as they drove away.

'Oh, I think it went all right, as far as one could judge. There

123

was plenty of applause—we shall see what is said to-morrow morning,' answered Harcourt, with a mighty yawn. 'They can't say that it wasn't magnificently staged,' he added, with complacency. 'And everything went like clockwork. I'll tell you what—I wish I could go to sleep for the next six months!'

'I believe I feel like that,' responded Lucian. 'Well, it is launched, at any rate.'

The old gentleman of the white beard and fur-lined cloak drove off in a private brougham, still nodding and blinking; the actor and the critic, lighting cigars, walked away together, and for some time kept silence.

'What do you really think?' said the actor at last. 'You're in rather a lucky position, you know, in respect of the fact that the Forum is a weekly and not a daily journal—it gives you more time to make up your mind. But you already have some notion of what your verdict will be?'

'Yes,' answered the critic. He puffed thoughtfully at his cigar. 'Well,' he said, 'I think we have heard some beautiful poetry, beautifully recited. But I confess to feeling a certain sense of incongruity in the attempt to mingle Greek art with modern stage accessories. I think Damerel's tragedy will read delightfully—in the study. But I counted several speeches to-night which would run to two and three pages of print, and I saw many people yawn. I fear that others will yawn.'

'What would you give it?' said the actor. 'The other ran for twelve months.'

'This,' said the critic, 'may run for one. But I think Harcourt will have to withdraw it within three weeks. I am bearing the yawns in mind.'

CHAPTER XXII

Lucian's tragedy ran for precisely seventeen nights. The 'attempt to revive Tragedy on the lines of pure Greek Art' was a failure. Everybody thought the poetry very beautiful, but there were too many long speeches and too few opportunities for action and movement to satisfy a modern audience, and Harcourt quickly discovered that not even magnificent scenery and crowds of supernumeraries arrayed in garments of white and gold and purple and green will carry a play through. He was in despair from the second night onwards, for it became evident that a great deal of cutting was necessary, and on that point he had much trouble with Lucian, who, having revised his work to the final degree, was not disposed to dock it in order to please the gods in the gallery. The three weeks during which the tragedy ran were indeed weeks of storm and stress. The critics praised the poetry of the play, the staging, the scenery, the beauty and charm of everything connected with it, but the public yawned. In Lucian's previous play there had been a warm, somewhat primitive human interest—it took those who saw it into the market-place of life, and appealed to everyday passions; in the new tragedy people were requested to spend some considerable time with the gods in Olympus amidst non-human characteristics and qualities. No one, save a few armchair critics like Mr. Chilverstone, wished to breathe this diviner air; the earlier audiences left the theatre cold and untouched. 'It makes you feel,' said somebody, 'as if you had been sitting amongst a lot of marble statues all night and could do with something warming to the blood.' In this way the inevitable end came. All the people who really wanted to see the tragedy had seen it within a fortnight; during the next few nights the audiences thinned and the advance bookings represented small future business, and before the end of the third week Harcourt had withdrawn the attempt to revive tragedy on the lines of pure Greek Art, and announced a revival of an adaptation from a famous French novel which had more than once proved its money-earning powers.

Lucian said little of this reverse of fortune—he was to all appearance unmoved by it; but Sprats, who could read his face as easily as she could read an open book, saw new lines write themselves there which told of surprise, disappointment, and anxiety, and she knew from his subdued manner and the unwonted reticence which he observed at this stage that he was thinking deeply of more things than one. In this she was right. Lucian by sheer force of circumstances had been dragged to a certain point of vantage whereat he was compelled to stand and look closely at the prospect which confronted him. When it became evident that the tragedy was a failure as a money-making concern, he remembered, with a sudden shock that subdued his temperamental buoyancy in an unpleasant fashion, that he had not foreseen such a contingency, and that he had confidently expected a success as great as the failure was complete. He sat down in his study and put the whole matter to himself in commendably brief fashion: for several months he and Haidee had been living and spending money on anticipation; it was now clear that the anticipation was not to be realised. The new volume was selling very slowly; the tragedy was a financial failure; very little in the way of solid cash would go from either to the right side of Lucian's account at Darlington's. And on the wrong side there must be an array of figures which he felt afraid to think of. He hurriedly cast up in his mind a vague account of those figures which memory presented to him; when he added the total to an equally vague guess of what Haidee might have spent, he recognised that he must be in debt to the bank to a considerable amount. He had never had the least doubt that the tragedy would prove a gold-mine—everybody had predicted it. Darlington had predicted it a hundred times, and Darlington was a keen, hard-headed business man. Well, the tragedy was a failure—to use the expressive term of the man in the street, 'there was no money in it.' It was to have replenished Lucian's coffers—it left them yawning.

Easy-going and thoughtless though he was, Lucian had a constitutional dislike of owing money to any one, and the thought that he was now in debt to his bankers irritated and annoyed him. Analysed to a fine degree, it was not that he was annoyed because he owed money, but because he was not in a position to cancel the debt with a few scratches of his pen, and so relieve himself of the disagreeable necessity of recognising his indebtedness to any one. He had a temperamental dislike of unpleasant things, and especially of things which did not interest him—his inherited view of life had caused him to regard it as a walk through a beautiful garden under perpetual sunshine, with full liberty to pluck whatever flower appealed to his eye, eat whatever fruit tempted his palate, and turn into whatever side-walk took his fancy. Now that he was beginning to realise that it is possible to wander out of such a garden into a brake full of thorns and tangles, and to find some difficulty in escaping therefrom, his dislike of the unpleasant was accentuated and his irritation increased. But there was a certain vein of method and of order in him, and when he really recognised that he had got somewhere where he never expected to be, he developed a sincere desire to find out at once just where he was. The present situation had some intellectual charm for him: he had never in all his life known what it was to want money; it had always come to his hand as manna came to the Israelites in the desert—he wondered, as these unwonted considerations for the present and the future filled him, what would develop from it.

'It will be best to know just where one really is,' he thought, and he went off to find his wife and consult with her. It was seldom that he ever conversed with her on any matter of a practical nature; he had long since discovered that Haidee was bored by any topic that did not interest her, or that she did not understand. She scarcely grasped the meaning of the words which Lucian now addressed to her, simple though they were, and she stared at him with puzzled eyes.

'You see,' he said, feeling that his explanation was inept and crude, 'I'd fully expected to have an awful lot of money out of the book and the play, and now, it seems, there won't be so much as I had anticipated. Of course there will be Robertson's royalties, and so on, but I don't think they will amount to very much for the half-year, and——'

Haidee interrupted him.

'Does it mean that you have spent all the money?' she asked. 'There was such a lot, yours and mine, together.'

Lucian felt powerless in the face of this apparently childish remark.

'Not such a lot,' he said. 'And you know we had heavy expenses at first—we had to spend a lot on the house, hadn't we?'

'But will there be no more to spend?' she asked. 'I mean, has it all been spent? Because I want a lot of things, if we are to winter in Egypt as you proposed.'

Lucian laughed.

'I'm afraid we shall not go to Egypt this winter,' he said. 'But don't be alarmed; I think there will be money for new gowns and so on. No; what I just wished to know was—have you any idea of what you have spent since I transferred our accounts to Darlington's bank?'

Haidee shrugged her shoulders. As a matter of fact she had used her cheque-book as she pleased, and had no idea of anything relating to her account except that she had drawn on it whenever she wished to do so.

'I haven't,' she answered. 'You told me I was to have a separate account, and, of course, I took you at your word.'

'Well, it will be all right,' said Lucian soothingly. 'I'll see about everything.'

He was going away, desirous of closing any discussion of the subject, but Haidee stopped him.

'Of course it makes a big difference if your books don't sell and people won't go to your plays,' she said. 'That doesn't bring money, does it?'

'My dear child!' exclaimed Lucian, 'how terribly perturbed you look! One must expect an occasional dose of bad luck. The next

127

book will probably sell by the tens of thousands, and the next play run for a hundred years!'

'They were saying at Lady Firmanence's the other afternoon that you had had your day,' she said, looking inquiringly at him. 'Do you think you have?'

'I hope I have quite a big day to come yet,' he answered quietly. 'You shouldn't listen to that sort of thing—about me.'

Then he left her and went back to his study and thought matters over once more. 'I'll find out exactly where I am,' he thought at last, and he went out and got into a hansom and was driven to Lombard Street—he meant to ascertain his exact position at the bank. When he entered, with a request for an interview with Mr. Eustace Darlington, he found that the latter was out of town, and for a moment he thought of postponing his inquiries. Then he reflected that others could probably give him the information he sought, and he asked to see the manager. Five minutes after entering the manager's private room he knew exactly how he stood with Messrs. Darlington and Darlington. He owed them close upon nine thousand pounds.

Lucian, bending over the slip of paper upon which the manager had jotted down a memorandum of the figures, trusted that the surprise which he felt was not being displayed in his features. He folded the paper, placed it in his pocket, thanked the manager for his courtesy, and left the bank. Once outside he looked at the paper again: the manager had made a distinction between Mr. Damerel's account and his wife's. Mr. Damerel's was about eighteen hundred pounds in debt; Mrs. Damerel's separate account had been drawn against to the extent of nearly seven thousand pounds. Lucian knew what had become of the money which he had spent, but he was puzzled beyond measure to account for the sums which Haidee had gone through within a few months.

Whenever he was in any doubt or perplexity as to practical matters Lucian invariably turned to Sprats, and he now called a hansom and bade the man drive to Bayswater. He knew, from long experience of her, that he could tell Sprats anything and everything, and that she would never once say 'I told you so!' or 'I knew how it would turn out!' or 'Didn't I warn you?' She might scold him; she would almost certainly tell him that he was a fool; but she wouldn't pose as a superior person, or howl over the milk which he had spilled—instead, she would tell him quietly what was the best thing to do.

He found her alone, and he approached her with the old boyish formula which she had heard a hundred times since he had discovered that she knew a great deal more about many things than he knew himself.

'I say, Sprats, I'm in a bit of a hole!' he began.

'And, of course, you want me to pull you out. Well, what is it?' she asked, gazing steadily at him and making a shrewd guess at the sort of hole into which he had fallen. 'Do the usual, Lucian, tell everything.'

When he liked to be so, Lucian was the most candid of men. He laid bare his soul to Sprats on occasions like these in a fashion which would greatly have edified a confessor. He kept nothing back; he made no excuses; he added no coat of paint or touch of white-wash. He set forth a plain, unvarnished statement, without comment or explanation; it was a brutally clear and lucid account of facts which would have honoured an Old Bailey lawyer. It was one of his gifts, and Sprats never had an instance of it presented to her notice without wondering how it was that a man who could marshal facts so well and put them before others in such a crisp and concise fashion should be so unpractical in the stern business of life.

'And that's just how things are,' concluded Lucian, 'What do you advise me to do?'

'There is one thing to be done at once,' she answered, without hesitation. 'You must get out of debt to Darlington; you must pay him every penny that you owe him as quickly as possible. You say you owe him nearly nine thousand pounds: very good. How much have you got towards paying that off?'

Lucian sighed deeply.

'That's just it!' he exclaimed. 'I don't exactly know. Let me see, now; well, look here, Sprats—you won't tell, of course—Mr. Pepperdine owes me a thousand—at least I mean to say I lent him a thousand, but then, don't you know, he has always been so good to me, that——'

'I think you had better chuck sentiment,' she said. 'Mr. Pepperdine has a thousand of yours. Very well—go on.'

'I've been thinking,' he continued, 'that I might now ask him for the money which my father left me. He has had full charge of that, you know. I've never known what it was. I dare say it was rather heavily dipped into during the time I was at Oxford, but there may be something left.'

'Has he never told you anything about it?' asked Sprats.

'Very little. Indeed, I have never asked him anything—I could trust him with everything. It's quite possible there may not be a penny; he may have spent it all on me before I came of age,' said Lucian. 'Still, if there is anything, it would go towards making up the nine thousand, wouldn't it?'

129

'Well, leave it out of the question at present,' she answered. 'What else have you coming in soon?'

'Harcourt has two hundred of mine, and Robertson about three hundred.'

'That's another five hundred. Well, and the rest?'

'I think that's the lot,' he said.

'There are people who owe you money,' she said. 'Come, now, Lucian, you know there are.'

Lucian began to wriggle and to study the pattern of the hearthrug.

'Oh! ah! well!' he said, 'I—I dare say I have lent other men a little now and then.'

'Better say given,' she interrupted. 'I was only wondering if there was any considerable sum that you could get in.'

'No, really,' he answered.

'Very well; then you've got fifteen hundred towards your nine thousand. That's all, eh?' she asked.

'All that I know of,' he said.

'Well, there are other things,' she remarked, with some emphasis. 'There are your copyrights and your furniture, pictures, books, and curiosities.'

Lucian's mouth opened and he uttered a sort of groan.

'You don't mean that I should—sell any of these?' he said, looking at her entreatingly.

'I'd sell the very clothes off my back before I'd owe a penny to Darlington!' she replied. 'Don't be a sentimental ass, Lucian; books in vellum bindings, and pictures by old masters, and unique pots and pans and platters, don't make life! Sell every blessed thing you've got rather than owe Darlington money. Pay him off, get out of that house, live in simpler fashion, and you'll be a happier man.'

Lucian sat for some moments in silence, staring at the hearthrug. At last he looked up. Sprats saw something new in his face—or was it something old? something that she had not seen there for years? He looked at her for an instant, and then he looked away.

'I should be very glad to live a simpler life,' he said. 'I dare say it seems rather sentimental and all that, you know, but of late I've had an awfully strong desire—sort of home-sickness, you know—for Simonstower. I've caught myself thinking of the old days, and—' he paused, laughed in rather a forced way, and sitting straight up in the easy-chair in which he had been lounging, began to drum on its arms with his fingers. 'What you say,' he continued presently, 'is quite right. I must not be in debt to Darlington—it has been a most

130

kind and generous thing on his part to act as one's banker in this fashion, but one mustn't trespass on a friend's kindness.'

Sprats flashed a swift, half-puzzled look upon him—he was looking another way, and did not see her.

'Yes,' he went on meditatively, 'I'm sure you are right, Sprats, quite right. I'll act on your advice. I'll go down to Simonstower to-morrow and see if Uncle Pepperdine can let me have that thousand, and if there is any money of my own, and when I come back I'll see if Robertson will buy my copyrights—I may be able to clear the debt off with all that. If not, I shall sell the furniture, books, pictures, everything, and Haidee and I will go to Italy, to Florence, and live cheaply. Ah! I know the loveliest palazzo on the Lung' Arno—I wish we were there already. I'm sick of England.'

'It will make a difference to Haidee, Lucian,' said Sprats. 'She likes England—and English society.'

'Yes,' he answered thoughtfully, 'it will make a great difference. But she gave up a great deal for me when we married, and she'll give up a great deal now. A woman will do anything for the man she loves,' he added, with the air of a wiseacre. 'It's a sort of fixed law.'

Then he went away, and Sprats, after spending five minutes in deep thought, remembered her other children and hastened to them, wondering whether the most juvenile of the whole brood were quite so childish as Lucian. 'It will go hard with him if his disillusion comes suddenly,' she thought, and for the rest of the day she felt inclined to sadness.

Lucian went home in a good humour and a brighter flow of spirits. He was always thus when a new course of action suggested itself to him, and on this occasion he felt impelled to cheerfulness because he was meditating a virtuous deed. He wrote some letters, and then went to his club, and knowing that his wife had an engagement of her own that night, he dined with an old college friend whom he happened to meet in the smoking-room, and to whom before and after dinner he talked in lively fashion. It was late when he reached home, and he was then more cheerful than ever; the picture of the old palazzo on the Lung' Arno had fastened itself upon the wall of his consciousness and compelled him to look at it. Haidee had just come in; he persuaded her to go with him into his study while he smoked a final cigarette, and there, full of his new projects, he told her what he intended to do. Haidee listened without saying a word in reply. Lucian took no notice of her silence: he was one of those people who imagine that they are addressing other people when they are in reality talking to themselves and require neither Yea nor Nay; he went on expatiating upon his

131

scheme, and the final cigarette was succeeded by others, and Haidee still listened in silence.

'You mean to do all that?' she said at last. 'To sell everything and go to Florence? And to live there?'

'Certainly,' he replied tranquilly; 'it will be so cheap.'

'Cheap?' she exclaimed. 'Yes—and dull! Besides, why this sudden fuss about owing Darlington money? It's been owing for months, and you didn't say anything.'

'I expected to be able to put the account straight out of the money coming from the book and the play,' he replied. 'As they are not exactly gold-mines, I must do what I can. I can't remain in Darlington's debt in that way—it wouldn't be fair to him.'

'I don't see that you need upset everything just for that,' she said. 'He has not asked you to put the account straight, has he?'

'Of course not!' exclaimed Lucian. 'He never would; he's much too good a fellow to do that sort of thing. But that's just why I must get out of his debt—it's taking a mean advantage of his kindness. I'm quite certain nobody else would have been so very generous.'

Haidee glanced at her husband out of the corners of her eyes: the glance was something like that with which Sprats had regarded him in the afternoon. He had not caught Sprats's glance, and he did not catch his wife's.

'By the bye, Haidee,' he said, after a short silence, 'I called at Darlington's to-day to find out just how we stand there, and the manager gave me the exact figures. You've rather gone it, you know, during the past half-year. You've gone through seven thousand pounds.'

Haidee looked at him wonderingly.

'But I paid for the diamonds out of that, you know,' she said. 'They cost over six thousand.'

'Good heavens!—did they?' said Lucian. 'I thought it was an affair of fifty pounds or so.'

'How ridiculous!' she exclaimed. 'Diamonds—like these—for fifty pounds! You are the simplest child I ever knew.'

Lucian was endeavouring to recall the episode of the buying of the diamonds. He remembered at last that Haidee had told him that she had the opportunity of buying some diamonds for a much less sum than they were worth. He had thought it some small transaction, and had bidden her to consult somebody who knew something about that sort of thing.

'I remember now,' he said. 'I told you to ask advice of some one who knew something about diamonds.'

'And so I did,' she answered. 'I asked Darlington's advice—he's an authority—and he said I should be foolish to miss the

132

chance. And then I said I didn't know whether I dare draw a cheque for such an amount, and he laughed and said of course I might, and that he would arrange it with you.'

'There you are!' said Lucian triumphantly; 'that's just another proof of what I've been saying all along. Darlington's such a kind-hearted sort of chap that he never said anything about it to me. Well, there's no harm done there, any way, Haidee; in fact, it's rather a relief to know that you've locked up six thousand in that way, because you can sell the diamonds and the money will go towards putting the account straight.'

Haidee looked at him narrowly: Lucian's eyes were fixed on the curling smoke of his cigarette.

'Sell my diamonds?' she said in a low voice.

'Yes, of course,' said Lucian; 'it'll be rather jolly if there's a profit on them. Oh yes, we must sell them. I can't afford to lock up six thousand in precious stones, you know, and of course we can't let Darlington pay for them. I wonder what they really are worth? What a lark if we got, say, ten thousand for them!'

Then he wandered into an account of how a friend of his had once picked up a ring at one of the stalls on the Ponte Vecchio in Florence, and had subsequently sold it for just ten times as much as he had given for it. He laughed very much in telling his wife this story, for it had certain amusing points in it, and Haidee laughed too, but if Lucian had been endowed with a better understanding of women he would have known that she was neither amused nor edified.

CHAPTER XXIII

Lucian came down to breakfast next morning equipped for his journey to Simonstower. He was in good spirits: the day was bright and frosty, and he was already dreaming of the village and the snow-capped hills beyond it. In dressing he had thought over his plans, and had decided that he was now quite reconciled to the drastic measures which Sprats had proposed. He would clear off all his indebtedness to Darlington, pay whatever bills might be owing, and make a fresh start, this time on the lines of strict economy, forethought, and prudence. He had very little conception of the real meaning of these important qualities, but he had always admired them in the abstract, and he now intended to form an intimate acquaintance with them.

'I've been thinking,' he said, as he faced Haidee at the breakfast-table and spread out the Morning Post, 'that when I have readjusted everything we shall be much better off than I thought. Those diamonds make a big difference, Haidee. In fact we shall have, or we ought to have, quite a decent little capital, and we'll invest it in something absolutely safe and sound. I'll ask Darlington's advice about that, and we'll never touch it. The interest and the royalties will yield an income which will be quite sufficient for our needs—you can live very cheaply in Italy.'

'Then you are still bent on going to Italy—to Florence?' she asked calmly.

'Certainly,' he replied. 'It's the best thing we can do. I'm looking forward to it. After all, why should we be encumbered as we are at present with an expensive house, a troop of servants, and all the rest of it? We don't really want them. Has it never occurred to you that all these things are something like the shell which the snail has to carry on his back and can't get away from? Why should a man carry a big shell on his back? It's all very well talking about the advantages and comforts of having a house of one's own, but it's neither an advantage nor a comfort to be tied to a house nor to anything that clogs one's action.'

Haidee made no reply to those philosophic observations.

'How long do you propose to stay in Italy?' she asked. 'Simply for the winter? I suppose we should return here for the season next year?'

'I don't think so,' answered Lucian. 'We might go into Switzerland during the very hot months—we couldn't stand Florence in July and August. But I don't intend returning to London for some time. I don't think I shall ever settle here again. After all, I am Italian.'

Then, finding that it was time he set out for King's Cross, he kissed his wife's cheek, bade her amuse and take care of herself during his absence, and went away, still in good spirits. For some time after he had gone Haidee remained where he had left her. She ate and drank mechanically, and she looked straight before her in the blank, purposeless fashion which often denotes intense concentration of thought. When she rose from the table she walked about the room with aimless, uncertain movements, touching this and that object without any reason for doing so. She picked up the Morning Post, glanced at it, and saw nothing; she fingered two or three letters which Lucian had left lying about on the breakfast-table, and laid them down again. They reminded her, quite suddenly, of a letter from Eustace Darlington which she had in her pocket, a trivial note, newly arrived, which informed her that he had made some purchase or other for her in Paris, whither he had gone for a week on business, and that she would shortly receive a parcel containing it. There was nothing of special interest or moment in the letter; she referred to it merely to ascertain Darlington's address.

After a time Haidee went into the study and sought out a railway guide. She had already made up her mind to join Eustace Darlington, and she now decided to travel by a train which would enable her to reach Paris at nine o'clock that evening. She began to make her preparations at once, and instructed her maid to pack two large portmanteaus. Her jewels she packed herself, taking them out of a safe in which they were usually deposited, and after she had bestowed them in a small handbag she kept the latter within sight until her departure. Everything was carried out with coolness and thoughtfulness. The maid was told that her mistress was going to Paris for a few days and that she was to accompany her; the butler received his orders as to what was to be done until Mrs. Damerel's return the next day or the day following. There was nothing to surprise the servants, and nothing to make them talk, in Haidee's proceedings. She lunched at an earlier hour than usual, drove to the station with her maid, dropped a letter, addressed to Lucian at Simonstower vicarage, into the pillar-box on the platform, and departed for Paris with an admirable unconcern. There was a choppy sea in the Channel, and the maid was ill, but Haidee acquired a hearty appetite, and satisfied it in the dining-car of the French train. She was one of those happily constituted people who can eat at the greatest moments of life.

She drove from the Gare du Nord to the Hôtel Bristol, and engaged rooms immediately on her arrival. A little later she inquired for Darlington, and then discovered that he had that day journeyed to Dijon, and was not expected to return until two days later. Haidee, in nowise disconcerted by this news, settled down to await his reappearance.

135

CHAPTER XXIV

Lucian arrived at the old vicarage towards the close of the afternoon. He had driven over from Oakborough through a wintry land, and every minute spent in the keen air had added to the buoyancy of his spirits. Never, he thought as he was driven along the valley, did Simonstower look so well as under its first coating of snow, and on the rising ground above the village he made his driver stop so that he might drink in the charm of the winter sunset. At the western extremity of the valley a shelving hill closed the view; on its highest point a long row of gaunt fir-trees showed black and spectral against the molten red of the setting sun and the purpled sky into which it was sinking; nearer, the blue smoke of the village chimneys curled into the clear, frosty air—it seemed to Lucian that he could almost smell the fires of fragrant wood which burned on the hearths. He caught a faint murmur of voices from the village street: it was four o'clock, and the children were being released from school. Somewhere along the moorland side a dog was barking; in the windows of his uncle's farmhouse, high above the river and the village, lights were already gleaming; a spark of bright light amongst the pine and fir trees near the church told him that Mr. Chilverstone had already lit his study-lamp. Every sound, every sight was familiar—they brought the old days back to him. And there, keeping stern watch over the village at its foot, stood the old Norman castle, its square keep towering to the sky, as massive and formidable as when Lucian had first looked upon it from his chamber window the morning after Simpson Pepperdine had brought him to Simonstower.

He bade the man drive on to the vicarage. He had sent no word of his coming; he had more than once descended upon his friends at Simonstower without warning, and had always found a welcome. The vicar came bustling into the hall to him, with no sign of surprise.

'I did not know they had wired to you, my boy,' he said, greeting him in the old affectionate way, 'but it was good of you to come so quickly.'

Lucian recognised that something had happened.

'I don't understand you,' he said. 'No one wired to me; I came down on my own initiative—I wanted to see my uncle on business.'

'Ah!' said the vicar, shaking his head. 'Then you do not know?—your uncle is ill. He had a stroke—a fit—you know what I mean—this very morning. Your Aunt Judith is across at the farm now. But come in, my dear boy—how cold you must be.'

136

Lucian went out to the conveyance which had brought him over, paid the driver, and bade him refresh himself at the inn, and then joined the vicar in his study. There again were the familiar objects which spelled Home. It suddenly occurred to him that he was much more at home here or in the farmhouse parlour along the roadside than in his own house in London, and he wondered in vague, indirect fashion why that should be so.

'Is my uncle dangerously ill, then?' he asked, looking at the vicar, who was fidgeting about with the fire-irons and repeating his belief that Lucian must be very cold.

'I fear so, I fear so,' answered Mr. Chilverstone. 'It is, I think, an apoplectic seizure—he was rather inclined to that, if you come to think of it. Your aunt has just gone across there. It was early this morning that it happened, and she has been over to the farm several times during the day, but this time I think she will find a specialist there—Dr. Matthews wished for advice and wired to Smokeford for some great man who was to arrive an hour ago. I am glad you have come, Lucian. Did you see Sprats before leaving?'

Lucian replied that he had seen Sprats on the previous day. He sat down, answering the vicar's questions respecting his daughter in mechanical fashion—he was thinking of the various events of the past twenty-four hours, and wondering if Mr. Pepperdine's illness was likely to result in death. Mr. Chilverstone turned from Sprats to the somewhat sore question of the tragedy. It was to him a sad sign of the times that the public had neglected such truly good work, and he went on to express his own opinion of the taste of the age. Lucian listened absent-mindedly until Mrs. Chilverstone returned with news of the sick man. She was much troubled; the specialist gave little hope of Simpson's recovery. He might linger for some days, but it was almost certain that a week would see the end of him. But in spite of her trouble Aunt Judith was practical. Keziah, she said, must not be left alone that night, and she herself was going back to the farm as soon as she had seen that the vicar was properly provided for in respect of his sustenance and comfort. Ever since her marriage Mrs. Chilverstone had felt that her main object in life was the pleasing of her lord; she had put away all thought of the dead hussar, and her romantic disposition had bridled itself with the reins of chastened affection. Thus the vicar, who under Sprats's régime had neither been pampered nor coddled, found himself indulged in many modes hitherto unknown to him, and he accepted all that was showered upon him with modest thankfulness. He thought his wife a kindly and considerate soul, and did not realise, being a truly simple man, that Judith was pouring out upon him the resources of a treasury which she had been stocking all her life. He was the first thing she had the chance of loving in a practical fashion; hence he began to live among rose-leaves. He protested now that Lucian and himself wanted for nothing. Mrs. Chilverstone, however, took the reins in hand, saw that the traveller was properly attended to and provided for, and did not leave the vicarage until the two men were comfortably seated at the dinner-table, the maids admonished as to lighting a fire in Mr. Damerel's room, and the vicar warned of the necessity of turning out the lamps and locking the doors. Then she returned to her brother's house, and for an hour or two Lucian and his old tutor talked of things nearest to their hearts, and the feelings of home came upon the younger man more strongly than ever. He began to wonder how it was that he had settled down in London when he might have lived in the country; the atmosphere of this quiet, book-lined room in a village parsonage was, he thought just then, much more to his true taste than that in which he had spent the last few years of his life. At Oxford Lucian had lived the life of a book-worm and a dreamer: he was not a success in examinations, and he brought no great honour upon his tutor. In most respects he had lived apart from other men, and it was not until the publication of his first volume had drawn the eyes of the world upon him that he had been swept out of the peaceful backwater of a student's existence into the swirling tides of the full river of life. Then had followed Lord Simonstower's legacy, and then the runaway marriage with Haidee, and then four years of butterfly existence. He began to wonder, as he ate the vicar's well-kept mutton, fed on the moorlands close by, and sipped the vicar's old claret, laid down many a year before, whether his recent life had not been a feverish dream. Looked at from this peaceful retreat, its constant excitement and perpetual rush and movement seemed to have lost whatever charm they once had for him. Unconsciously Lucian was suffering from reaction: his moral as well as his physical nature was crying for rest, and the first oasis in the desert assumed the delightful colours and soft air of Paradise.

Later in the evening he walked over to the farmhouse, through softly falling snow, to inquire after his uncle's condition. Mrs. Chilverstone was in the sick man's room and did not come downstairs; Miss Pepperdine received him in the parlour. In spite of the trouble that had fallen upon the house and of the busy day which she had spent, Keziah was robed in state for the evening, and she sat bolt upright in her chair plying her knitting-needles as vigorously as in the old days which Lucian remembered so well. He sat down and glanced at Simpson Pepperdine's chair, and wished the familiar figure were occupying it, and he talked to his aunt of her brother's illness, and the cloud which hung over the house weighed heavily upon both.

'I am glad you came down, Lucian,' said Miss Pepperdine, after a time. 'I have been wanting to talk to you.'

'Yes,' he said. 'What about?'

Keziah's needles clicked with unusual vigour for a moment or two.

'Simpson,' she said at last, 'was always a soft-hearted man. If he had been harder of heart, he would have been better off.'

Lucian, puzzled by this ambiguous remark, stared at Miss Pepperdine in a fashion indicative of his amazement.

'I think,' continued Miss Pepperdine, with pointed emphasis, 'I think it is time you knew more than you know at present, Lucian. When all is said and done, you are the nearest of kin in the male line, and after hearing the doctors to-night I'm prepared for Simpson's death at any moment. It's a very bad attack of apoplexy— if he lived he'd be a poor invalid all his life. Better that he should be taken while in the full possession of his faculties.'

Lucian gazed at the upright figure before him with mingled feelings. Miss Pepperdine used to sit like that, and knit like that, and talk like that, in the old days—especially when she felt it to be her duty to reprimand him for some offence. So far as he could tell, she was wearing the same stiff and crackly silk gown, she held her elbows close to her side and in just the same fashion, she spoke with the same precision as in the time of Lucian's youth. The sight of her prim figure, the sound of her precise voice, blotted out half a score of years: Lucian felt very young again.

'It may not be so bad as you think,' he said. 'Even the best doctors may err.'

Miss Pepperdine shook her head.

'No,' she said, 'it's all over with Simpson. And I think you ought to know, Lucian, how things are with him. Simpson has been a close man, he has kept things to himself all his life; and of late he has been obliged to confide in me, and I know a great deal that I did not know.'

'Yes?' said Lucian.

'Simpson,' she continued, 'has not done well in business for some time. He had a heavy loss some years ago through a rascally lawyer whom he trusted—he always was one of those easy-going men that will trust anybody—and although the old Lord Simonstower helped him out of the difficulty, it ultimately fell on his own shoulders, and of late he has had hard work to keep things going. Simpson will die a poor man. Not that that matters—Judith and myself are provided for. I shall leave here, afterwards. Judith, of course, is married. But as regards you, Lucian, you lent Simpson some money a few months ago, didn't you?'

'My dear aunt!' exclaimed Lucian, 'I——'

'I know all about it,' she said, 'though it's only recently that I have known. Well, you mustn't be surprised if you have to lose it, Lucian. When all is settled up, I don't think there will be much, if anything, over; and of course everybody must be paid before a member of the family. The Pepperdines have always had their pride, and as your mother was a Pepperdine, Lucian, you must have a share of it in you.'

'I have my father's pride as well,' answered Lucian. 'Of course I shall not expect the money. I was glad to be able to lend it.'

'Well,' said Miss Pepperdine, with the air of one who deals out justice impartially, 'in one way you were only paying Simpson back for what he had laid out on you. He spent a good deal of money on you, Lucian, when you were a boy.'

Lucian heard this news with astonished feelings.

'I did not know that,' he said. 'Perhaps I am careless about these things, but I have always thought that my father left money for me.'

'I thought so too, until recently,' replied Miss Pepperdine. 'Your father thought that he did, too, and he made Simpson executor and trustee. But the money was badly invested. It was in a building society in Rome, and it was all lost. There was never a penny piece from it, from the time of your father's death to this.'

Lucian listened in silence.

'Then,' he said, after a time, 'my uncle was responsible for everything for me? I suppose he paid Mr. Chilverstone, and bought my clothes, and gave me pocket-money, and so on?'

'Every penny,' replied his aunt. 'Simpson was always a generous man.'

'And my three years at Oxford?' he said inquiringly.

'Ah!' replied Miss Pepperdine, 'that's another matter. Well—I don't suppose it matters now that you should know, though Simpson wouldn't have told you, but I think you ought to know. That was Lord Simonstower—the old lord. He paid every penny.'

Lucian uttered a sharp exclamation. He rose from his chair and took a step or two about the room. Miss Pepperdine continued to knit with undiminished vigour.

'So it would seem,' he said presently, 'that I lived and was educated on charity?'

'That is how most people would put it,' she answered, 'though, to do them justice, I don't think either Lord Simonstower or Simpson Pepperdine would have called it that. They thought you a

140

promising youth and they put money into you. That's why I want you to feel that Simpson was only getting back a little of his own in the money that you lent him, though I know he would have paid it back to the day, according to his promise, if he'd been able. But I'm afraid that he would not have been able, and I think his money affairs have worked upon him.'

'I wish I had known,' said Lucian. 'He should have had no anxiety on my account.'

He continued to pace the floor; Miss Pepperdine's needles clicked an accompaniment to his advancing and retreating steps.

'I thought it best,' she observed presently, 'that you should know all these things—they will explain a good deal.'

'Yes,' he answered, 'it is best. I should know. But I wish I had known long ago. After all, a man should not be placed in a false position even by his dearest friends. I ought to have been told the truth.'

Miss Pepperdine's needles clicked viciously.

'So I always felt—after I knew, and that is but recently,' she answered. 'But, as I have said to you before, Simpson Pepperdine is a soft-hearted man.'

'He has been a kind-hearted man,' said Lucian. He was thinking, as he walked about the room, glancing at the well-remembered objects, that the money which he had wasted in luxuries that he could well have done without would have relieved Mr. Pepperdine of anxiety and trouble. And yet he had never known, never guessed, that the kindly-hearted farmer had anything to distress him.

'I think we all seem to walk in darkness,' he said, thinking aloud. 'I never had the least notion of this. Had I known anything of it, Uncle Simpson should have had all that I could give him.'

Miss Pepperdine melted. She had formed rather hard thoughts of Lucian since his marriage. The side-winds which blew upon her ears from time to time represented him as living in a style which her old-fashioned mind did not approve: she had come to consider him as extravagant, frivolous, and unbalanced. But she was a woman of sound common sense and great shrewdness, and she recognised the genuine ring in Lucian's voice and the sincerity of his regret that he had not been able to save Simpson Pepperdine some anxiety.

'I'm sure you would, my boy,' she said kindly. 'However, Simpson has done with everything now. I didn't tell Judith, because she frets so, but the doctors don't think he'll ever regain consciousness—it will only be a matter of a few days, Lucian.'

'And that only makes one wish that one had known of his

anxieties sooner,' he said. 'Five years ago I could have helped him substantially.'

He was thinking of the ten thousand pounds which had already disappeared. Miss Pepperdine did not follow his line of thought.

'Yes, I've heard that you've made a lot of money,' she said. 'You've been one of the lucky ones, Lucian, for I always understood that poets generally lived in garrets and were half-starved most of their time. I'm sure one used to read all that sort of thing in books; but perhaps times have changed, and so much the better. Simpson always read your books as soon as you sent them. Upon my word, I'm sure he never understood what it was all about, except perhaps some of the songs and ballads, but he liked the long words, and he was very proud of these little green books—they're all in his bureau there, along with his account-books. Well, as I was saying, I understand you've made money, Lucian. Take care of it, my boy, for you never know when you may want it, and want it badly, in this world. There's one thing I want you to promise me. I don't yet know how things will be when Simpson's gone, but if he is a bit on the wrong side of the ledger, it must be made up by the family, and you must do your share. It mustn't be said that a Pepperdine died owing money that he couldn't pay. I've already talked it over with Judith, and if there is money to be found, she and I and you must find it between us. If need be, all mine can go,' she added sharply. 'I can get a place as a housekeeper even at my age.'

Lucian gave her his promise readily enough, and immediately began to wonder what it might imply. But he agreed with her reasoning, and assured himself that, if necessary, he would live on a crust in order to carry out her wishes. And soon afterwards he set out for the vicarage, promising to return for news of Mr. Pepperdine's condition at an early hour in the morning.

As he walked back over the snow Lucian was full of thought. The conversation with Miss Pepperdine had opened a new world to him. He had always believed himself independent: it now turned out that for years and years he had lived at other men's charges. He owed his very food to the charity of a relative; another man, upon whom he had no claim, had lavished generosity upon him in no unstinted fashion. He was full of honest gratitude to these men, but he wished at the same time that he had known of their liberality sooner. He felt that he had been placed in a false position, and the feeling lowered him in his own estimation. He thought of his father, who earned money easily and spent it freely, and realised that he had inherited his happy-go-lucky temperament. Yet he had never doubted that his father had made provision for him, for he

142

remembered hearing him tell some artist friends one afternoon in Florence that he had laid money aside for Lucian's benefit, and Cyprian Damerel had been a man of common sense, fond of pleasure and good living and generous though he was. But Lucian well understood the story of the Roman building society—greater folk than he, from the Holy Father downwards, had lost money out of that feverish desire to build which has characterised the Romans of all ages. No doubt his father had been carried away by some wave of enthusiasm, and had put all his eggs into one basket, and they had all been broken together. Still, Lucian wished that Mr. Pepperdine had told him all this on his reaching an age of understanding—it would have made a difference in many ways. 'I seem,' he thought, as he plodded on through the snow, 'I seem to have lived in an unreal world, and to have supposed things which were not!' And he began to recall the days of sure and confident youth, when his name was being extolled as that of a newly risen star in the literary firmament, and his own heart was singing with the joy of pride and strength and full assurance. He had never felt one doubt of the splendour of his career, never accepted it as anything but his just due. His very certainty on these matters had, all unknown to himself, induced in him an unassuming modesty, at which many people who witnessed his triumphs and saw him lionised had wondered. Now, however, he had tasted the bitterness of reverse; he had found that Fortune can frown as easily as she can smile, and that it is hard to know upon what principle her smiles and frowns are portioned out. To a certain point, life for Lucian had been a perpetual dancing along the primrose way—it was now developing into a tangle wherein were thorns and briars.

He was too full of these thoughts to care for conversation, even with his old tutor, and he pleaded fatigue and went to bed. He lay awake for the greater part of the night, thinking over his talk with Miss Pepperdine, and endeavouring to arrange his affairs so that he might make good his promise to her, and when he slept, his sleep was troubled by uneasy dreams. He woke rather late in the morning with a feeling of impending calamity hanging heavily upon him. As he dressed, Mr. Chilverstone came tapping at his door—something in the sound warned Lucian of bad news. He was not surprised when the vicar told him that Simpson Pepperdine had died during the night.

He walked over to the farm as soon as he had breakfasted, and remained there until noon. Coming back, he overtook the village postman, who informed him that the letters were three hours late that morning in consequence of the heavy fall of snow, which had choked up the roads between Simonstower and Oakborough.

'It'll be late afternoon afore I've finished my rounds,' he added, with a strong note of self-pity. 'If you're going up to the vicarage, sir, it 'ud save me a step if you took the vicar's letters—and there's one, I believe, for yourself.'

Lucian took the bundle of letters which the man held out to him, and turned it over until he found his own. He wondered why Haidee had written to him—she had no great liking for correspondence, and he had not expected to hear from her during his absence. He opened the letter in the vicar's study, without the least expectation of finding any particular news in it.

It was a very short letter, and, considering the character of the intimation it was intended to make, the phrasing was commendably plain and outspoken. Lucian's wife merely announced that his plans for the future were not agreeable to her, and that she was leaving home with the intention of joining Eustace Darlington in Paris. She further added that it was useless to keep up pretences any longer; she had already been unfaithful, and she would be glad if Lucian would arrange to divorce her as quickly as possible, so that she and Darlington might marry. Either as an afterthought, or out of sheer good will, she concluded with a lightly worded expression of friendship and of hope that Lucian might have better luck next time.

It is more than probable that Haidee was never quite so much her true self in her relation to Lucian as when writing this letter. It is permitted to every woman, whatever her mental and moral quality, to have her ten minutes of unreasoning romance at some period of her life, and Haidee had hers when she and Lucian fell in love with each other's beauty and ran away to hide themselves from the world while they played out their little comedy. It was natural that they should tire of each other within the usual time; but the man's sense of duty was developed in Lucian in a somewhat exceptional way, and he was inclined to settle down to a Darby and Joan life. Haidee had little of that particular instinct. She was all for pleasure and the glory of this world, and there is small wonder that the prospect of exile in a land for which she had no great liking should have driven her to the salvation of her diamonds and herself by recourse to the man whom she ought to have married instead of Lucian. There was already a guilty bond between them; it seemed natural to Haidee to look to it as a means of drawing her away from the dangers which threatened her worldly comfort. It was equally natural to her to announce all these things to Lucian in pretty much the same terms that she would have employed had she been declining an invitation to some social engagement.

Lucian read the letter three times. He gave no sign of whatever emotion it called up. All that he did was to announce in

144

quiet, matter-of-fact tones that he must return to London that afternoon, and to beg the loan of the vicar's horse and trap as far as Wellsby station. After that he lunched with Mr. and Mrs. Chilverstone, and if they thought him unusually quiet, there was good reason for that in the fact that Simpson Pepperdine was lying dead in the old farmhouse behind the pine groves.

CHAPTER XXV

Haidee, waiting for Darlington in Paris, spent the time in a state of perfect peace, amused herself easily and successfully, and at the same time kept clear of such of her acquaintance as she knew to be in the French capital at that moment. On the morrow Darlington would return, and after that everything would be simple. She had arranged it all in her own mind as she travelled from London, and she believed—having a confident and sanguine disposition—that the way in which the affair presented itself to her was the only way in which it could possibly present itself to any one. It had been a mistake to marry Lucian. Well, it wasn't too late to rectify the mistake, and one was wise, of course, in rectifying it. If you find out that you are on the wrong road—why, what more politic and advisable than to take the shortest cut to the right one? She was sorry for Lucian, but the path which he was following just then was by no means to her own taste, and she must leave him to tread it alone. She was indeed sorry for him. He had been an ardent and a delightful lover—for a while—and it was a pity he was not a rich man. Perhaps they might be friends yet. She, at any rate, would bear no malice—why should she? She was fond enough of Lucian in one way, but she had no fondness for a quiet life in Florence or Pisa or anywhere else, and she had been brought up to believe that a woman must be good to the man who can best afford to be good to her, and she felt as near an approach to thankfulness as she had ever felt in her life when she remembered that Eustace Darlington still cherished a benevolent disposition towards her.

Darlington did not return to Paris until nearly noon of the following day. When he reached his hotel he was informed by his valet, whom he had left behind, that Mrs. Damerel had arrived, and had asked for him. Darlington felt no surprise on hearing this news;

nothing more serious than a shopping expedition occurred to him. He sent his man to Haidee's rooms with a message, and after changing his clothes went to call upon her himself. His manner showed her that he neither suspected nor anticipated anything out of the common, but his first question paved the way for her explanation. It was a question that might have been put had they met in New York or Calcutta or anywhere, a question that needed no definite answer.

'What brings you here? Frills, or frocks, or something equally feminine, I suppose?' he said carelessly, as he shook hands with her. 'Staying long?'

The indifference of his tone sounded somewhat harshly in Haidee's hearing. It was evident that he suspected nothing and had no idea of the real reason of her presence. She suddenly became aware that there might be difficulties in the path that had seemed so easy.

'Lucian here?' asked Darlington, with equal carelessness.

'No,' she said. Then, in a lower tone, she added, 'I have left Lucian.'

Darlington turned quickly from the window, whither he had strolled after their greeting. He uttered a sharp, half-suppressed exclamation.

'Left him?' he said. 'You don't mean——'

His interrogative glance completed the sentence. There was something in his eyes, something stern and businesslike, that made Haidee afraid. Her own eyes turned elsewhere.

'Yes,' she said.

Darlington put his hands in his pockets and came and stood in front of her. He looked down at her as if she had been a child out of whom he wished to extract some information.

'Quarrelling, eh?' he said.

'No, not quarrelling at all,' she answered.

'Then—what?'

'He has spent all the money,' she said, 'and lots beside, and he is going to sell everything in the house in order to pay you, and then he wanted me to go and live cheaply—cheaply, you understand?—in Italy; and—and he said I must sell my diamonds.'

'Did he?' said Darlington. 'And he is going to sell everything in order to pay me, is he? Well, that's honest; I didn't think he'd the pluck. He's evidently not quite such an utter fool as I've always thought him. Well?'

'And, of course, I left him.'

'That "of course" is good. Of course, being you, you did, "of course." Yes, I understand that part, Haidee. But'—he looked

146

around him with an expressive glance at her surroundings, 'why—here?' he inquired sharply.

'I came to you,' she said in a low and not too confident voice.

Darlington laughed—a low, satirical, cynical laughter that frightened her. She glanced at him timidly; she had never known him like that before.

'I see!' he said. 'You thought that I should prove a refuge for the fugitive wife? But I'm afraid that I am not disposed to welcome refugees of any description—it isn't my métier, you know.'

Haidee looked at him in astonishment. Her eyes caught and held his: he saw the growing terror in her face.

'But——' she said, and came to a stop. Then she repeated the word, still staring at him with questioning eyes. Darlington tore himself away with a snarl.

'Look here!' he said, 'I'm not a sentimental man. If I ever had a scrap of sentiment, you knocked it out of me four years ago. I was fond of you then. I'd have made you a kind husband, my girl, and you'd have got on, fool as you are by nature. But you threw me over for that half-mad boy, and it killed all the soft things I had inside me. I knew I should have my revenge on both of you, and I've had it. He's ruined; he hasn't a penny piece that isn't due to me; and as for you—listen, my girl, and I'll tell you some plain truths. You're a pretty animal, nice to play with for half an hour now and then, but you're no man's mate for life, unless the man's morally blind. I once heard a scientific chap say that the soul's got to grow in human beings. Well, yours hasn't sprouted yet, Haidee. You're a fool, though you are a very lovely woman. I suppose—'—he came closer to her, and looking down at her astonished face smiled more cynically than ever—'I suppose you thought that I would run away with you and eventually marry you?'

'I—yes—of course!' she whispered.

'Well,' he said, 'if I, too, had been a fool, I might have done that. But I am not a fool, my dear Haidee. Perhaps I'm hard, brutal, cynical—the world and its precious denizens have made me so. I'm not going to run away with the woman who ran away with another man on the very eve of her marriage to me; and as to marrying you, well—I'm plain spoken enough to tell you that I made up my mind years ago that whatever other silliness I might commit, I would never commit the crowning folly of marrying a woman who had been my mistress.'

Haidee caught her breath with a sharp exclamation. If she had possessed any spirit she would have risen to her feet, said things, done things: having none, like most of her sort, she suddenly buried her face in her hands and sobbed.

147

'I dare say it doesn't sound nice,' said Darlington, 'but Lord knows it's best to be plain spoken. Now, my girl, listen to me. Go home and make the best of your bargain. I'll let Lucian Damerel off easily, though to tell you the truth I've always had cheerful notions of ruining him hopelessly. If he wants to live cheaply in Italy, go with him—you married him. You have your maid here?—tell her to pack up and be ready to leave by the night train. I dare say Damerel thinks you have only run over here to buy a new gown; he never need know anything to the contrary.'

'B-b-b-but I have t-t-told him!' she sobbed. 'He knows!'

'Damn you for a fool!' said Darlington, between his teeth. He put his hands in his pockets again and began rattling the loose money there. For a moment he stood staring at Haidee, his face puckered into frowning lines. He came up to her. 'How did you tell him?' he said. 'You didn't—write it?'

'Yes,' she answered. 'I did—I wrote him a letter.'

Darlington sighed.

'Oh, well!' he said, 'it doesn't matter, only he'll be able to get heavy damages, and I wanted to clear him out. It's the fortune of war. Well, I'm going. Good-day.'

He had walked across to the door and laid his hand upon the latch ere Haidee comprehended the meaning of his words. Then she sprang up with a scream.

'And what of me?' she cried. 'Am I to be left here?'

'You brought yourself here,' he retorted, eyeing her evilly. 'I did not ask you to come.'

She stared at him open-mouthed as if he were some strange thing that had come into her line of vision for the first time. Her breath began to come and go in gasps. She was an elementary woman, but at this treatment from the man she had known as her lover a natural indignation sprang up in her and she began to find words.

'But this!' she said, with a nearer approach to honesty than she had ever known, 'this is—desertion!'

'I am under no vow to you,' he said.

'You have implied it. I trusted you.'

'As Lucian trusted you,' he sneered.

She became speechless again. Something in her looks brought Darlington back from the door to her side.

'Look here, Haidee,' he said, not unkindly, 'don't be a little fool. Go home quickly and settle things with your husband. Tell him you wrote that letter in a fit of temper; tell him—oh, tell him any of the lies that women invent so easily on these occasions! It's absolutely hopeless to look to me for protection, absolutely impossible for me to give it——'

He stopped. She was staring at him in a strange way—the way in which a dumb animal might stare if the butcher who was about to kill it condescended to try to explain to it why it was necessary that he should presently cut its throat. Darlington hummed and ha'd when he caught that look. He cast a furtive glance at the door and half turned away from Haidee.

'Yes, quite impossible,' he repeated. 'The fact is—well, you may as well knew it now as hear it later on—I am going to be married.'

She nodded her head as if she quite understood his meaning, and he, looking full at her again, noticed that she was trying to moisten her lips with the tip of her tongue, and that her eyes were dilated to an unusual degree.

'You can't say that I've treated you badly,' he said. 'After all, you had the first chance, and it wasn't my fault if you threw it away. There, now, be sensible and go back to London and make it up with Damerel. You can easily get round him—he'll believe anything you tell him. Say you were upset at the thought of going to Italy with him, and lost your head. Things will come all right if you only manage your cards properly. Well, I'm going—good-day.'

He turned slowly from her as if he were somewhat ashamed of his desertion. They had been standing by the side of a table, littered about on which were several odds and ends picked up by Haidee on the previous day. Amongst them was an antique stiletto, sharp as a needle, which had taken her fancy at a shop in the Palais Royal. She had thought of using it as a hat-pin, and was charmed when the dealer suggested that it had probably tasted the heart's-blood of more than one victim. Its glitter caught her eye now, and she picked it up and struck furiously at Darlington's back.

At that moment Lucian was being conducted to his wife's room by a courteous manager. At the threshold they paused, brought to a simultaneous standstill by a wild scream. When they entered the room, Darlington lay crumpled up and dead in the centre of the floor, and Haidee, gazing spellbound at him from the furthest corner, was laughing—a long, low ripple of laughter that seemed as if it would never cease. The stiletto, thrown at her feet, flashed back a ray of sunlight from the window.

CHAPTER XXVI

That afternoon Saxonstowe arrived in town from Yorkshire with a grim determination in his heart to have it out once and for all with Sprats. He had tried to do his duty as a country squire and to interest himself in country life and matters: he had hunted the fox and shot pheasants, sat on the bench at petty and at quarter sessions, condoled with farmers on poor prices and with old women on bad legs, and he was still unsatisfied and restless and conscious of wanting something. The folk round about him came to the conclusion that he was not as other young men of his rank and wealth—he seemed inclined to bookishness, he was a bit shy and a little bit stand-offish in manner, and he did not appear to have much inclination for the society of neighbours in his own station of life. Before he succeeded to the title Saxonstowe had not been much known in the neighbourhood. He had sometimes visited his predecessor as a schoolboy, but the probability of his becoming the next Lord Saxonstowe was at that time small, and no one had taken much notice of Master Richard Feversham. When he came back to the place as lord and master, what reputation he had was of a sort that scarcely appealed to the country people. He had travelled in some fearsome countries where no other man had ever set foot, and he had written a great book about his adventures, and must therefore be a clever young man. But he was not a soldier, nor a sailor, and he did not particularly care for hunting or shooting, and was therefore somewhat of a hard nut to crack. The honest gentlemen who found fox-hunting the one thing worth living for could scarcely realise that even its undeniable excitements were somewhat tame to a man who had more than once taken part in a hunt in which he was the quarry, and they were disposed to regard the new Viscount Saxonstowe as a bit of a prig, being unconscious that he was in reality a very simple-minded, unaffected young man who was a little bit embarrassed by his title and his wealth. As for their ladies, it was their decided opinion that a young peer of such ancient lineage and such great responsibilities should marry as soon as possible, and each believed that it was Lord Saxonstowe's bounden duty to choose a wife from one of the old north-country families. In this Saxonstowe agreed with them. He desired a wife, and a wife from the north country, and he knew where to find her, and wanted her so much that it had long been evident to his sober judgment that, failing her, no other woman would ever call him husband. The more he was left alone, the more deeply he sank in the sea of love. And at last he felt that life was too short to be trifled with, and he went back to Sprats and asked her firmly and insistently to marry him.

Sprats was neither hurt nor displeased nor surprised. She listened silently to all he had to say, and she looked at him with her usual frankness when he had finished.

'I thought we were not to talk of these matters?' she said. 'We were to be friends—was there not some sort of compact?'

'If so, I have broken it,' he answered—'not the friendship—that, never!—but the compact. Besides, I don't remember anything about that. As to talking of this, well, I intend to go on asking you to marry me until you do.'

'You have not forgotten what I told you?' she said, eyeing him with some curiosity.

'Not at all. I have thought a lot about it,' he answered. 'I have not only thought, but I have come to a conclusion.'

'Yes?' she said, still curious. 'What conclusion?'

'That you are deceiving yourself,' he answered. 'You think you love Lucian Damerel. I do not doubt that you do, in a certain way, but not in the way in which I would wish you, for instance, to love me, and in which I believe you could and would love me—if you would let yourself.'

Sprats stared at him with growing curiosity and surprise. There was something masterful and lordly about his tone and speech that filled her heart with a great sense of contentment—it was the voice of the superior animal calling to the inferior, of the stronger to the weaker. And she was so strong that she had a great longing to be weak—always providing that something stronger than herself were shielding her weakness.

'Well?' was all she could say.

'You have always felt a sense of protection for him,' continued Saxonstowe. 'It was in you from the first—you wanted something to take care of. But isn't there sometimes a feeling within you that you'd like to be taken care of yourself?'

'Who taught you all this?' she asked, with puzzled brows. 'You seem to have acquired some strange knowledge of late.'

'I expect it's instinct, or nature, or something,' he said. 'Anyhow, have I spoken the truth?'

'You don't expect me to confess the truth to you, do you?' she answered. 'You have not yet learned everything, I see.' She paused and regarded him for some time in silence. 'I don't know why,' she said at last, 'but this seems as if it were the prelude to a fight. I feel as I used to feel when I fought with Lucian—there was always a lot of talk before the tearing and rending began. I feel talky now, and I

151

also feel that I must fight you. To begin with, just remember that I am a woman and you're a man. I don't know anything about men—they're incomprehensible to me. To begin with, why do you wish to marry me?—you're the first man who ever did. I want to know why—why—why?'

'Because you're the woman for me and I'm the man for you,' he replied masterfully. 'You are my mate.'

'How do you know?'

'I feel it.'

'Then why don't I feel it?' she asked quickly.

'Are you dead certain you don't?' he said, smiling at her. 'I think, perhaps, that if you could just get deep down into yourself, you do.'

'But that doesn't explain why you want to marry me,' she said inconsequently. 'You tell me that what I have always felt for Lucian is not what I ought to feel for the man I love. Well, if I analyse what I feel for Lucian, perhaps it is what you say it is—a sense of protection, of wanting to help, and to shield; but then, you say that that is the sort of love you have for me.'

'Did I?' he said, laughing quietly. 'You forget that I have not yet told you what sort of love I have for you—we have not reached the love-making stage yet.'

Sprats felt femininity assert itself. She knew that she blushed, and she felt very hot and very uncomfortable, and she wished Saxonstowe would not smile. She was as much a girl and just as shy of a possible lover as in her tom-boy days, and there was something in Saxonstowe's presence which aroused new tides of feeling in her. He had become bold and masterful; it was as if she were being forced out of herself. And then he suddenly did a thing which sent all the blood to her heart with a wild rush before it leapt back pulsing and throbbing through her body. Saxonstowe spoke her name.

'Millicent!' he said, and laid his hand very gently on hers. 'Millicent!'

She drew away from him quickly, but her eyes met his with courage.

'My name!' she said. 'No one ever called me by my name before. I had half forgotten it.'

'Listen,' he said. 'I want you to think all this over, like the woman you are. Don't waste your life on a dream or a delusion. Come to me and be my wife and friend so long as God lets us live. You are a true woman—a woman in a thousand. I would not ask you else. I will be a true man to you. And you and I together can do great things, for others. Think, and tell me your thoughts—afterwards.'

152

'Yes, afterwards,' she said. She wanted him to go, and he saw it and went, and Sprats sat down to think. But for the first time in her life she found it impossible to think clearly. She tried to marshal facts and to place them before her in due sequence and proper order, but she discovered that she was pretty much like all other women at these junctures and that a strange confusion had taken possession of her. For the moment there was too much of Saxonstowe in her mental atmosphere to enable her to think, and after some time she uttered an impatient exclamation and went off to attend to her duties. For the remainder of the afternoon she bustled about the house, and the nursing-staff wondered what it was that had given their Head such a fit of vigorous research into unexplored corners. It was not until evening that she allowed herself to be alone again, and by that time she was prepared to sit down and face the situation. She went to her own room with a resolute determination to think of everything calmly and coolly, and there she found evening newspapers lying on the table, and she picked one up mechanically and opened it without the intention of reading it, and ere she knew what was happening she had read of the tragedy in Paris. The news stamped itself upon her at first without causing her smart or pain, even as a clean shot passes through the flesh with little tearing of the fibres. She sat down and read all that the telegrams had to tell, and searched each of the newspapers until she was in possession of the latest news.

She had gone into her room with the influence of Saxonstowe's love-making still heavy upon her womanhood; she left it an unsexed thing of action and forceful determination. In a few moments she had seen her senior nurse and had given her certain orders; in a few more she was in her outdoor cloak and bonnet and at the door, and a maid was whistling for a hansom for her. But just as she was running down the steps to enter it, another came hurriedly into the square, and Saxonstowe waved his hand to her. She paused and went back to the open door; he jumped from his cab and joined her, and they went into the house together, and into the room which she had just left.

'I was going to you' she said, 'and yet I might have known that you would come to me.'

'I came as soon as I knew,' he answered.

She looked at him narrowly: he was watching her with inquiring eyes.

'We must go there at once,' she said. 'There is time to catch the night train?'

'Yes,' he said, 'plenty of time. I have already made some arrangements—I thought you would wish it.'

153

She nodded in answer to this, and began to take some things out of a desk. Saxonstowe noticed that her hand was perfectly steady, though her face was very pale. She turned presently from packing a small handbag and came up to him.

'Listen,' she said; 'it is you and I who are going—you understand?'

He looked at her for a moment in silence, and then bowed his head. He had not understood, but he felt that she had come to some determination, and that that was no time to question her. In a few moments more they had left the house and set out on their journey to Paris.

CHAPTER XXVII

Our neighbours on the other side of the Channel are blessed with many qualities which were not given to us who reside in these islands, and amongst them is one which most Englishmen would not pay a penny for if it were on sale in market overt. This is the quality of sentiment—a thing which we others strive to choke at its birth, and to which at any time we give but an outside corner of the hearth of life. It is a quality of which one may have too much, but in its place it is an excellent and a desirable quality, for it tends to the establishment of a fitting sense of proportion, and makes people polite and considerate at the right moment. Had the tragedy of Haidee and Darlington occurred in England, there would have been much vulgar curiosity manifested, for amongst us we often fail to gauge the niceties of a situation. In Paris, sentiment fixed the affaire Damerel at its right value in a few hours. It was a veritable tragedy—one to be spoken of with bated breath—one of those terrible dramas of real life which far transcend anything that can be placed upon the stage. The situations were pathetic, the figures of the chief actors of a veritable notability. The young husband, great as a poet and handsome as a Greek god; the young wife, beautiful and charming; the plutocrat lover, of whom death forbade to speak—they were all of a type to attract. Then the intense tragedy of the final situation! Who could tell what had occurred between the lover and the wife in that last supreme scene, since he was dead and she bereft of reason? It had all the elements of greatness, and greatness demands respect.

Therefore, instead of being vulgarised, as it would have been in unsentimental England, the affaire Damerel was spoken of with a tender respect and with few words. It was an event too deplorable to merit common discussion.

Lucian had swept through London to Paris intent on killing Darlington with his own hands. His mental balance had been destroyed, and he himself rendered incapable of hearing or seeing reason long before he reached the French capital. The courteous manager who replied to Lucian's calm inquiries for Mrs. Damerel did not realise that the composure of the distinguished-looking young gentleman was that of the cunning madman. Inside Lucian's breast nestled a revolver—his fingers were itching to get at it as he followed his guide up the stairs, for he had made up his mind to shoot his faithless wife and his treacherous enemy on sight.

The sight of Haidee, mopping and mowing in her corner, the sound of her awful laughter, brought Lucian back to sanity. Living and moving as if he were in some fearful dream, he gave orders and issued directions. The people of the hotel, half paralysed by the strangeness of the tragedy, wondered at his calmness; the police were astonished by the lucidity of the statement which he gave to them. His one great desire was to shield his wife's name. The fierce resentment which he had felt during his pursuit of her had completely disappeared in presence of the tragedy. Before the end of the afternoon some curious mental process in him had completely rehabilitated Haidee in his estimation: he believed her to have been deeply wronged, and declared with emphasis that she must have killed Darlington in a fit of desperation following upon some wickedness of his own. Her incriminating letter he swept aside contemptuously—it was a sure proof, he said, that the poor child's mind was already unhinged when it was written. He turned a blind eye to undoubted facts. Out of a prodigal imagination and an exuberant fancy he quickly built up a theory which presently assumed for him the colours of absolute truth. Haidee had been tempted in secret by this devil who had posed as friend; he had used his insidious arts to corrupt her, and the temptation had fallen upon her at the very moment when he, Lucian, was worrying her with his projects of retrenchment. She had taken flight, the poor Haidee who had lived in rose-leaf luxury all her days, and had fled from her exaggerated fears to the man she believed her friend and Lucian's. Then, when she had found out his true character, she—in a moment of awful fear or fright, most probably—had killed him. That was the real story, the poor, helpless truth. He put it before Sprats and Saxonstowe with a childlike belief in its plausibility and veracity that made at least one of them like to weep—he had shown them the letter which Haidee had written to Lucian before leaving town, and they knew the real truth of the whole sorry business. It seemed best, after all, thought Sprats, and said so to Saxonstowe when she got the chance, that Lucian should cherish a fiction rather than believe the real truth. And that he did believe his fiction was soon made evident.

'It is all my fault—all!' he said to Sprats, with bitter self-reproach. 'I never took care of her as I should have done, as I had vowed to do. You were right, Sprats, in everything that you said to me. I wonder what it is that makes me so blind to things that other people see so clearly? I ought not to have let the poor child be exposed to the temptations of that arch-devil; but I trusted him implicitly. He always made the most sincere professions of his friendship for both of us. Then again, how is it, why is it, that people so constantly deceive me? I believe every man as I expect every man to believe me. Do you think I ever dreamt of all this, ever dreamt of what was in that scoundrel's mind? Yet I ought to have foreseen—I ought to have been guided by you. It is all my fault, all my fault!'

It was useless to argue with him or to condole with him. He had persuaded himself without an effort that such and such things were, and the only thing to be done with him was to acquiesce in his conclusions and help him as judiciously as possible. The two faithful friends who had hurried to his side remained with him until the troubled waters grew calm again. That was now an affair of time. Haidee was certainly insane, and the physicians held out little hope of her recovery. By their advice she was removed to a private institution within easy distance of Paris, and Lucian announced his intention of settling down in the gay city in order to be near her. He talked of her now as if she had been a girl-bride, snatched away from him by ruthless fate, and it was plain to see that he had obliterated the angry thoughts that had filled him during his frenzy of resentment, and now cherished nothing but feelings of chastened and tender regret. For Haidee, indeed, frailest of frail mortals, became apotheosised into something very different. Lucian, who never did anything by halves and could not avoid extremes, exalted her into a sort of much-wronged saint; she became his dream, and nobody had the heart to wake him.

Sprats and Saxonstowe worked hard for him at this time, one relieving him of much trouble in making the necessary arrangements for Haidee, the other of a large part of the business affairs brought into active operation by the recent tragedy. Saxonstowe, working untiringly on his behalf, was soon able to place Lucian's affairs in order. Lucian gave him full power to act, and ere long had the satisfaction of knowing that the liability to

Darlington and Darlington had been discharged, that Miss Pepperdine's mind had been set at rest as to the preservation of the family honour, and that he owed money to no one. He would be able to surround the stricken Haidee with every comfort and luxury that one in her condition could enjoy, and he himself need never feel a moment's anxiety. For the affaire Damerel had had its uses. Lucian came again in the market. Mr. Robertson began to sell the thin green-clad volumes more rapidly than ever before; even the portly epic moved, and finally began racing its sister competitors for the favour of the fickle public. Mr. Harcourt, with a rare sense of fitness, revived Lucian's first play to crowded houses; an enterprising Frenchman went over to London and witnessed a performance, and within a few weeks presented a version of it at one of the Parisian theatres. French translations of Lucian's works followed, and sold like hot cakes; the Italian translations received a fillip, and people in the United States became interested. Nothing, said Mr. Robertson, could have been better, from a trade point of view.

Lucian accepted all this with indifference and equanimity. All his thoughts were centred on the quiet house in the little village outside Paris, where Haidee laughed at her own fingers or played with dolls. Every afternoon he left his appartement and travelled into the country to inquire after his wife's health. He always carried some little gift with him—flowers, fruit, a child's picture-book, a child's toy, and the nurse to whom these things were given used to weep over them, being young and sentimental, and very much in love with Lucian's face and hair, which was now turning a pretty and becoming grey at the temples. Sometimes he saw the doctor, who was sympathetic, and guarded in his answers, and sometimes he walked in the garden with an old abbé who used to visit the place, and exchanged pious sentiments with him. But he never saw Haidee, for the doctors feared it, and thus his conception of her was not of the madwoman, but of the young beauty with whom he had made an impetuous runaway marriage. He used to walk about Paris in those days with eyes that wore a far-away expression, and the women would speak of his beauty with tears in their eyes and shake their heads over the sadness of his story, which was well known to everybody, and in pecuniary value was worth a gold-mine.

CHAPTER XXVIII

When they had done everything that could be done for him at that time, Sprats and Saxonstowe left Lucian in Paris and returned together to London. He appeared to have no particular desire that they should remain with him, nor any dread of being alone. Sprats had seen to the furnishing of his rooms and to the transportation of his most cherished books and pictures; he was left surrounded with comfort and luxury, and he assured his friends that he wanted for nothing. He intended to devote himself to intense study, and if he wanted a little society, well, he already had a considerable acquaintance amongst authors and artists in Paris, and could make use of it if need were. But he spoke of himself as of an anchorite; it was plain to see that he believed that the joie de vivre existed for him no longer. It was also plain that something in him wished to be clear of the old life and the old associations. He took an affectionate farewell of Sprats and of Saxonstowe at the Gare du Nord, whither he accompanied them on their departure, but Sprats was keenly aware of the fact that there was that in him which was longing to see the last of them. They were links of a chain that bound him to a life with which he wished to have no further connection. When they said good-bye, Sprats knew that she was turning down a page that closed a long chapter of her own life.

She faced the problem bravely and with clear-headedness. She saw now that much of what she had taken to be real fact had been but a dream. Lucian had awakened the mother-instinct in her by his very helplessness, but nothing in him had ever roused the new feeling which had grown in her every day since Saxonstowe had told her of his love. She had made the mistake of taking interest and affection for love, and now that she had found it out she was contented and uneasy, happy and miserable, pleased and furious, all at once. She wanted to run away from Saxonstowe to the very ends of the earth, but she also cherished a secret desire to sit at his feet and be his slave, and would rather have torn her tongue out than tell him of it.

While they were father-and-mother-ing Lucian in Paris, Saxonstowe had remained solid and grim as one of the Old Guard, doing nothing but his duty. Sprats had watched him with keen observation, and had admired his stern determination and the earnest way in which he did everything. He had taken hold of Lucian as a big brother might take a little one, and had been gentle and firm, kindly and tactful, all at once. She had often longed to

158

throw her arms round him and kiss him for his good-boy qualities, but he had sunk the lover in the friend with unmistakable purpose, and she was afraid of him. She began to catch herself looking at him out of her eye-corners when he was not looking at her, and she hated herself. Once when he came suddenly into a room, she blushed so furiously that she could have cried with vexation, and it was all the more aggravating, she said, because she had just happened to be thinking of him. Travelling back together, she was very subdued and essentially feminine. Her manner invited confidence, but Saxonstowe was stiff as a ramrod and cold as an icicle. He put her into a hansom at Charing Cross, and bade her good-bye as if she had been a mere acquaintance.

But he came to her the next afternoon, and she knew from his face that he was in an urgent and a masterful mood. She recognised that she would have to capitulate, and had a happy moment in assuring herself that she would make her own terms. Saxonstowe wasted no time. He might have been a smart young man calling to collect the water-rate.

'The night that we went to Paris together,' he said, 'you made an observation which you thought I understood. I didn't understand it, and now I want to know what you meant.'

'What I said. That we were going—you and I—together,' she answered.

'But what did that mean?'

'Together,' she said, 'together means—well, of course, it means—together.'

Saxonstowe put his hands on her shoulders; she immediately began to study the pattern of the hearthrug at their feet.

'Will you marry me, Millicent?' he said.

She nodded her head, but her eyes still remained fixed on his toes.

'Answer me,' he commanded.

'Yes,' she said, and lifted her eyes to his.

A moment later she disengaged herself from his arms and began to laugh.

'I was going to extract such a lot of conditions,' she said. 'Somehow I don't care about them now. But will you tell me just what is going to happen?'

'You knew, I suppose, that I should have already mapped everything out. Well, so I have. We shall be married at once, in the quietest possible fashion, and then we are going round the world in our own way. It is to be your holiday after all these years of work.'

She nodded, with perfect acquiescence in his plans.

'At once?' she said questioningly.

'A week from to-day,' he said.

The notion of such precipitancy brought the blood into her face.

'I suppose I ought to say that I can't possibly be ready in a week,' she said, 'but it so happens that I can. A week to-day, then.'

Mr. Chilverstone came up from Simonstower to marry them. It was a very quiet wedding in a quiet church. Lady Firmanence, however, was there, and before the bride and bridegroom left to catch a transatlantic liner for New York she expressed a decided opinion that the fourth Viscount Saxonstowe had inherited more than his share of the good sense and wise perception for which their family had always been justly famous.

CHAPTER XXIX

Lucian settled down into a groove-like existence. He read when he liked and worked when he felt any particular inclination to do so; he amused himself at times with the life which a man of his temperament may live in Paris, but always with the air of one who looks on. He made a few new friends and sometimes visited old ones. Now and then he entertained in a quiet, old-fashioned way. He was very indulgent and caressing to a certain coterie of young people who believed in him as a great master and elevated his poetry to the dignity of a cult. He was always a distinguished figure when he showed himself at the opera or the theatre, and people still pointed him out on the boulevards and shook their heads and said what a pity it was that one so young and handsome and talented should carry so heavy a burden. In this way he may be said to have become quite an institution of Paris, and Americans stipulated with their guides that he should be pointed out to them at the first opportunity.

Whatever else engaged Lucian's attention or his time, he never forgot his daily visit to the quiet house in the suburbs where Haidee still played with dolls or laughed gleefully at her attendants. He permitted nothing to interfere with this duty, which he regarded as a penance for his sins of omission to Haidee in days gone by. Others might forsake Paris for the sea or the mountains; Lucian remained there all the year round for two years, making his daily pilgrimage. He saw the same faces every day, and heard the same report, but he never saw his wife. Life became curiously even and regular, but it never oppressed him. He had informed himself at the very beginning of this period that this was a thing to be endured, and he endured it as pleasantly and bravely as possible. During those two years he published two new volumes, of a somewhat new note, which sold better in a French translation than in the English original, and at Mr. Harcourt's urgent request he wrote a romantic drama. It filled the Athenæum during the whole of a London season, and the financial results were gratifying in a high degree, for the glamour and mystery of the affaire Damerel were still powerful, and Lucian had become a personality and a force by reason of his troubles.

At the end of two years, the doctor to whose care Haidee had been entrusted called Lucian into his private room one day and told him that he had grave news to communicate. His patient, he said, was dying—slowly, but very surely. But there was more than that: before her death she would recover her reason. She would probably recall everything that had taken place; it was more than possible that she would have painfully clear recollections of the scene, whatever it might be, that had immediately preceded her sudden loss of sanity. It was but right, said the doctor, that Mr. Damerel should know of this, but did Mr. Damerel wish to be with his wife when this development occurred? It might be a painful experience, and death must soon follow it. It was for Mr. Damerel to decide. Lucian decided on the instant. He had carried an image of Haidee in his mind for two years, and it had become fixed on his mental vision with such firmness that he could not think of her as anything but what he imagined her to be. He told the doctor that he would wish to know as soon as his wife regained her reason—it was his duty, he said, to be with her. After that, every visit to the private asylum was made with anxious wonder if the tortured brain had cleared.

It was not until the following spring—two and a half years after the tragedy of the Bristol—that Lucian saw Haidee. He scarcely knew the woman to whom they took him. They had deluged him with warnings as to the change in her, but he had not expected to find her a grey-haired, time-worn woman, and he had difficulty in preserving his composure when he saw her. He did not know it, but her reason had returned some time before, and she had become fully cognisant of her surroundings and of what was going to happen. More than that, she had asked for a priest and had enjoyed ghostly consolation. She gazed at Lucian with a curious wistfulness, and yet there was something strangely sullen in her manner.

'I wanted to see you,' she said, after a time. 'I know I'm going

161

to die very soon, and there are things I want to say. I remember all that happened, you know. Oh yes, it's quite clear to me now, but somehow it doesn't trouble me—I was mad enough when I did it.'

'Don't speak of that,' he said. 'Forget it all.'

She shook her head.

'Never mind,' she went on. 'What I wanted to say was, that I'm sorry that—well, you know.'

Lucian gazed at her with a sickening fear creeping closely round his heart. He had forced the truth away from him: he was to hear it at last from the lips of a dying woman.

'You were to blame, though,' she said presently. 'You ought not to have let me go alone on his yacht or to the Highlands. It was so easy to go wrong there.'

Lucian could not control a sharp cry.

'Don't!' he said, 'don't! You don't know what you're saying. It can't be that—that you wrote the truth in that letter? It was—hallucination.'

She looked at him out of dull eyes.

'I want you to say you forgive me,' she said. 'The priest—he said I ought to ask your forgiveness.'

Lucian bowed his head.

'Yes,' he said, 'I forgive all you wish. Try not to think of it any more.'

He was saying over and over to himself that she was still disordered of mind, that the sin she was confessing was imaginary; but deeper than his insistence on this lay a dull consciousness that he was hearing the truth. He stood watching her curiously. She suddenly looked up at him, and he saw a strange gleam in her eyes.

'After all,' she said, half spitefully, 'you came between him and me at the beginning.'

Lucian never saw his wife again. A month later she was dead. All the time of the burial service he was thinking that it would have been far better if she had never recovered her reason. For two years he had cherished a dream of her that had assumed tender and pathetic tones. It had become a part of him; the ugly reality of the last grim moments of her life stood out in violent contrast to its gentleness and softness. When the earth was thrown upon the coffin, he was wondering at the wide difference which exists between the real and the unreal, and whether the man is most truly blessed who walks amongst stern verities or dreams amidst the poppy-beds of illusion. One thing was certain: the face of truth was not always beautiful, nor her voice always soothing to the ear.

CHAPTER XXX

After Haidee's death Lucian left Paris, and during the rest of the spring and summer of that year went wandering hither and thither about Europe. His mind was at this time in a state of quiescence; he lounged from one place to another, faintly interested and lazily amused. He was beginning to be a little bored by life, and a little tempted to drift with its stream. It was in this frame of mind that he returned to London in the following autumn. There, soon after his return, he sprang into unwonted activity.

It was on the very eve of the outbreak of the war in South Africa. Men were wondering what was going to happen. Some, clearer of vision than their fellows, saw that nothing but war would solve the problem which had assumed vast proportions and strange intricacies because of the vacillating policy of a weak Government of twenty years before; the Empire was going to pay now, with millions of its treasure and thousands of its men, for the fatal error which had brought the name of England into contempt in the Transvaal and given the Boers a false notion of English strength and character. Others were all for a policy of smoothing things over, for spreading green boughs over pitfalls—not that any one should fall into them, but in order to make believe that the pitfalls were not there. Others again, of a breed that has but lately sprung into existence in these islands, advocated, not without success, a policy of surrender to everybody and everything. There was much talking at street corners and in the market-place; much angry debate and acrimonious discussion. Men began to be labelled by new names, and few took the trouble to understand each other. In the meantime, events developed as inevitable consequence always develops them in such situations. Amidst the chattering of tiny voices the thunders of war burst loud and clear.

Lucian was furious with indignation. Fond as he was of insisting on his Italian nationality, he was passionately devoted to England and the English, and had a great admiration for the history and traditions of the country of his adoption. There had once been a question in his mind as to whether he should write in English or in Italian—he had elected to serve England for many reasons, but chiefly because he recognised her greatness and believed in her destiny. Like all Italians, he loved her for what she had done for Greece and for Italy. England and Liberty were synonymous names; of all nations in the world, none had made for freedom as England had. His blood had leapt in his veins many a time at the thought of

163

the thousand and one great things she had done, the mighty battles she had fought for truth and liberty; he had drunk in the notion from boyhood that England stood in the very vanguard of the army of deliverance. And now she was sending out her armies, marshalling her forces, pouring out her money like water, to crush a tiny folk, a nation of farmers, a sturdy, simple-minded race, one of the least amongst the peoples of the earth! He shook his head as if he had been asleep, and asked himself if the nation had suddenly gone mad with lust of blood. It was inconceivable that the England of his dreams could do this thing. He looked for her, and found her nowhere. The streets were hot all day with the tramping of armed men. The first tidings of reverse filled the land with the old savage determination to fight things out to the end, even though all the world should range itself on the other side.

Lucian flung all his feelings of rage, indignation, sorrow, and infinite amazement into a passionate sonnet which appeared next morning in large type, well leaded and spaced, in the columns of a London daily newspaper that favoured the views of the peace-at-any-price party. He followed it up with others. At first there was more sorrow and surprise than anything else in these admonitions; but as the days went on their tone altered. He had endeavoured to bring the giant to his senses by an appeal to certain feelings which the giant was too much engaged to feel at that moment; eliciting no response, he became troublesome, and strove to attract the giant's attention by pricking him with pins. The giant paid small attention to this; he looked down, saw a small thing hanging about his feet with apparently mischievous intentions, and calmly pushed it away. Then Lucian began the assault in dead earnest. He could dip his pen in vitriol with the best of them, and when he realised that the giant was drunk with the lust of blood he fell upon him with fury. The vials of poetic wrath had never been emptied of such a flood of righteous anger since the days wherein Milton called for vengeance upon the murderers of the Piedmontese.

It is an ill thing to fight against the prevalent temper of a nation. Lucian soon discovered that you may kick and prick John Bull for a long time with safety to yourself, because of his good nature, his dislike of bothering about trifles, and his natural sluggishness, but that he always draws a line somewhere, and brings down a heavy fist upon the man who crosses it. He began to find people fighting shy of his company; invitations became less in number; men nodded who used to shake hands; strong things were said in newspapers; and he was warned by friends that he was carrying things too far.

'Endeavour,' said one man, an acquaintance of some years'

164

standing, for whose character and abilities he had a great regard, 'endeavour to get some accurate sense of the position. You are blackguarding us every day with your sonorous sonnets as if we were cut-throats and thieves going out on a murdering and marauding expedition. We are nothing of the sort. We are a great nation, with a very painful sense of responsibility, engaged in a very difficult task. The war is bringing us together like brothers—out of its blood and ashes there will spring an Empire such as the world has never seen. You are belittling everything to the level of Hooliganism.'

'What is it but Hooliganism?' retorted Lucian. 'The most powerful nation in the world seizing one of the weakest by the throat!'

'It is nothing of the sort,' said the other. 'You know it is your great curse, my dear Lucian, that you never get a clear notion of the truth. You have a trick of seeing things as you think they ought to be; you will not see them as they are. Just because the Boers happen to be numerically small, to lead a pastoral life, and to have gone into the desert like the Israelites of old, you have brought that far too powerful imagination of yours to bear upon them, and have elevated them into a class with the Swiss and the Italians, who fought for their country.'

'What are the Boers fighting for?' asked Lucian.

'At present to grab somebody else's property,' returned the other. 'Don't get sentimental about them. After all, much as you love us, you're only half an Englishman, and you don't understand the English feeling. Are the English folk not suffering, and is a Boer widow or a Boer orphan more worthy of pity than a Yorkshire lass whose lad is lying dead out there, or a Scottish child whose father will never come back again?'

Lucian swept these small and insignificant details aside with some impatience.

'You are the mightiest nation the world has ever seen,' he said. 'You have a past—such a past as no other people can boast. You have a responsibility because of that past, and at present you have thrown all sense of it away, and are behaving like the drunken brute who rises gorged with flesh and wine, and yells for blood. This is an England with vine-leaves in her hair—it is not the England of Cromwell.'

'I thank God it is not!' said the other man with heartfelt reverence. 'We wish for no dictatorship here. Come, leave off slanging us in this bloodthirsty fashion, and try to arrive at a sensible view of things. Turn your energies to a practical direction—write a new romantic play for Harcourt, something that will cheer

165

us in these dark days, and give the money for bandages and warm socks and tobacco for poor Tommy out at the front. He isn't as picturesque—so it's said—as Brother Boer, but he's a man after all, and has a stomach.'

But Lucian would neither be cajoled nor chaffed out of his rôle of prophet. He became that most objectionable of all things—the man who believes he has a message, and must deliver it. He continued to hurl his philippics at the British public through the ever-ready columns of the peace-at-any-price paper, and the man in the street, who is not given to the drawing of fine distinctions, called him a pro-Boer. Lucian, in strict reality, was not a pro-Boer—he merely saw the artistry of the pro-Boer position. He remembered Byron's attitude with respect to Greece, and a too generous instinct had led him to compare Mr. Kruger to Cincinnatus. The man in the street knew nothing of these things, and cared less. It seemed to him that Lucian, who was, after all, nothing but an ink-slinger, a blooming poet, was slanging the quarter of a million men who were hurrying to Table Bay as rapidly as the War Office could get them there. To this sort of thing the man in the street objected. He did not care if Lucian's instincts were all on the side of the weaker party, nor was it an excuse that Lucian himself, in the matter of strict nationality, was an Italian. He had chosen to write his poems in England, said the man in the street, and also in the English language, and he had made a good thing out of it too, and no error, and the best thing he could do now was to keep a civil tongue in his head, or, rather, pen in his hand. This was no time for the cuckoo to foul the nest wherein he had had free quarters for so long.

The opinion of the man in the street is the crystallised common-sense of England, voiced in elementary language. Lucian, unfortunately, did not know this, and he kept on firing sonnets at the heads of people who, without bluster or complaint, were already tearing up their shirts for bandages. The man in the street read them, and ground his teeth, and waited for an opportunity. That came when Lucian was ill-advised enough to allow his name to be printed in large letters upon the placard of a great meeting whereat various well-intentioned but somewhat thoughtless persons proposed to protest against a war which had been forced upon the nation, and from which it was then impossible to draw back with either safety or honour. Lucian was still in the clouds; still thinking of Byron at Missolonghi; still harping upon the undoubted but scarcely pertinent facts that England had freed slaves, slain giants, and waved her flag protectingly over all who ran to her for help. The foolishness of assisting at a public meeting whereat the nation was

166

to be admonished of its wickedness in daring to assert itself never occurred to him. He was still the man with the message.

He formed one of a platform party of whom it might safely have been said that every man was a crank, and every woman a faddist. He was somewhat astonished and a little perplexed when he looked around him, and realised that his fellow-protestants were not of the sort wherewith he usually foregathered; but he speedily became interested in the audience. It had been intended to restrict admission to those well-intentioned folk who desired peace at any price, but the man in the street had placed a veto upon that, and had come in large numbers, and with a definite resolve to take part in the proceedings. The meeting began in a cheerful and vivacious fashion, and ended in one dear to the English heart. The chairman was listened to with some forbearance and patience; a lady was allowed to have her say because she was a woman. It was a sad inspiration that led the chairman to put Lucian up next; a still sadder one to refer to his poetical exhortations to the people. The sight of Lucian, the fashionably attired, dilettante, dreamy-eyed poet, who had lashed and pricked the nation whose blood was being poured out like water, and whose coffers were being depleted at a rapid rate, was too much for the folk he essayed to address. They knew him and his recent record. At the first word they rose as one man, and made for the platform. Lucian and the seekers after peace were obliged to run, as rabbits run to their warrens, and the enemy occupied the position. Somebody unfurled a large flag, and the entire assemblage joined in singing Mr. Kipling's invitation to contribute to the tambourine fund.

In the school of life the teacher may write many lessons with the whitest chalk upon the blackest blackboard, and there will always be a child in the corner who will swear that he cannot see the writing. Lucian could not see the lesson of the stormed platform, and he continued his rhyming crusade and made enemies by the million. He walked with closed eyes along a road literally bristling with bayonets: it was nothing but the good-natured English tolerance of a poet as being more or less of a lunatic that kept the small boys of the Strand from going for him. Men at street corners made remarks upon him which were delightful to overhear: it was never Lucian's good fortune to overhear them. His nose was in the air.

He heard the truth at last from that always truthful person, the man in liquor. In the smoking-room of his club he was encountered one night by a gentleman who had dined in too generous fashion, and whose natural patriotism glowed and scintillated around him with equal generosity. He met Lucian face to face, and he stopped and looked him up and down with a fine and eminently natural scorn.

'Mr. Lucian Damerel,' he said, with an only slightly interrupted articulation; 'Mr. Lucian Damerel—the gentleman who spills ink while better men spend blood.' Then he spat on the ground at Lucian's feet, and moved away with a sneer and a laugh.

The room was full of men. They all saw, and they all heard. No one spoke, but every one looked at Lucian. He knew that the drunken man had voiced the prevalent sentiment. He looked round him, without reproach, without defiance, and walked quietly from the room and the house. He had suddenly realised the true complexion of things.

Next morning, as he sat over a late breakfast in his rooms, he was informed that a young gentleman who would give no name desired earnestly to see him. He was feeling somewhat bored that morning, and he bade his man show the unknown one in. He looked up from his coffee to behold a very young gentleman upon whom the word subaltern was written in very large letters, whose youthful face was very grim and earnest, and who was obviously a young man with a mission. He pulled himself up in stiff fashion as the door closed upon him, and Lucian observed that one hand evidently grasped something which was concealed behind his back.

'Mr. Lucian Damerel?' the young gentleman said, with polite interrogation.

Lucian bowed and looked equally interrogative. His visitor glowered upon him.

'I have come to tell you that you are a damned scoundrel, Mr. Lucian Damerel,' he said, 'and to thrash you within an inch of your beastly life!'

Lucian stared, smiled, and rose lazily from his seat.

The visitor displayed a cutting-whip, brandished it, and advanced as seriously as if he were on parade. Lucian met him, seized the cutting-whip in one hand and his assailant's collar in the other, disarmed him, shook him, and threw him lightly into an easy-chair, where he lay gasping and surprised. Lucian hung the cutting-whip on the wall. He looked at his visitor with a speculative gaze.

'What shall I do with you, young sir?' he said. 'Throw you out of the window, or grill you on the fire, or merely kick you downstairs? I suppose you thought that because I happen to be what your lot call "a writin' feller," there wouldn't be any spunk in me, eh?'

The visitor was placed in a strange predicament. He had expected the sweet savour of groans and tears from a muscleless, flabby ink-and-parchment thing: this man had hands which could

168

grip like steel and iron. Moreover, he was cool—he actually sat down again and continued his breakfast.

'I hope I didn't squeeze your throat too much,' said Lucian politely. 'I have a nasty trick of forgetting that my hands are abnormally developed. If you feel shaken, help yourself to a brandy and soda, and then tell me what's the matter.'

The youth shook his head hopelessly.

'Y—you have insulted the Army!' he stammered at last.

'Of which, I take it, you are the self-appointed champion. Well, I'm afraid I don't plead guilty, because, you see, I know myself rather better than you know me. But you came to punish me? Well, again, you see you can't do that. Shall I give you satisfaction of some sort? There are pistols in that cabinet—shall we shoot at each other across the table? There are rapiers in the cupboard—shall we try to prick each other?'

The young gentleman in the easy-chair grew more and more uncomfortable. He was being made ridiculous, and the man was laughing at him.

'I have heard of the tricks of foreign duellists,' he said rudely.

Lucian's face flushed.

'That was a silly thing to say, my boy,' he said, not unkindly. 'Most men would throw you out of the window for it. As it is, I'll let you off easy. You'll find some gloves in that cupboard—get them out and take your coat off. I'm not an Englishman, as you just now reminded me in very pointed fashion, but I can use my fists.'

Then he took off his dressing-gown and rolled up his sleeves, and the youngster, who had spent many unholy hours in practising the noble art, looked at the poet's muscles with a knowing eye and realised that he was in for a very pretty scrap. He was a little vain of his own prowess, and fought for all he was worth, but at the end of five minutes he was a well-licked man, and at the expiration of ten was glad to be allowed to put on his coat and go.

Lucian flung his gloves into the corner of the room with a hearty curse. He stroked the satiny skin under which his muscle rippled smoothly. He had the arm of a blacksmith, and had always been proud of it. The remark of the drunken man came back to him. That was what they thought of him, was it?—that he was a mere slinger of ink, afraid of spilling his blood or suffering discomfort for the courage of his convictions? Well, they should see. England had gone mad with the lust of blood and domination, and after all he was not her son. He had discharged whatever debt he owed her. To the real England, the true England that had fallen on sleep, he would explain everything, when the awakening came. It would be no crime to shoulder a rifle and strap a bandolier around one's

169

shoulders in order to help the weak against the strong. He had fought with his pen, taking what he believed to be the right and honest course, in the endeavour to convert people who would not be converted, and who regarded his efforts as evidences of enmity. Very well: there seemed now to be but one straight path, and he would take it.

It was remembered afterwards as a great thing in Lucian's favour that he made no fuss about his next step. He left London very quietly, and no one knew that he was setting out to join the men whom he honestly believed to be fighting for the best principles of liberty and freedom.

CHAPTER XXXI

When the war broke out, Saxonstowe and his wife, after nearly three years of globe-trotting, were in Natal, where they had been studying the conditions of native labour. Saxonstowe, who had made himself well acquainted with the state of affairs in South Africa, knew that the coming struggle would be long and bitter. He and his wife entered into a discussion as to which they were to do: stay there, or return to England. Sprats knew quite well what was in Saxonstowe's mind, and she unhesitatingly declared for South Africa. Then Saxonstowe, who had a new book on hand, put his work aside, and set the wires going, and within a few hours had been appointed special correspondent of one of the London newspapers, with the prospect of hard work and exciting times before him.

'And what am I to do?' inquired Lady Saxonstowe, and answered her own question before he could reply. 'There will be sick and wounded—in plenty,' she said. 'I shall organise a field-hospital,' and she went to work with great vigour and spent her husband's money with inward thankfulness that he was a rich man.

Before they knew where they were, Lord and Lady Saxonstowe were shut up in Ladysmith, and for one of them at least there was not so much to do as he had anticipated, for there became little to record but the story of hope deferred, of gradual starvation, and of death and disease. But Sprats worked double tides, unflinchingly and untiringly, and almost forgot that she had a

170

husband who chafed because he could not get more than an occasional word over the wires to England. At the end of the siege she was as gaunt as a far-travelled gypsy, and as brown, but her courage was as great as ever and her resolution just as strong. One day she received an ovation from a mighty concourse that sent her, frightened and trembling, to shelter; when she emerged into the light of day again it was only to begin reorganising her work in preparation for still more arduous duties. The tide of war rolled on northwards, and Sprats followed, picking up the bruised and shattered jetsam which it flung to her. She had never indulged in questionings or speculations as to the rights or wrongs of the war. Her first sight of a wounded man had aroused all the old mothering instinct in her, and because she had no baby of her own she took every wounded man, Boer or Briton, into her arms and mothered him.

CHAPTER XXXII

A huddled mass of fugitives—men, women, children, horses, cattle—crowded together in the dry bed of a river, seeking shelter amongst rocks and boulders and under shelving banks, subjected continually to a hurricane of shot and shell, choked by the fumes of the exploding Lyddite, poisoned by the stench of blood, saturated all through with the indescribable odour of death. Somewhere in its midst, caged like a rat, but still sulkily defiant, the peasant general fingered his switch as he looked this way and that and saw no further chance of escape. In the distance, calmly waiting the inevitable end, the little man with the weather-beaten face and the grey moustaches listened to the never-ceasing roar of his cannon demanding insistently the word of surrender that must needs come.

Saxonstowe, lying on a waterproof sheet on the floor of his tent, was writing on a board propped up in front of him. All that he wrote was by way of expressing his wonder, over and over again, that Cronje should hold out so long against the hell of fire which was playing in and around his last refuge. He was trying to realise what must be going on in the river bed, and the thought made him sick. Near him, writing on an upturned box, was another special correspondent who shared the tent with him; outside, polishing tin

171

pannikins because he had nothing else to do, was a Cockney lad
whom these two had picked up in Ladysmith and had attached as
body-servant. He was always willing and always cheerful, and had a
trick of singing snatches of popular songs in a desultory and
disconnected way. His raucous voice came to them under the
booming of the guns.

> 'Ow, 'ee's little but 'ee's wise,
> 'Ee's a terror for 'is size,
> An' 'ee does not hadvertise:
> Do yer, Bobs?'

'What a voice that chap has!' said Saxonstowe's companion.
'It's like a wheel that hasn't been oiled for months!'

> 'Will yer kindly put a penny in my little tambourine,
> For a gentleman in khaki ordered sou-outh?'

chanted the polisher of tin pans.
'They have a saying in Yorkshire,' remarked Saxonstowe, 'to
the effect that it's a poor heart that never rejoices.'
'This chap must have a good 'un, then,' said the other. Give us
a pipeful of tobacco, will you, Saxonstowe? Lord! will those guns
never stop?'

> 'For the colonel's lady and Judy O'Grady,
> Are sisters hunder their skins,'

sang the henchman.
'Will our vocalist never stop?' said Saxonstowe, handing over
his pouch. 'He seems as unconcerned as if he were on a Bank
Holiday.'

> 'We wos as 'appy as could be, that dye,
> Dahn at the Welsh 'Arp, which is 'Endon—'

The raucous voice broke off suddenly; the close-cropped
Cockney head showed at the open flap of the tent.
'Beg pardon, sir,' said the Cockney voice, 'but I fink there's
somethin' 'appened, sir—guns is dyin' orf, sir.'
Saxonstowe and his fellow scribe sprang to their feet. The roar
of the cannon was dying gradually away, and it suddenly gave place
to a strange and an awful silence.

172

Saxonstowe walked hither and thither about the bed of the river, turning his head jerkily to right and left.

'It's a shambles!—a shambles!—a shambles!' he kept repeating. He shook his head and then his body as if he wanted to shake off the impression that was fast stamping itself ineffaceably upon him. 'A shambles!' he said again.

He pulled himself together and looked around him. It seemed to him that earth and sky were blotted out in blood and fire, and that the smell of death had wrapped him so closely that he would never breathe freely again. Dead and dying men were everywhere. Near him rose a pile of what appeared to be freshly slaughtered meat—it was merely the result of the bursting of a Lyddite shell amongst a span of oxen. Near him, too, stood a girl, young, not uncomely, with a bullet-wound showing in her white bosom from which she had just torn the bodice away; at his feet, amongst the boulders, were twisted, strange, grotesque shapes that had once been human bodies.

'There's a chap here that looks like an Englishman,' said a voice behind him.

Saxonstowe turned, and found the man who shared his tent standing at his elbow, and pointed to a body stretched out a yard or two away—the body of a well-formed man who had fallen on his side, shot through the heart. He lay as if asleep, his face half hidden in his arm-pit; near him, within reach of the nerveless fingers that had torn out a divot of turf in his last moment's spasmodic feeling for something to clutch at, lay his rifle: round his rough serge jacket was clasped a bandolier well stored with cartridges. His broad-brimmed hat had fallen off, and half his face, very white and statuesque in death, caught the sunlight that straggled fitfully through the smoke-clouds which still curled over the bed of the river.

'Looks like an Englishman,' repeated the special correspondent. 'Look at his hands, too—he hasn't handled a rifle very long, I'm thinking.'

Saxonstowe glanced at the body with perfunctory interest—there were so many dead men lying all about him. Something in the dead man's face woke a chord in his memory: he went nearer and bent over him. His brain was sick and dizzy with the horrors of the blood and the stink of the slaughter. He stood up again, and winked his eyes rapidly.

'No, no!' he heard himself saying. 'No! It can't be—of course it can't be. What should Lucian be doing here? Of course it's not he—it's mere imagination—mere im-ag-in-a-tion!'

'Here, hold up, old chap!' said his companion, pulling out a flask. 'Take a nip of that. Better? Hallo—what's going on there?'

He stepped on a boulder and gazed in the direction of a wagon round which some commotion was evident. Saxonstowe, without another glance at the dead man, stepped up beside him.

He saw a roughly built, rugged-faced man, wrapped in a much-worn overcoat that had grown green with age, stepping out across the plain, swishing at the herbage with a switch which jerked nervously in his hand. At his side strode a muscular-looking woman, hard of feature, brown of skin—a peasant wife in a faded skirt and a crumpled sun-bonnet. Near them marched a tall British officer in khaki; other Boers and British, a group of curious contrasts, hedged them round.

'That's Cronje,' said the special correspondent, as he stepped down from the boulder. 'Well, it's over, thank God!'

The conquered was on his way to the conqueror.

www.ingramcontent.com/pod-product-compliance
Lightning Source LLC
Chambersburg PA
CBHW011505170626
46812CB00008B/2980

* 9 7 8 1 6 4 4 3 9 3 6 9 7 *